In his debut novel, *Taken*, B. D. Eas... [barcode obscures text] ...
of a swift and explosive adventure. Readers will follow ...
his sister, Tiffany, and his younger twin brothers, Mason and
Austin, into mysterious ruins, eerie catacombs, and a creepy
castle that defies imagination. One part Swiss Family Robinson,
one part Indiana Jones, *Taken* is a riveting tale of just how far
mankind is willing to go for the ultimate prize.

—**Wayne Thomas Batson**, best-selling author of
The Door Within Trilogy, The Berinfell Prophecies, and
The Dark Sea Annals

Don't even touch this book unless you plan to read it at once.
Taken wastes no time thrusting its readers headlong into the
beginning of what promises to be an epic saga. Exploding with
mystery and high-stakes adventure, this book is masterfully
crafted to awaken even the most stubborn of imaginations.
And yet perhaps the most impressive feat is Mr. Eastman's
ability to punctuate all of it with a deep and powerful message
of faith. A job well done.

—**Christopher Miller**, coauthor of the multi-award-
winning Codebearers series

My buddy Brock Eastman has a winner here! Take fascinating
characters, put them on a fantastical adventure, and tell the
story at a page-turning pace, and you've got *Taken*, the first
volume of his forthcoming, five-book series titled The Quest
for Truth. Oh, and parents, don't forget his solid emphasis on
Christian principles. Tell you what: get this book for your kids,
and they'll enjoy it so much that I bet you'll end up reading
it too! Way to go Brock!

—**Frank Pastore**, host of *The Frank Pastore Show* on
KKLA 99.5 FM in Los Angeles, Author of *Shattered: Struck
Down, But Not Destroyed*

Taken is awesome! People of any age will enjoy it. I can't wait for the rest of the series!

—**Ruth Santoyo**, age 14

The Wikks' adventures kept me at the edge of my seat throughout the whole book!

—**Cody Lugovskiy**, age 13

The book kept me very interested and I was really excited when I got to read it! It was one of the best books I've ever read. I would definitely recommend it!

—**Nicole Blunier**, age 10

Taken is a fast-paced, fun, easy-to-read book. It allowed my imagination and mind to get lost in the story. I enjoyed it and can't wait to read the next Quest for Truth book!

—**Brooke Harrell**, age 13

Finally, something new, exciting, and original! Brock Eastman has written a page-turner that will definitely make you want to read the sequel.

—**Jonathan Maiocco**, age 17

TAKEN

THE QUEST FOR TRUTH

TAKEN

THE FIRST ADVENTURE IN
THE QUEST FOR TRUTH

BROCK EASTMAN

P&R
PUBLISHING
P.O. BOX 817 • PHILLIPSBURG • NEW JERSEY 08865-0817

Printed in the United States of America

Library of Congress Control Number: 2011931138

To my wife:

When God gave me you,
he gave me all I needed to succeed.
You complete the threefold cord that God designed for my life.

Without you I would be lost.

Contents

Acknowledgments

A few well-deserved thanks.

To my wife, Ashley, for allowing me to write and dream. For the time you allowed me to have, but was truly yours. And for encouraging me to finally be "done." I needed someone to tell me.

To my daughters, Kinley Grace and Elsie Mae. Mommy and I love you so much.

To my dad, Dave, and mom, Diane. Thanks for helping me to dream big and for your flexibility. You always gave me the tools I needed to succeed. You've been there for me, and continue to be there for my family. I know that at a moment's notice you'll make the thousand-mile trip to be here.

To my sister, Tiffany, for all the fun we had growing up and what our combined imaginations could produce. I still haven't found that gorilla. And to my brother-in-law, Tyler, who stands firm in the Word and is an example to me. To my nieces, Autumn, Madison, and baby Knapp. You guys are so cute; whenever my Kinley is around you she learns something new.

To my grandparents, Bill and Dotty. You guys have been nothing less than a solid foundation for me.

To my cousin Matthew. You read *Taken* in two days, and your desire to know what happens next has continued to push me forward.

To Emily and Tom. You guys bought and read the book before anyone else. Sorry for the grammar and the missing page numbers.

To Marianne. You took a chance on me and encouraged me to finish. Without your honest editing, teaching, and commitment, I'm not sure what condition this manuscript would be in.

To Melissa for having a vision for my book finding a home with P&R. You e-mailed me with praise for *Taken* far before I'd shown any proposals. Thanks.

To my friends Taylor and Alex. You guys rock! Thanks for keeping me young.

Most of all to the God who keeps us all in His hands. You've set a path before me, and even when I get lost You bring me back. You provide, You protect, and You are always there. To the Creator of Truth.

Prologue

"I implore you not to do it." The man clasped his hands before him as he pleaded with his friend. "It isn't—"

"It's entirely my fault. I should have kept it. I might have saved her," his friend rambled. He was out of his wits, lost to all sense of reason. "It's the only way. She must be preserved," he murmured.

"She's dying. You must let her go. Your grief is consuming you, and what you seek cannot be found," the first man warned. "She didn't want—"

"Don't say it!" the second man cut him off. "She didn't know what she wanted. She was sick." Fear and anger shook his body as he spoke.

"It's not natural."

"But it's possible, and it's the only hope I have."

"No, there is a greater hope, if only you would listen to me."

"Enough of your foolishness, Samuel! I want to be alone with my wife."

"Just think of her and what she would want."

The grieving man placed his face in his hands and began to sob. Samuel stepped forward to comfort him. Had he been able to get through? He placed a hand on his friend's back.

"No, I want you to leave! I've made my decision!" the man yelled and stood to his full height. "Leave me!"

Samuel turned to leave. If only his friend would listen. What he'd discovered would not produce the results he wanted. Samuel understood the fullness of the text, but his grieving friend would not listen. He'd asked how Samuel knew, and Samuel replied, "Faith in the Truth."

Faith was not something his friend understood. He needed solid evidence; he needed something tangible, something *real*.

TOP SECRET:
PHOENIX
E4: 32

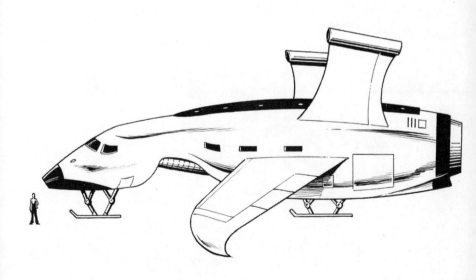

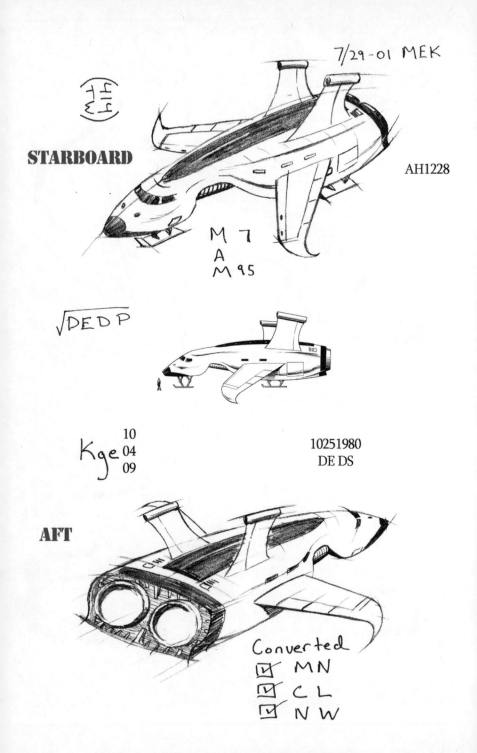

7/29-01 MEK

STARBOARD

AH1228

M 7
A
M 95

√DEDP

Kge 10
04
09

10251980
DE DS

AFT

Converted
☑ MN
☑ CL
☑ NW

12282007

EME$^6_{11}$

ANK
OCT
10/07

826P + R10

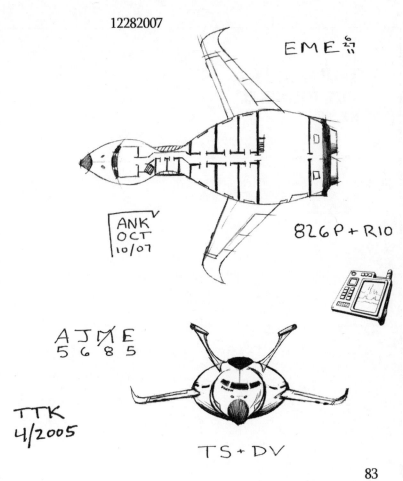

AJME
5 6 8 5

TTK
4/2005

TS + DV

83

9-4-5

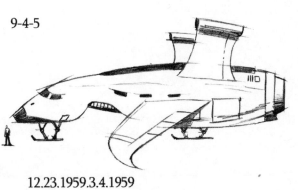

12.23.1959.3.4.1959

TOP SECRET:
THE PHOENIX
E4: 32

Commissioned October 25th, 1580, to the
federal diplomatic exchange bureau.

Transfer of vessel approved on September
4th, 1590, to ~~Archaeological research~~
~~Foundation~~.

P.O.,
Implemented tracking Sync.
Networked to BEAM use
Sequence 12-28-07 to activate.
— S.K.

3.3.88.6.23.88.1.12.90.1.12.90.5.17.91.11.4.92.12.21.93.1.20.95.8.28.96.10.28.97.
12.30.98.12.30.98.4.21.0.7.7.1.11.15.2.5.23.4.10.11.5.8.2.7.12.18.8.10.8.9.12.10.9

Shock

Oliver stood alone beneath the endless night sky, pondering what lay ahead. In a few minutes his family would leave on an expedition to begin an archeological dig. Normally this meant they'd be neck deep in ruins and ancient artifacts. But his parents were hiding something, and Oliver didn't know why. They weren't usually this secretive.

Three soft beeps sounded from a device on his wrist. For the seventh time in as many minutes, Oliver glanced at his mTalk. It was already midnight. Not surprisingly, his parents were behind schedule. He sighed, realizing he'd have to finish packing by himself. His family was scheduled to launch at 12:30, and there was still a lot to do.

Oliver hurried back into the cargo bay and started stacking the many crates of supplies. One by one he set them in place and strapped them down. As he inspected his work, he wiped the sweat from his face on his sleeve and noticed his bicep bulge beneath the fabric. He'd just turned seventeen and had spent the last year under the physical training regiment of the Academy. He wondered whether he could have completed this task by himself a year ago. He subconsciously rubbed his fingers over the Academy Squadron badge stitched on the sleeve of his t-shirt. A feeling of belonging and pride came over him.

Something clattered in the hall of the upper deck. Oliver scowled. Mason and Austin were probably fighting. At eleven years old, they were adept at finding opportunities for mischief. Their sister, Tiffany, was supposed to keep an eye on them, but she'd probably fallen asleep reading. Why was he the only responsible one? he wondered, irritated.

Oliver's boots clanked against the metal stairs as he climbed to the balcony overlooking the cargo bay. As he looked through the raised cargo door, the wind blew a variety of autumn leaves into the open bay. The breeze gave him an eerie feeling and he shivered. Something felt wrong. Where were his parents?

Walking down the corridor, Oliver stopped and looked into the research lab. Sure enough Tiffany was asleep on a couch. Her hand grasped their mom's Archeos e-journal, its screen still glowing. Oliver understood his parents' need to document every minute detail of their archeology digs in the journal, but he didn't understand his sister's obsession with reading through the myriad of notes—boring descriptions of glass shards, scraps of metal, and soil samples. Oliver glared at his sister and gave voice to a sigh, hoping to wake her, but it didn't work. She had one job: watch the twins. Oliver felt the warmth in his cheeks; his temper was rising. He'd been making strides in controlling it recently, but when it came to his siblings, he had to work extra hard at keeping it in check.

Oliver crept toward the twins' cabin. He was sure they'd be jumping on their bunks or throwing things at each other. He couldn't wait to nail them and make them clean the galley or lavatories for misbehaving. Surprisingly, their cabin was silent as he approached. The boys were fast asleep, Mason on the bottom bunk and Austin on the top, one leg hanging limply over the side. With a disgusted glance at the messy cabin, Oliver pulled the door shut. He had grown accustomed to the rigorous order kept at the Academy. Oliver glanced at his mTalk. A quarter past midnight! What was keeping his parents?

He stomped back to the cargo bay in frustration. A lot had changed since he'd been gone. His parents were acting differently. Were they mad at him for going to the Academy? He really didn't have a choice since all males had to serve at some point. They should be proud of him for being admitted early at sixteen, a truly rare privilege. And how long had they been hiding things from him? he wondered. The more he thought, the more bizarre his parents' behavior seemed. They'd picked him up from the Academy in an unmarked, expensive silver ship. While it wasn't unusual for Oliver's family to inhabit a ship for expeditions, it was strange that they hadn't mentioned the *Phoenix* earlier. And who had beefed up their budget so they could afford it? He didn't even know where they were going on their current expedition. That was very odd. And there was no sign that anyone from Archeos, the society his parents worked for, would be joining them on this trip.

Oliver flexed his muscles, reminding himself of the physical strides he had made over the past year. He stepped outside and tapped on his mTalk to call his dad. Mr. Wikk's picture appeared on the screen while the mTalk tried to reach him. The call was rejected and the screen went blank. He couldn't believe it. Not only were they late, but now they were ignoring him. Oliver felt his temper rising again. He'd have to fly back to the house and see what was holding them up. They were never going to leave on time.

His black sky scooter hovered outside the *Phoenix*, waiting to take Oliver wherever he needed to go. He swung a leg over, and with a twist on the throttle, the craft quietly darted forward. Ten minutes later Oliver could see his home, a collection of seven connected domes. The quiet night ride had calmed him, even though he was still anxious to get going.

Suddenly, Oliver heard a strange sound. What in the world? Letting off the throttle, he killed the engine. It was men shouting. Voices he didn't recognize. What was happening? He pulled the sky scooter off the main trail and slid off the seat. Oliver cautiously crept up the trail toward his house. There was a large black transport ship hovering over his front yard. Ropes hung from the sides. There was more shouting. Someone was issuing orders to search the house and grounds.

The backyard was empty, so Oliver was able to race to the garage unobserved. Once inside, he locked the door behind him and approached the next door that led into the kitchen. With a slow turn of the handle, Oliver pushed the door open a crack just large enough to see through. His dad and mom were there, but they weren't alone.

A stranger stood in front of his parents. His face was shadowed by a black pilot cap, but Oliver could see the faint line of a scar on the man's cheek. He wore a black uniform, covered by a long black trench coat. Three silver stripes decorated the upper part of his coat sleeves—that meant he was a captain. Directly above them was a patch with a silver skull and the word Übel. Übel? Oliver had never heard of them. What was going on? His parents seemed confused too, or maybe shocked. They'd definitely been caught off guard at this man's arrival. And the men shouting? Something was wrong. This guy wasn't a guest; he was an intruder.

"What brings you here at this late hour, Captain Vedrik?" Elliot Wikk asked. Oliver's dad held his hand behind him, and his mom grasped it. Even in the midst of this frightening intrusion, their love was evident. They drew strength from each other.

"You know why I'm here." Captain Vedrik's voice was low and raspy, like a snake's hiss before it strikes. He approached Oliver's parents and looked around the kitchen. A satisfied smile slipped across his lips. "You weren't expecting us until tomorrow."

Mr. Wikk nodded. "We hoped it would be a few days."

"It would have been easier if you'd accepted our offer," Vedrik said with a scowl. "But I suppose we're past that now."

He rolled his shoulders and exhaled. "Where are your children?" Mr. Wikk straightened. Standing protectively in front of Oliver's mom, he remained silent.

Vedrik smirked and narrowed his eyes. "We know that you picked up Oliver from the Academy, and Tiffany and the twins from Bewaldeter." Oliver's chest tightened when Vedrik said his name. He didn't like the idea of this man knowing so much about his family. What else did he know? Oliver knew he had to stop him. Maybe he could knock him out and help his parents escape, but he had to find the right moment, a moment of surprise.

Vedrik shouted over his shoulder. "Search the house! There should be four children somewhere around here." Oliver scowled. He was not a child.

Footsteps echoed down the hall as the house was searched. This was his chance. He was ready. Oliver grasped the door handle, but almost as instantly he stopped, and his grip eased. He remembered what he'd learned about balance of forces at the Academy. He was clearly outnumbered and would likely be captured if he attempted a rescue. Taking a deep calming breath, Oliver waited and watched. His heart drummed rapidly.

Mr. Wikk shifted backward. He was purposely blocking something from Vedrik's view. Of course, it was the book! Oliver's parents had shown the book to him when he returned. It was the one thing they had shared with him. Covered in crimson leather, the book was the prize find of their last dig. Mr. Wikk hadn't let it leave his side. Now it sat exposed on the kitchen table like a beacon calling to be seen.

Vedrik moved toward the garage like a fox on the hunt. Mr. Wikk looked toward the door and made eye contact with Oliver. His expression tightened with fear. Fear for his son, not for himself.

Mr. Wikk stepped forward abruptly. Vedrik spun around. "Don't try anything stupid. The compound is surrounded. There is no escape," the captain hissed.

Oliver felt his heart drop to his stomach. What could he possibly do? He had to act soon, or even he would be captured.

Vedrik sighed and leaned against the kitchen counter. "My superiors are quite interested in your work, you know. For some reason they feel you are essential to our destiny." He smiled haughtily. "You should have accepted their generous offer and saved me the trip to this scrap of a planet."

Oliver's mom, Laura Wikk, spoke up boldly, "We can't be bribed."

Vedrik's eyebrows narrowed, and an unsettling darkness crept across his face. "It wasn't a bribe. You should have considered it your salary." He held out a hand and tightened the strap of his glove. "People can always be bought." As quickly as the darkness came, it disappeared. The captain shrugged. "There is no choice now."

"There was never a choice," Mr. Wikk said.

"True, I suppose, but a willing partner is always better than an unwilling one. Regardless, I've been assigned to escort you on this expedition." Vedrik's chin rose proudly. "Together we will discover the truth."

A soldier walked into the kitchen and waited for the captain to acknowledge him. The man shuddered under Vedrik's annoyed glare. "What is it?"

Clearing his throat, the soldier lowered his head. "Sir, all the bedrooms are empty."

Vedrik slammed his fist on the counter. The darkness had reappeared. "Where are the children?"

"They aren't here," Mr. Wikk admitted.

The captain looked like a wild animal choosing its prey. His eyes bored into Mrs. Wikk. "Where are they?"

Mrs. Wikk responded with confidence and strength. "It's true. They're not here."

Vedrik angrily turned to the soldier. "Search the woods behind the house! These people never lie, it's against some code they follow." The soldier went into the living room and issued new orders.

Oliver took a deep breath. He had to act now or the woods would be swarming with Übel soldiers. He looked around the garage for a weapon but found nothing. They had taken everything to the *Phoenix*. Oliver heard Vedrik's serpentine voice again.

"We know that your recent discovery has revealed the whereabouts of Ursprung."

"You're mistaken," replied Mrs. Wikk

"As our report stated," Mr. Wikk clarified, "the discovery at Dabnis Castle leads no farther than the last known location of the Gläubigers."

Vedrik began to pace. "You speak truthfully, but there is more to the story." He turned his back on Oliver's parents. The captain carelessly opened a cabinet and then slammed it shut, continuing his seemingly unfocused yet persistent search. Oliver remained frozen; only an inch of wood separated him and the captain, who was but five steps away.

"What do you mean?" asked Mr. Wikk, trying to hold Vedrik's focus.

"Well," turning back toward Mr. Wikk, "it was previously believed that the Gläubigers had nothing to do with Ursprung. But we know differently now, don't we?" Captain Vedrik laughed menacingly. "You underestimate my resources."

Vedrik moved to the table and took the leather-bound book in his gloved hand. He held it out and cackled. "And what have we here? I saw the book the moment I walked in, but watching your efforts to block it has been amusing! As if you could hide it from me." A sarcastically sympathetic smile crossed his lips. "This book, this priceless book, is how I know the Gläubigers are linked. The existence of this book was revealed to me just four days ago." Vedrik looked at Oliver's parents, who were stunned. It was clear they had not expected this. "And now I find it lying unprotected on your kitchen table."

Oliver felt anger boiling up inside him, but not at Vedrik this time. Had Oliver's dad shared with him the danger they were in, he could have helped protect the book. Instead, it was clear to him that his parents had been careless.

Mr. and Mrs. Wikk recovered their composure. Their family's safety was all that mattered.

Mr. Wikk inhaled. "Well, now that you have what you need, kindly leave."

Vedrik smiled deviously as he wagged his gloved finger. "No, I don't think so. You see, we still need you!" The finger now pressed against Mr. Wikk's chest. "As you know, it's believed that in an earlier time the Federation prohibited research into Ursprung, and with a single key stroke all electronic records that mentioned our origin were deleted."

So this Übel group wasn't part of the Federal forces; they were something else—rogues, mercenaries, thieves, something dark.

Vedrik stepped away from Mr. Wikk and shook the book with his hand. "Discovering ancient artifacts like this book is the only way we can re-create the information that was lost."

Oliver understood. His parents were renowned archeologists who specialized in the field of origins. These villains needed their expertise.

Mr. Wikk shook his head. "It could take hundreds if not thousands of years to explore all the abandoned settlements scattered throughout the Federation. You'd need hundreds of teams working for you."

Vedrik set the book on the counter. "We don't need to explore every settlement." And raising his eyebrows, he continued, "We already know where the fabled path began. It started at Dabnis Castle. The second waypoint is at the coordinates you discovered in the underground chamber. The very same place you were planning on leaving for tonight."

Oliver clenched his fists. This man knew more of his parents' plans than he did. He was furious. How could they keep this from him?

"As archeology experts, you are essential to our mission," Vedrik continued. "Your expertise will be needed many times during this expedition."

."We didn't accept the money, and our decision hasn't changed," Mr. Wikk clarified.

Mrs. Wikk nodded her head. "Money has never been a motivation for our work."

"How noble," he sneered.

Mrs. Wikk stared into Vedrik's cold, black eyes. "We search for truth, and its discovery is our reward."

Vedrik stared with boredom at Oliver's mom and then ran his finger across the book's cover. "My superiors believe, as do I, that Ursprung holds many answers. Answers that validate legends that became myths just a few centuries ago and were historical facts only a millennium before that. You see, my society's desires are not much different from yours."

Oliver could see that his parents weren't buying Vedrik's motives, and neither did he. Übel was after more than just the truth, but what?

Vedrik continued his proclamation. "There is no greater mystery to be solved than where we humans came from—our origin. The rewards garnered from any truths that you've discovered thus far cannot compare to what Ursprung can unlock." The darkness crept back across Vedrik's face, and his fist rose in anger. "And you know that!" shouted Vedrik, consumed with rage. Then a clever smile crossed his face, washing away the anger and darkness. "Perhaps I should share something with you," Vedrik said.

Walking across the kitchen, Vedrik turned to face Oliver's parents. "Many years ago one of my superiors came across an artifact from a long-abandoned city. Do you know what was written on that artifact?"

Mr. and Mrs. Wikk just waited silently, paralyzed with anticipation as they cautiously observed the disturbed man before them.

Vedrik looked toward the ceiling. "And I give unto them eternal life; and they shall never perish." He spoke as if the words were tattooed on his innermost soul. "Do you understand those words?" But the captain didn't give them a chance to answer. "The secret to living forever is within our grasp. The secret to eternal youth."

The handle on the other door to the garage rattled as someone, likely a soldier, attempted to come inside. Oliver turned to see and shifted awkwardly on his left foot. It twisted slightly and his shoulder nudged the door to the kitchen. He looked back to the captain instantly, but it was too late. Vedrik abruptly turned toward the garage door.

A streak of fear bolted through Oliver. His stomach seemed to turn over, and his mind went numb. Captain Vedrik's cold black eyes were all he could see, and they were locked on him.

Pursuit

Vedrik's gasp seemed to suck the air from the room; Oliver couldn't breathe. The captain's shadowy black eyes were drilling into him and holding him in place.

"In here! They're in here!" Vedrik roared. Oliver's legs were useless. His mind was frantically telling him to run, but nothing was happening.

Vedrik lunged for the door. Mr. Wikk intercepted him in midair, bringing him to the ground with a thud. Holding the captain down, he called to Oliver, "Run! Get your sister and brothers out of here. Go!"

Vedrik's face twisted with rage. With his free hand he reached into his jacket and then jabbed a small black object into Mr. Wikk's side. Oliver saw a blue spark and heard a sizzling buzz as the Zapp-It came to life and surged energy into Elliot Wikk. Oliver's dad slumped.

"No!" cried Oliver.

The captain shoved Mr. Wikk's limp body aside. Fear swept over Mrs. Wikk's face. Tears began to stream down her cheeks as she knelt next to her husband. For a split second the world seemed out of focus, and then Oliver's adrenaline kicked in.

"Dad!" shouted Oliver. Just as he reached to swing the door open and rush upon the captain, Oliver saw his dad's arm move and then his eyes open. He was alive.

Mrs. Wikk looked to the door. "Run, Oliver!"

Oliver's legs came to life, and he turned to escape. With a backward kick, he slammed the kitchen door shut in the face of the captain as he scrambled to his feet.

He looked to the garage door, but it was no good—the shadow of a soldier was silhouetted in the window. The door handle shook violently under the intruder's grasp before the sound of his shoulder bashing into the door thundered through the garage. It wouldn't hold for long.

Oliver searched the garage for another exit. A charging cable for the sky scooters dangled from the ceiling. It was his only hope. He grabbed the cable and pulled himself up onto the rafters.

The captain entered the garage. The charging cable still writhed in the air like a snake, and Vedrik looked up. Glaring with rage at Oliver, the captain pulled his pistol from the harness and aimed it. A small red dot appeared on Oliver's chest. It was over. He flinched as he saw the captain's finger press the trigger.

Nothing happened. Vedrik clicked the trigger several more times. Oliver watched with curiosity as the captain turned the gun over in his hands. The power cell was missing. "Blast! You won't get away, boy. Come down before you hurt yourself." The garage door burst open, and two more men charged into the garage.

The garage skylight was still open. Could he get to it in time? He sprang from rafter to rafter and climbed out onto the roof.

Vedrik's voice echoed in the garage. "He's on the roof! Hurry!"

Glazed with dew, the domed roof was as slick as a frozen lake. Oliver fell to his back and slid down it; he dug in his heels, but there was nothing to grip. He awkwardly dropped off the roof, arms flailing, and his body crashed into the unforgiving ground. Oliver picked himself up and groaned, shaking out his limbs. Nothing felt broken.

Soldiers appeared out of the darkness and surrounded him like a pack of hungry wolves. Step by step he backed away from them. Something pricked the back of his neck. A row of thorny brambles created a wall behind him. He was trapped again. Or was he?

Teeth clenched, Oliver twisted and dove into the underbrush. Thorns tore at his exposed forearms and poked through his clothes, pricking his flesh. He rolled to his feet and popped up, ready to run.

An argument erupted among the soldiers. "You. Go after the boy!"

"I'm a pilot. Send one of your men."

Oliver heard the man grunt. "You two, after him!"

The voices faded as Oliver blazed forward. He came across a narrow path and recognized it as the twins' bike trail. Hope trickled into his heart. Oliver knew the woods well. The path wound among the dark shadows of tall pines; it would lead to the *Phoenix*. The night air echoed with heavy breathing. Pine needles crunched under lumbering feet. The soldiers were nearing. Oliver looked over his shoulder, searching for his pursuers, but the thick forest shrouded them. They could be anywhere.

Oliver crouched and listened. The breathing had ceased. The howl of the wind through the pines was the only sound. They were waiting for him. Crack! A branch splintered above Oliver's head. Something had pierced the wood.

"Cruz, set your gun to stun! The captain wants him alive!"

A green streak zipped past, lighting the underside of the trees with a mystical glow. At least they weren't trying to kill him anymore, thought Oliver, somewhat relieved. He still had to escape, however, so he got to his feet and ran. Whoomp! The weapon unleashed another glowing green shot. Oliver dove and then scrambled to his feet again. Each time he heard the telltale *whoomp* of the weapon, he dodged left or right.

"Stop now, and we won't hurt you!" snarled Cruz, but then laughed.

"Yeah, we'll be sure to take good care of you," the other man jeered.

Needles snagged in Oliver's short brown hair as a branch grazed the top of his head. Just a bit farther, he urged himself. A fallen tree, a casualty of last year's windstorm, created a bridge across the chasm that separated Oliver from the *Phoenix*. This was his path to freedom. Broken branches and house-size boulders littered the trail, but they wouldn't stop him. The obstacle course at the Academy had prepared him. Oliver scrambled among the debris and found himself free of its clutches. He could hear the roar of the river coursing the depths of the chasm ahead. Almost there, he thought, and then something rustled in the bushes to his right.

Wham! Oliver's torso burned as he hit the ground, gasping for breath. A moment passed before he caught his breath and another before he realized what had knocked him off his feet.

He'd been outmaneuvered. Oliver's arms were pinned to the ground by a soldier. The man stared into Oliver's face with a sinister grin. A drop of sweat fell from the man's brow and landed on Oliver's face; it trickled to his lips. Oliver shuddered at the salty taste.

"I've got you now," the soldier sneered. His hot breath smelled like sewage.

"Hold him, Frank!" The second soldier, Cruz, was gasping for air a few yards away, bent over, hands on his knees.

Self-defense lessons flashed through Oliver's mind. In an instant he knew what to do. He thrust his knee up, catching his captor in the ribs. A roar of pain erupted from the soldier, and he rolled to his back, holding his chest, breathless. Oliver clambered to his feet, scattering dry pine needles. Cruz wearily lifted his gun and shot several stuns. Whoomp. Whoomp. Whoomp. Oliver jumped, rolled, and ran. With a quick look backward, he saw the heavier soldier, Cruz, pulling his comrade to his feet.

The log was close now. Just seventy feet . . . fifty feet . . . thirty feet . . . ten feet . . . the log.

Oliver stepped foot over foot. Adrenaline coursed through his body, heightening his senses. Through the soles of his shoes, he could feel every knob and pit in the wood beneath his feet. The log groaned under his weight. Would it hold? A sharp wind wrapped around Oliver's body, tugging at his clothes. Arms out straight, he caught his balance. Whoomp, whoomp. More stuns whizzed by him. The soldiers hesitated at the log as Oliver dismounted.

Pushing on the wood, Oliver felt the soft bark crumble under his palms. He took a deep breath, and then pushed on the rotting log again. Stun shots blasted the earth, leaving black divots. Grunting loudly, Oliver gave one final push, and the end of the log swung over the side of the ravine. The dead tree teetered for a moment, and then gravity did the rest, pulling it into the dark crevice. Echoes filled the forest as the timber rebounded off the chasm walls. A faint splash marked the bridge's arrival to the water below. Oliver smiled. The only other crossing was a mile away. Judging by Cruz's condition, it would take the two soldiers a half hour to make the round trip to the *Phoenix*.

Oliver recklessly charged through the pine forest as branches tore at his exposed skin. He had one mission. Get to the *Phoenix* and escape.

An ambient blue glow filtered through the branches, creating an eerie, iridescent scene. Through gaps in the canopy Oliver saw a bright aqua ball streaming upward. It burst, illuminating the exposed bits of cold night sky. Flares! The soldiers were signaling their comrades.

Oliver slid down a slope blanketed with brown pine needles. A branch caught him in the face, snapping his upper body backward. His left cheek pulsed with pain. Oliver slid past several more tree trunks before his aching body came to rest at the bottom of the slope. Oliver touched his cheek and felt the moistness of blood. He'd fix it later. First, he had to get to the ship.

In front of him the forest ended, opening into a large clearing. There was the ship, his escape from the villains who were stalking him as their prey. A warm breeze blew through the cloudless sky and rustled the branches of the encompassing forest. The *Phoenix* sat silently. Its large wings swept forward from the engines to the bridge. The ship's silver skin reflected the brilliant moonlight above, illuminating the clearing with a heavenly ambience. The serenity of the setting didn't match the emotions raging within Oliver.

In moments, soldiers would be swarming the area. To launch the *Phoenix* Oliver needed time, something he had little of. Oliver winced as he saw the twins standing in the ship's small side hatch. What were they doing? "Get inside!" he shouted.

"What's with the fireworks," groaned Mason, the older of the twins. He brushed his sandy blond hair from his blue eyes and yawned.

"They're not fireworks!" Oliver broke into a sprint for the ship. The twins stood barefoot in their pajamas, clueless to the danger that lurked in the woods around them.

The younger twin, Austin, stepped out from the hatch, his green eyes half open. "Why are you running?"

"Get in the ship! Where's Tiffany?" Oliver demanded.

"I'm right here." The girl's soft voice came from behind the twins. "Why are you shouting?"

"Get in the ship!" he commanded again. It was as if his orders were falling on deaf ears.

The night sky glowed blue. A flare sailed quietly upward and exploded with a loud thunderclap. A shower of blue sparks rained down. Austin stepped back, bumping into his sister. She grasped his shoulders uncertainly.

Tiffany reached out her hand. "Oliver, your cheek is bleeding."

He ignored her. He had closed the gap to the ship. Mason fell to the ground with a thud as Oliver pulled him in through the hatch. Taking no time to help his younger brother up, he turned and slammed his fist against the button, closing the door. A yellow light flashed and the airlock lowered, closing with a loud thump. With two clicks it locked.

"Austin, Mason, go to the bridge and strap yourselves in."

"What's the bridge?" asked Austin as he pulled Mason to his feet.

The older twin began brushing himself off, looking very put off by Oliver's abrasive behavior. "It's where Dad flies—" Mason started.

There was no time. Oliver cut him off. "Tiffany I need you to load up the NavCom."

Tiffany scowled. "Why are we—?"

Oliver didn't hear the rest of her sentence. Their silhouettes faded as he charged down the dark corridor toward the engine room. His head was pounding from being hit with the tree branch. His stomach was in knots. He'd only been at the Academy for one year and hadn't flown anything as large as the *Phoenix*. But he had to show courage for his family.

1.3

Getaway

Tiffany waited in the copilot's seat. She tapped one of the three screens of the *Phoenix's* navigation console, known as the NavCom, and it came to life. One screen displayed a three-dimensional globe that represented their home planet of Tragiws. Tiffany swiped her fingers across the screen, and the globe expanded. She centered the screen on a small blue dot, which marked the *Phoenix's* location. A thin green line rotated around the blue icon like the hand on an old clock. With the line's every cycle, Tiffany saw glowing green dots—representing objects—moving closer to the *Phoenix*. If their parents were on the way, why would Oliver lock them out? Tiffany counted twelve dots. Who else was with them . . . or coming after them?

Her mind was still fuzzy with sleep. It wasn't thunder that had woken her, but exploding flares. Plus, Oliver was out of control. He had come crashing from the woods like a savage, bleeding and crazy. She looked at the middle screen of the NavCom, which showed the status of the *Phoenix's* systems. Engines were online. Reactors were powering up. The communications system was activated. All airlocks were sealed. Oliver was really going to launch the *Phoenix*—without their parents.

Tiffany glanced back at her brothers. They looked nervous sitting in their seats, all strapped in. And why shouldn't they be nervous? Had Oliver ever flown something as powerful as the *Phoenix*? Her parents, skilled pilots, had run into a myriad of problems flying even a small craft.

The last screen displayed route and destination information. The destination was a planet called Jahr des Eises, and her dad had already programmed the variables for the flight. That provided her some comfort.

The seconds ticked by. The dots moved closer. Then Oliver burst into the bridge. "Tiffany, are all the systems loaded?"

"Oliver! Where are—?"

"No questions!" Her brother scrambled into the pilot's chair and strapped in. "Soldiers are coming!"

"Soldiers!" Tiffany, Mason, and Austin shouted in varying tones of concern.

Oliver ignored them and tapped one of the pilot's consoles. With a few more taps, a thundering buzz filled the air. The overhead lights flickered as the engines drained power from the reactors. The *Phoenix* began to shake while the engines fought to produce enough thrust to lift its weight. Oliver gave a hard pull on the flight controls, and the nose of the ship rose slowly. The shaking grew more intense, and then all was dark.

Oliver brought the nose of the *Phoenix* down. The bridge glowed ominously each time the console screens flashed on and off.

"Oliver, what about Mom and Dad?" Tiffany cried.

Oliver was silent. Tiffany started at a bright blue flash. It lit the cabin, and a loud boom rang throughout the ship. More flares exploded outside. The *Phoenix* lurched forward as Oliver adjusted the vector of the thrusters. A scraping noise pierced the bridge as the tops of pines scratched the sleek, silver underside of the ship.

As the *Phoenix* gained altitude and speed, it slid smoothly into the cloudless night sky. But the peaceful travel lasted only a moment. Acceleration immobilized the kids in their seats as Oliver yanked the flight controls backward. The *Phoenix* vibrated, shuddered, and then shook violently, pointing straight up.

"A little longer," Oliver pushed the throttle forward with all his might. The *Phoenix* needed every ounce of thrust.

"My head's spinning," Mason whined from his seat in the second row.

Austin looked at his twin. "It feels like someone's tightening a rope around my chest."

Oliver tapped the screen to raise the ship's cabin pressure. A siren rang out.

Tiffany looked at the copilot's radar screen. "Star fighters!"

"How many are there?" Oliver asked.

"Two."

Oliver turned the controls hard to the right. The *Phoenix* rolled, and then dived. Tiffany gasped as her body was thrown sideways. She grasped the armrests of her seat. "What are you doing!"

"UTE!" Oliver stared forward with an iron grip on the controls.

"What's UTE?" asked Mason.

"Urgent Tactical Evasion," Oliver explained. "Hold on! I'm taking us into the canyon!"

"What?" yelled the twins.

A deep narrow chasm littered with outcroppings stretched through the woods behind their home. It was the same crevice Oliver had crossed to lose the soldiers.

"But it's too narrow for the *Phoenix*!" Mason exclaimed.

Oliver shook his head. "Not for me! I've flown several canyon missions."

"Weren't you in a simulator?" asked Austin.

"Where the worst consequence was 'Failure' flashing across the screen in red letters?" Mason added.

"Yes, but I only failed twice."

The twins looked at each other with mirrored expressions of anxiety.

As the *Phoenix* dived, the canyon walls swept up around the silver ship. Oliver yanked the controls left, spinning the *Phoenix* and narrowly missing a boulder. Tiffany gasped and gripped the armrests on her seat more tightly, her nails digging into the leather padding.

Only one of the fighters followed into the canyon. The other remained overhead.

"Why haven't they fired on us?" asked Austin.

"Because Mom and Dad are—" Suddenly Oliver twisted the controls, spinning the ship to avoid a large protruding rock.

"Oliver! The canyon is narrowing," Tiffany yelled.

"I know."

Oliver waited until the last moment and spun the *Phoenix* on its side, squeezing through the narrow gap. The pursuing pilot didn't have time to react, and the wings of his star fighter were ripped off.

Oliver looked at a screen showing the view behind the *Phoenix*. He saw the pilot eject while the star fighter plummeted into the river. A parachute opened and the pilot floated down to the water. He wouldn't be chasing them any longer.

"One down!"

Hovering above the canyon, the second fighter waited for the *Phoenix* to emerge.

"Oliver, the canyon ends up ahead!" Tiffany screamed. With every second, the solid rock face grew larger.

"There's an opening, and it's just large enough for the *Phoenix*," Oliver explained.

"What?" Tiffany turned to Oliver. "In there?"

"It's the only way to lose him."

As they approached the cave, Oliver slowed the *Phoenix*. "That pilot's going to have to decide between three options. Wait at the entrance of the cave, fly to the other side, or fly through behind us. I'm hoping he follows." Tiffany looked at

Oliver in disbelief. He had a plan, but would they die while carrying it out? Oliver dropped the *Phoenix's* altitude, almost grazing the water below. The fighter above dived. The chase was on!

A giant mouth, teeth bared, was open before them. Tiffany still couldn't believe her brother was really going for it. The black void swallowed the *Phoenix* smoothly. Tiffany switched on the ship's lights, illuminating the darkness and revealing hundreds of stalactites and stalagmites.

"Hold on, everyone!" Oliver ordered.

"Turn around!" Tiffany shouted.

"We can't. This is our best chance to lose him."

The hourglass-shaped formations approached. The *Phoenix* was yards away when Oliver jerked the controls hard right. The ship spun onto its back. The seat harnesses dug into the kids' shoulders, as gravity tried to smash them against the ceiling. The cabin pressure wasn't high enough. The *Phoenix* shuddered fiercely, and Oliver's sweaty hands slipped from the controls. There was a loud crash, and a siren rang out.

"What happened?" asked Tiffany.

Oliver cocked an eyebrow. "The left wing rubbed against a rock."

"Rubbed?" Tiffany accused. "That felt more like a direct hit, Oliver!"

She touched a red icon flashing on the console before her. Several alerts flashed across the screen: "Left wing impacted! Communication transponders offline! Stability sensors offline! Wing integrity compromised!"

"Oliver, there's a lot of damage!" Tiffany exclaimed.

"Can't—worry—now!" Oliver pulled hard on the controls, barely making it around a large bend in the cave. The ship shook violently as he tried to straighten it.

Her knuckles white, Tiffany's hands burned as she retightened her grip on the armrests. "What's wrong?"

"There's some variance in the controls."

"Seems like more than variance," called Mason from the second row.

Oliver hoped his brother was mistaken.

Tiffany watched the small fighter come around the corner. "He made it through."

"That's all right. I'm going to lose him up here."

"How?" asked Austin.

"We're approaching a cavern with several waterfalls."

"How do you know?" asked Tiffany.

"Dad brought me here once." Flying into an expansive cavern, Oliver pulled back on the controls and the *Phoenix* obeyed, slowing. He pointed to a waterfall pouring from a narrow crevice, high in the cavern wall. "There's our escape."

"That gap looks too narrow," called Mason.

"We aren't going in. We just need the waterfall." Oliver increased the *Phoenix's* thrust. Austin leaned forward in his seat, eagerly awaiting Oliver's next move. Mason closed his eyes and crossed his arms protectively over his chest.

"Here we go!"

"Where?" asked Tiffany.

"Up," Oliver answered.

"Up the waterfall?" Mason squawked.

"Awesome!" Austin cried, and pulled his harness straps tighter. Tiffany closed her eyes.

The nose of the ship brushed the falling water. Oliver pulled back the controls and angled it upward. Water plastered the windshield, and the *Phoenix's* speed dropped suddenly. Oliver moved the thrusters to full to fight the impact of the water. The *Phoenix* deflected the water into a spray, leaving a clear path for the smaller ship to follow. Oliver counted down quietly to himself until his pursuer was directly underneath.

With a swift pull on the controls, the *Phoenix* flew out of the falling water. The full force of the waterfall pounded the star fighter, sending it into a powerless downward spin. As it slammed into the pool below, water erupted into the air. The small glass canopy opened, and the pilot climbed out before the craft was swallowed by the water.

Tiffany and the twins broke into cheers and praised Oliver. The *Phoenix* circled the cavern once, and Oliver gave a wave to the soaked pilot below. Then he made a U-turn and headed back toward the cave entrance.

"Why are we going back?" asked Austin.

"If there are reinforcements, they'll probably try to cut us off on the other side."

A few minutes later, the *Phoenix* and all aboard were out of the cave and into the canyon.

"Let's get out of here!" Pulling back on the controls, Oliver took the silver star cruiser high into the sky. The *Phoenix* began to shake, fighting gravity's hold on it. Higher and higher it climbed into the midnight air, and the dark blue night sky slowly turned pure black. Millions of tiny lights twinkled ahead. And with a final shudder, the *Phoenix* broke free of Tragiws. Oliver instinctively activated the ship's artificial gravity.

Seemingly free from danger, Tiffany ferociously interrogated Oliver. "What's going on? Where are Mom and Dad?"

Frowning, Oliver looked her in the eyes and shook his head. "We aren't safe yet."

1.4

Hyper Flight

Tiffany scowled. "Safe from what? The soldiers?"

Oliver tried to deflect her questions. "Tiffany, bring up the coordinates for Dad and Mom's destination. They're probably preprogrammed."

"They are," she said, then rounded on him again. "Did you do something at the Academy?"

Oliver glared angrily. "No! They aren't federal soldiers."

"Who are they?" Tiffany shouted in frustration. He'd been acting like a hotshot ever since he returned from officer training.

"Please! We just need to get away from here," Oliver's voice cracked. Tiffany stopped her onslaught. What was going on? Not federal soldiers? She'd wait, but she'd get her answers.

The twins chattered excitedly behind them. "Mason—" Oliver cleared his throat. "—I need you and Austin to get Mom's journal. Tiffany, can you tell them where you left it?"

"It's in the research lab on the circle table," she said harshly. Her frustration with Oliver was impossible to contain.

Unfazed by his sister's attitude, Austin hopped out of his seat and disappeared through the doorway. Mason wobbled when he stood. "Whoa! My legs feel funny." Gripping the back of the chair, he shook his legs. He took a couple of steps and then ran for the library. "Hey, Aus. Are your legs tingly?" he shouted as he disappeared through the hatch.

"OK, they're gone," Tiffany said. "Will you tell me what's going on now?" Didn't Oliver understand how frightening it was not to know what was happening? She took a cleansing breath. "Oliver—"

"Tiffany, I will tell you once we're safe. I have to concentrate. I . . ." Oliver hesitated, "I've never done what we're about to do. I've never made a jump into hyper flight."

Tiffany instantly understood. Oliver was scared. He really didn't know what was happening. She had to let him concentrate and try to help. She trusted he would explain things later, but it was still hard not to be angry at the situation. Using every ounce of her will, she exhaled quickly and forcefully and asked, "Oliver, what can I do?"

"I need those coordinates," Oliver said.

"Right." Tiffany nodded her head. A single tap brought up the coordinates. A small green globe with swirling purple blotches appeared and rotated on the screen. Several statistics about the planet popped up next to the moving image, including a name.

"The destination is Jahr des Eises. Dad entered the flight plan yesterday at—" Tiffany looked at the screen "—three."

"That'll make this a lot easier, but do you know why we might be headed there?" Oliver asked.

"No, I don't," Tiffany said. She was curious. "I figured we'd be heading to Enerazan. After all, that's where the Archeos Alliance headquarters is. If Dad and Mom were headed to a dig site, they'd rendezvous with their colleagues at Archeos."

"This ship doesn't have any Archeos markings, so I don't think this expedition was being funded by them. I think Dad and Mom found something—something big."

"What makes you say that?" asked Tiffany.

"They've been withholding things from me. For example, they never mentioned the *Phoenix*. And this trip—usually I know where we're headed, who we're going with, and for how long. I suppose they shared all of that with you though," Oliver said.

Tiffany shook her head. "No, Oliver, they haven't told me anything. That's why I was so interested in their journal entries," she explained. "They haven't said much over the last nine months."

Oliver was skeptical of his sister. "So they haven't told you anything?"

"Nothing except for the usual, 'We're doing good. We're looking forward to seeing you soon.'"

Oliver exhaled. "Well, whoever attacked tonight must be the cause for their secrecy."

"Attacked?"

"Well not attacked, but broke into our house. That's why I took off. Mom and Dad ordered me to escape with you and the boys," Oliver explained. "But seeing as neither you nor I know anything of our parents' plans, I don't know where we're escaping to."

"Shouldn't we contact someone?" Tiffany asked. Certainly the authorities could help them, she thought.

"Who? We don't know these men or what they're capable of. Our ship isn't linked to Archeos, which makes me think we shouldn't contact them," Oliver said.

"So what do we do?"

"For now we head to the coordinates Dad programmed. He and Mom had a reason to go there. We'll have to piece it together."

Tiffany dragged the image of the revolving globe to a box on the screen labeled *primary display*. "I just sent you the coordinates."

Oliver moved the numbers to a flashing blue icon that would activate the hyper flight sequence.

"Please confirm the coordinates, 123.34 x, 342.30 y, 863.22 z, Jahr des Eises," a computerized voice repeated.

"Yes," Oliver responded nervously. He gave Tiffany a half smile.

"Hyper flight sequence engaged. Plotting course," said the computer.

Several applications popped up on the screen, displaying each step the flight computer was taking for the *Phoenix's* hyper flight.

"Tiffany, will you see if the twins have found anything?" Oliver's tone was friendlier, but he didn't look up from the screen. "We're going to go into hyper flight shortly, so have the twins come back. And hurry!"

"All right." Tiffany unstrapped herself and headed for the library.

Mason and Austin were busy searching the library's cabinets and shelves. "It's not here," Austin said, clipping a strap back into place.

"Keep looking. It has to be somewhere," Mason said. "Where was it that Tiffany said she left it?"

"I don't remember," Austin said, falling into one of the comfy chairs in the middle of the room. "Something circle, I think."

"Did you check the table?" Mason asked.

"Yeah, I'm looking at it right now."

"Well?" Mason turned around and saw Austin relaxing, his feet on the circle table. "Don't just sit there, help me!"

"I'm tired," Austin complained. "I was awoken from a deep sleep, and rather rudely I might add."

"Austin, we were just being chased by star fighters and Dad and Mom aren't with us. Something is very wrong!"

Austin got to his hands and knees and began to search the floor. "Are you worried?"

Mason paused, looking away from Austin. "No." The thought of his parents put a knot in his stomach, but now was not the time to be scared. "Oliver's got everything under control."

"Do you think our parents are dead?" asked Austin.

Mason froze. That his parents might be dead hadn't occurred to him. But before he could even consider it, Austin shouted, "I think I found it!"

Mason hurried over to his brother, who was using the table to pull himself up. With one look, he knew it was the journal. "That's it!"

The twins' mom used the e-journal for everything. Her extensive notes outlined past archeological digs and contained contact information and a myriad of other items. It was their parents' personal encyclopedia. If there was any tool that could help the kids, this was it. Austin smiled proudly and handed it to Mason, who pushed a button on its front. The device opened like a book, revealing two dark computer screens.

Austin leaned close to Mason in excitement. "Turn it on!"

"I don't see a switch anywhere."

"Maybe you tap the screen like the computers on the bridge," Austin suggested.

He should have thought of that. Mason tapped, but nothing happened.

"Hey, guys," Tiffany said as she entered the room.

"We found the e-journal!" Austin exclaimed, bouncing on his toes.

"But we can't figure it out," Mason admitted, and handed it to Tiffany.

She took the stylus and began tapping on the left screen. Once in the upper left corner, once in the lower right corner, and then twice more in the upper left corner. The journal's screens glowed to life. "Good job, boys, but we're getting ready to jump into hyper flight so we need to hurry back to the bridge. We'll look at this later," Tiffany said.

Wondering whether Oliver knew how to perform a hyper flight, Mason turned to Austin anxiously, but his twin was gone. "Where did—?" but Mason didn't need to finish his question. He could hear Austin shouting excitedly as he ran down the corridor and toward the bridge. "Are you ready, sis?" Mason hoped she'd tell him if she was scared, or if she had any new information from Oliver.

Instead, Tiffany grabbed Mrs. Wikk's tan canvas pack from the floor and took a quick look around the cabin. "Is everything secured?" she asked as she slid the journal into the pack.

"I think so," Mason responded.

"Then let's go."

Although disappointed at her shortness, Mason followed Tiffany to the bridge without any questions.

"Austin told me he found the journal," Oliver said as Tiffany and Mason entered the bridge. Austin was already strapped into his seat.

"Yes, he did." Tiffany took the copilot seat. Mason strapped his harnesses across his chest and looked at Austin, who was beaming.

"Everyone strapped in?" Oliver asked. Tiffany and the twins confirmed, just as a red strobe light began to flash.

"Confirm hyper flight sequence initialization. Projected course is clear," the computer stated. Oliver touched an icon that flashed the word *jump*. Instantly, large blue numbers appeared on the screens, starting a countdown. Oliver hoped he'd done everything right. If not there would be little left of them in a matter of seconds.

The computer spoke again. "Ten seconds to jump." The twins double-checked their harnesses, and Tiffany gripped her armrests. Oliver tapped the screen again, and titanium heat shields slid down to cover the three sections of the windshield. The shields were meant for entry to an atmosphere, but also protected the family against the intense blasts of radiation that often flared up during hyper flight.

"Eight seconds . . ."

"Hold on guys." Tiffany turned back to look at the twins.

"Six seconds . . ."

"All right; here we go." Oliver looked at the screen.

"Oliver, what are those red blips?" Tiffany asked.

"Other ships." Oliver thought of his parents, wondering whether they were on one of them.

"Five . . . four . . . three . . . two . . . one."

Instantly the kids were smashed against their seats. A whistling noise filled the cabin.

Austin covered his ears to block it out. The whistling ceased and the pressure slackened. The kids felt the invisible hold release them.

"Hyper flight stabilized," the computer informed them.

Austin exhaled as he slumped down in his seat, and then smiled at Mason, "What a rush." Mason nodded, bent over, and stroked back his shaggy hair. He looked like he was going to throw up.

For almost a minute, everyone was silent. The only noise was the soft hum of energy running through the thousands of wires overhead. Oliver sighed and looked at Tiffany and then the twins. He was finally ready to recount the awful truth.

1.5

Übel

So much had happened, and Oliver was ready to let it all out. He swiveled his chair to face his younger sister and brothers. Bits of the last hour flashed in Oliver's mind.

"Our parents have been taken!" Oliver blurted, more bluntly than he had wanted.

"Taken?" cried the three siblings. Their faces all turned pale with fear.

Mason sniffled. "Who took them?"

"Some men called the Übel," answered Oliver.

"The who?" asked Tiffany.

"The Übel. I've never heard of them," Oliver explained.

"Neither have I," said Tiffany.

"Where did they go?" asked Austin.

"I'm not sure. But they wanted to take us too," Oliver confessed.

"Well, wouldn't that have been better than being separated from Mom and Dad?" asked Mason.

Oliver's nostrils flared, but he caught himself. "These were bad men, and Dad and Mom ordered me to leave with you. Dad even tackled this captain guy to help me escape."

"So you were with them?" asked Tiffany.

"Not quite, I was hidden until the last minute."

"Are Mom and Dad all right?" asked Tiffany.

"I think so—I mean yes."

The questions were coming out slowly as if it pained them to speak.

"Let me start from the very beginning," Oliver said.

Tiffany and the twins nodded.

"I'd been waiting for Dad and Mom to return from the compound. They had gone back to lock up. But now I think they just needed a moment together to say goodbye to our home." Oliver stopped.

"Goodbye?" Tiffany asked.

"I don't know, but I get the feeling that we aren't going back."

Tiffany looked at him with curiosity.

"I got tired of waiting, and it was almost time to take off, so I headed back to see what was holding them up. I heard shouting as I neared home, and a large black shuttle was floating overhead like a thundercloud. Something was clearly wrong." Austin was hanging on Oliver's every word, almost falling out of his seat. Mason sat back completely still, his face pale. Tiffany's hand covered her mouth as she listened.

"I snuck into the garage and heard someone talking to Dad and Mom—the captain of the invasion. They called him Vedrik." Oliver cracked his knuckles. The thought of the man in black interrogating his parents in their own kitchen made his blood boil. "The captain had learned of Dad and Mom's recent discoveries."

"Anyone could have done that," Tiffany interrupted. "Mom and Dad publish their finds to the Archeos data network daily."

"Yes," Oliver continued, "but this guy knew things Dad and Mom hadn't told anyone."

"How do you know?" Tiffany asked.

"Vedrik knew about the book."

Tiffany stiffened. "What else did he know?"

"The captain claimed it was the missing link, the key to unlocking the path to some place. Apparently, most people believe it to be a myth. He said that his boss had come across an artifact with an inscription on it, something about living forever. I can't remember it. But this guy was strange; he'd lose control and then just snap out of it like nothing had happened. I couldn't tell whether he was crazy or just plain evil." Oliver shuddered as he recalled Vedrik's odd darkness. "It was shortly after this that he spotted me. Dad tried to stop him and bought me just enough time to escape." Oliver decided to leave out that his dad had received a nasty jolt from the captain's strange device. "I was chased through the woods, but I lost the soldiers at that old log. Sorry boys, but I destroyed your bridge. I had to push it into the ravine to escape."

Austin and Mason frowned. "That's all right. It doesn't sound like we'll be going back anyhow," Austin said. Mason nodded glumly in agreement.

"Can you tell us more about the Übel?" asked Tiffany.

"Not too much. The captain wore a silver patch on the side of his sleeve that had a skull and the word *Übel*."

"Pirates!" blurted Austin. "I bet they are. Taking hostages, pillaging artifacts, a skull insignia." Austin sat back with a smug look on his face.

Oliver shook his head. "No, I don't think so. These guys were more like a militia than some mangy pirates. They were clearly soldiers of some sort. I wish I could show you what I'm talking about."

A small whimper turned the boys' attention to their sister. Tears rolled down her face. "These men broke into our house and kidnapped our parents. How?"

Oliver looked at his sister. "That's what we have to figure out."

"I'll tell you how. They busted down the—" Austin began.

"Not how did they break in—how were they allowed to do it?" Oliver explained.

Austin scowled. "Why didn't you stop them? You're a cadet at the Academy. Why'd you run?"

Cheeks red, Oliver turned to Austin, his fists clenched. "I was about to attack the Captain—"

"But you didn't!" Austin interrupted accusingly.

Tiffany and Mason looked nervously at Oliver as if he were going to explode. Oliver's temper was boiling. Oliver cleared his throat. "I was waiting for the right moment."

"And it never came!" Austin shouted and raised his arms angrily. "If I'd been there, I'd have stopped the Captain and anybody else who stood in my way."

Oliver flew to his feet, about to demonstrate to Austin what he had wanted to do to Vedrik. Suddenly, he felt the soft grasp of his sister's hand on his arm. She was at his side, tears still rolling down her face. "Oliver, you did the right thing. Had you not been cautious, we'd all be captured," Tiffany admitted.

Oliver exhaled a long deep breath. His sister's words calmed him, but he feared that what Austin had said was true. He had waited too long. If he had just struck immediately, he could have caught the Captain off guard.

Austin was on his feet as well; whether to fight or to run, it was unclear. Oliver slowly sat back down. He needed to remain in control, and losing it on his eleven-year-old brother would destroy any authority he had.

"She's right. You did the best thing you could. What did you do after the Captain saw you?" Mason asked. Austin and Tiffany sat again to hear more.

Oliver stroked back his usually spiky hair, now matted with sweat, blood, dirt, and pine needles. "I used one of the sky scooter charging cables to climb through a skylight in the garage. Then I jumped off the back. There were soldiers everywhere." Oliver felt his forehead for scratches and winced at the fresh wounds. "I dove through some brambles and—"

"Let me put something on those," Tiffany interrupted. She grabbed a small medical kit from one of the many compartments and took out a swab and ointment. As she started to apply it, she said, "Continue."

"Two soldiers chased me until I lost them at the bridge. After that I was clear the rest of the way, except for a run-in with a tree." He winced as Tiffany swept the cotton tip across the wound. "When I got here, I knew we only had minutes before the soldiers would arrive."

Tiffany clapped her hand to her mouth.

"What is it?" asked Mason.

"As I was loading up the NavCom, green dots peppered the screen. There must have been a dozen soldiers on their way," Tiffany explained.

"That was close," admitted Mason.

"Couldn't we have used the ship to take out the soldiers?" asked Austin.

"This is an unarmed cruiser; at least I think it's unarmed. Honestly, I don't know much about the *Phoenix*; Dad and Mom didn't tell me about it. I'm just glad I was able to fly it."

"Well you did a good job," Austin praised him sheepishly.

This was an apology. Oliver knew his youngest brother; apologies weren't his specialty.

"Thanks," Oliver said. But Austin wouldn't look him in the eyes.

"So it's just us. We're all alone." Mason's voice faded as he looked down at the floor. Reality was setting in and everyone became quiet. The only noise was the hum of the lights and the low rumble of the engines for several minutes.

Tiffany stared at Oliver, shaking her head slowly. "I don't understand. Why didn't Mom and Dad tell us we were in danger?"

Mason looked like he might cry. "Are those men going to hurt them?" Oliver looked into his little brother's blue eyes, but before he could answer, Austin interrupted.

"Are they after us right now? How are we going to fight them off?"

Oliver turned to Austin. "I don't think they could have tracked us into hyper flight." He had to keep everyone calm. He didn't have the answers they wanted, and he didn't know what lay ahead. "We all need to try to relax."

"Relax? Our parents were taken by some mysterious organization and you want me to be calm? We don't even know where we're going!" Tiffany sighed and dropped her head into her lap. Her long brown hair closed like a curtain over her face.

Mason moved to the armrest of Tiffany's chair and placed his hand on her back. He was scared too, and looked to Oliver for support.

"The Übel obviously need Dad and Mom," Oliver said honestly. "Our parents are too valuable to them. Whatever it is they want, they believe they need our parents to get it."

Tiffany raised her head and pulled her hair back. Wiping her eyes, she looked at Mason appreciatively and patted his leg.

"We're going to be okay, and we're going to rescue Dad and Mom," Oliver declared. It was true, he could feel it. "We just need to figure out what they had planned, then we can head them off at their first location."

With these words of direction, the expressions on his siblings' faces changed. He'd thought of it that moment, but it wasn't a bad plan. They had to start somewhere.

Tiffany pointed to Oliver's head. "There are some pine needles in your hair."

To Oliver's surprise, a small smile appeared on her lips. Pulling several green needles from his head, he chuckled. "I forgot what it was like to have hair. This is the first time it's grown back since basic training." He scrubbed his head with his fingers to see if anything else might fall out. "I need a shower."

Tiffany bit her lower lip in thought. Oliver always knew when his sister was thinking deeply, which was often. She was the logical one, the smart one; she could solve most problems with the right information and a little bit of time. He knew he could rely on her to piece together their parents' unrealized plans. "I'm trying to remember what mom mentioned about the upcoming trip. Are you sure we can't contact Archeos?" Tiffany asked.

"I don't know," Oliver said.

"After all, they may know who did this, and they would have the resources to track down these soldiers," Tiffany explained.

Tiffany made sense, but Oliver didn't feel very comfortable with this idea. His parents always worked with Archeos, so it bothered him that this time was different. It seemed important, but he couldn't put his finger on why. Plus, saving his parents was within his ability. He'd just escaped soldiers, outflown two star fighters, and successfully launched into hyper flight.

"No, we can't contact the Alliance!" Mason shouted suddenly.

"Why not?" asked Tiffany.

"Because of what Oliver said about the captain knowing more than he should have." Mason stood up from the armrest. "You said that he knew about the book, and that information was not public. That means there is a mole somewhere in Archeos. We know that none of us have told anyone, but someone at Archeos might have."

"Do you really think they have someone on the inside?" Tiffany asked Oliver.

"Someone has to have been providing information to these soldiers—to Vedrik," Mason explained. "If we go to Archeos, we might be handing ourselves over to the Übel."

"Yes, but Mason, we need help. We're just kids." Tiffany looked to Oliver for support.

Oliver scoffed. "We aren't just kids. We're already on our way to Jahr des Eises." Besides, he wasn't a kid; he'd just turned seventeen and was a legal adult.

Tiffany sighed as she realized her mistake. "I didn't mean . . . I appreciate what you've done."

Oliver cleared his throat, and his voice came off deeper than usual. "Mason, that was great thinking about Vedrik." He smiled at his little brother and shook his head. "I should have made the connection. We could have walked into a trap if it wasn't for you. Good listening."

"That was very perceptive, Mason," Tiffany agreed. But even though Mason was probably right, she hated the idea of attempting a rescue without help.

Austin raised an eyebrow and looked a little confused at Mason's deduction. "I don't get it yet, but good job bro. So what now?"

Oliver nodded. It was time to claim his role, to cement his authority as their leader. "Everything has happened very quickly. I'm sure it's all as much a shock to you as it is to me," Oliver said solemnly. "It's going to take some time to digest it, but we have to act now if we want to rescue our parents. I'm the oldest and therefore responsible for you three. So for now, we're headed to Jahr des Eises." Tiffany looked at Oliver anxiously. Oliver shook his head. "Until we learn something that provides a better option, this is our plan. Right now, we have the advantage of surprise."

Mason backed toward his seat and sat down. "Maybe I was wrong with what I discovered."

Oliver shook his head. "No, I think you were absolutely right, and since we've agreed on a destination—"

"Ha," Tiffany scoffed. "Agreed?"

Oliver turned to her and scowled. "I'm sorry you don't agree, but Mason's right. This is our plan!" Oliver looked at his little brother, and Mason sunk lower in his chair, his blue eyes fearful. Oliver gave a half smile. "Well, I'm going to change into some clean clothes. Maybe I'll take a quick shower too."

"I'm going to get a snack," said Austin.

"How much time do we have?" Mason asked.

"About five hours," Oliver answered.

Shortly after Oliver and Austin disappeared into the corridor, Mason looked at Tiffany. "It was great how Oliver handled the escape and all, but I don't think we can rescue our parents. We need an adult. What happens if we get caught?"

"I don't know, but we should listen to Oliver," Tiffany answered to Mason's surprise, and even a little to her own. She'd been offended by Oliver's assertive behavior, but she knew the two of them needed to remain unified for the twins' sake. "If these men can just break into someone's home and take them without any worry that they'll be caught, they must be working for someone very powerful. We don't know what capabilities the Übel might have or who they are in contact with," Tiffany explained. "Besides, Oliver's learned a lot at the Academy. Let's give him a chance."

Mason nodded slowly. "If you say so, sis."

1.6

e-Journal

ustin finished his snack—a peanut butter and raspberry jam sandwich. Raspberry jam was a specialty of his family. His parents had discovered raspberry plants growing wild in some ruins several years ago. The berries' identity was discovered in a book found in one of the ancient houses. It contained a recipe for something called raspberry jam. His parents had taken a sprig from the bush and began growing their own in the greenhouse at home. They'd made a lot of jam, and Austin was happy to see the cupboards in the galley (the ship's kitchen) stocked with several jars. It was time to head back to the bridge, where Tiffany was monitoring the ship's progress.

He'd wiped his mouth with his sleeve, when Oliver stepped out of the lavatory. Oliver had put on grey pants and a blue hooded sweatshirt with the Federal Star Fleet Academy logo across the chest. He looked refreshed and very different from the dirty, sweaty, bloody teenager who had come screaming out of the woods and maniacally taken the silver star cruiser barreling through a canyon.

"Hey, Austin." He stood and waited for Austin to reach him. "You know, I think you were right. I should have acted immediately, maybe then we'd—"

"No," Austin interrupted. "I was wrong. We're free because of you." He knew he'd been out of line. "You're a really great pilot. The diving into the canyon, the speeding through the cave around those big ceiling-to-floor rocks, and then up the waterfall." Austin's face was wild with excitement. "You took out two fighters without using any weapons." Oliver smiled appreciatively, humbled by his younger brother's admiration. "It was all so quick I didn't have a chance to be scared," Austin continued, and then added in his toughest voice, "Not that I would have been scared. I was going to offer to fly the ship if you didn't think you could. But obviously you did. Maybe sometime you can show me how to fly like that?" Austin bent down to tie his shoe.

"Yeah, sure."

Austin glanced at Oliver hopefully. "Maybe tomorrow?"

"How about we wait until you're at least fourteen."

"But that's three years from now!"

"It takes time, Aus." Oliver laughed. "I promise I'll teach you someday." He pulled his brother up and put his arm around him.

Austin looked up at Oliver as they walked toward the bridge. "Do you think you can teach me to fly up a waterfall too? That was really cool."

"Sure, little buddy."

"Everything all right?" Tiffany asked, as Oliver and Austin entered the bridge.

"Yeah. Everything is as good as it can be considering we're hurtling through space with no parents, while being chased by evil pirates, I mean soldiers," Austin said sarcastically.

Tiffany gave a small laugh. "I meant between you two."

"Yeah, we're okay," Oliver said.

"So how much longer?" asked Austin.

"We'll be in hyper flight for at least four hours and thirty-one minutes. We should just try to rest while we can," Oliver suggested.

Tiffany opened her mom's e-journal and tapped the screen, causing it to light up. She selected the most recent entries for their last expedition and began reading quietly to herself.

Oliver was in the pilot's seat checking the status of the *Phoenix's* systems.

"Everything all right?" Tiffany asked.

"Yeah, so far so good. Everything seems to be running fine. I'm going to check the cargo manifest."

"I'm reading about Dad and Mom's recent expedition to Dabnis Castle." She looked at Oliver and then turned to the twins. "Would you guys like me to read it aloud?"

"How about we go to the galley to get some food, and Tiffany can read it there. I have to admit I'm a bit hungry," said Oliver. At that moment, his stomach growled loud enough for everyone to hear.

"All right," Tiffany agreed, getting up from her chair.

"Yeah, I'm hungry too," said Austin.

"Didn't you just eat something?" asked Tiffany.

"I'm a growing boy," Austin stated matter-of-factly.

Cabinets and counters lined three of the galley walls, interrupted only by a nanocook, cryostore, and thermaclean. The remaining wall had a video monitor as well as the door they'd entered. In the middle of the room was a long table with twelve swivel chairs around it.

Oliver got into the cryostore and pulled out a cold bottle of Energen, but then put it back. "I'll need to get some sleep eventually." He settled on a bottle of milk, and then placed a macaroni pack into the nanocook for ten seconds. Once the timer beeped, he grabbed a spork and took a seat at the head of the table. Mason opened the bottom drawer of the cryostore and took out a small bag of carrots. Austin searched through the cabinets and found a box of animal crackers. Excellent. Austin sat down with his prize. He opened the package and removed several animals. The legs of the crackers were first to go, followed by the heads.

Tiffany watched him curiously, observing the young male behavior as if in a laboratory. "Violent and oddly cruel," she remarked as if making a mental note.

Austin growled at her and stuffed three more cookies into his mouth. Oliver almost choked as he laughed at his little brothers' antics. Mason replied by sticking two carrots in his mouth to make fangs and growling back at Austin.

Tiffany raised her eyebrows. "Well then, now that we're all settled let me start from the top." Tiffany tapped the screen a couple times. "We are settled, right?"

The boys all nodded their heads, entertained by their sister's lack of amusement.

"OK, the last entries are titled "Dabnis Castle" and were created just fourteen days ago." Tiffany cleared her throat and began.

October 29th, 1600.

We made our first discovery today. Elliot was taking pictures in the courtyard of the castle. The stone floor of the courtyard resembled a pie cut into twelve slices. Large pillars stood at the outside end of each slice, each adorned with a single ruby. Each ruby was etched with its own unique symbol. Instead of removing these beautiful jewels, Elliot photographed them, moving from pillar to pillar.

As he took the picture of the last ruby, the ground began to shake. The twelve pillars began wobbling, and Elliot ran out of the courtyard to stand behind the surrounding hedge. One by one the pillars fell inward toward the center of the circular courtyard. The top mantle of each pillar smashed into the center of its corresponding slice of the stone pie, splitting it in half. The inner half of each slice slid backward into a trench, causing the center of the courtyard to separate and the point of each slice to rise skyward, revealing a hidden circular room underneath.

After some investigation, we realized that each time Elliot stepped on a slice of the pie to photograph a ruby he set off a trigger. When all twelve were activated, the pillars fell.

We found that each slice had been teetering on a stone wall and the impact from the pillar caused the stone to tilt into the trench that surrounded the room. The stone slices looked like petals on a half-open flower and the room was like the pistil.

Elliot called Rand, Jen, and me, and the four of us climbed down into the room. The grey stones that made up the walls of the room had become overgrown with thick green moss, which was now coated with a thin layer of dust from the collapse.

In the center of the circular room stood a full size statue of a man. The figure wore a robe and had a stern look on his face. A sword was sheathed on his side, while one arm was outstretched holding a small dark-green sphere. The sphere stood out because it was carved of jade, while the statue was of ordinary grey stone. An engraving rimmed the base of the statue. It read, "At life's highest point, you are going nowhere unless you see the symbol of truth among the trinity." I took a picture of the engraving on the statue, as the stone man was too large to take with us. We collected the rubies, now lying loose, and took the sphere back to the *Phoenix* for analysis.

The sphere was inscribed with the word *Evad,* which is the name of a planet we visited in October of 1599. It also was inscribed with two numbers, but we searched the database and neither of the numbers, 71.54 or 165.23, matched any of the three coordinates for Evad. We believe the numbers are the longitude and latitude of a place on Evad. We wanted to leave for Evad immediately, but decided the castle may have a few more secrets.

Tiffany stopped. "That's interesting. Why were they heading to Jahr des Eises, if Evad was where the clue led them?"

"They haven't found the book yet. Maybe they learn something more when they discover it," Oliver suggested.

"I agree; read the next entry," Mason asked. Tiffany continued.

October 31st, 1600.

We found another set of artifacts today. I was exploring the tallest of the eight castle towers in hope that it was what the inscription on the statue was referring to. However, as I peered out over the castle, I did not see anything significant that might represent truth. What I did find was an inscription on the stone mantle of the fireplace. The inscription read, "Light the way to the truth." I took a picture of it and thought how interesting it was that this engraving was over a fireplace.

In the fireplace was a metal frame to set logs in, but there were no logs to be seen. I noticed a small rope at the back of the hearth. As I examined it, I realized it was a fuse.

Upon lighting it, the flame sped up the back of the stone chimney. About five feet up, the fire raced out openings in each side of the chimney. As the flames followed a path along the middle of the wall, it ignited several other fuses. These fuses led straight to the ceiling. As each disappeared through small holes in the slate roof, I heard a creak and then the sound of something sliding down the slanted roof of the tower. I assumed the objects had fallen to the ground off the roof.

As I headed down the five-story spiral staircase, I contacted Elliot to have him meet me. As we walked around the exterior of the tower, we found twelve capsules with planks inside. The planks were of different lengths and each had its own unique symbol carved into it. I took pictures of the carvings and then packed the planks of wood away for further examination.

"Wait, I saw those on the cargo manifest." Oliver turned and tapped the screen, then swiped his finger across. "Here it is: Crate 8.23.1601-DC-B contains twelve capsules with planks. And 8.21.1601-DC-A contains the jade sphere and the rubies."

"So we have a bunch of the artifacts?" Austin asked.

"It seems so," said Oliver.

"I wonder if the artifacts are tools to unlock the next clue?" Tiffany asked.

"That might mean that the Übel needs us, or at least what we have, as much as they need our parents," exclaimed Mason.

"You might be right," Oliver said hopefully.

"Tiffany, read on," Austin said. He was clearly excited. "We still haven't gotten to the book."

"All right. The next entry."

November 5th, 1600.

We spent the last five days scouring the remaining eighty-three rooms of the castle. Elliot and I will have to depart in just a few days to pick Oliver up from the Academy* and Tiffany, Mason, and Austin up from Bewaldeter. But today was the last day we would need. We discovered what might be the most significant clue to the existence of Ursprung ever found.

"Here we go!" shouted Austin.

Tiffany cleared her throat, "As I was saying,"

When we made this discovery, Elliot was in an old library empty of books. The library stretched three stories high with balconies lining the second and third floors. It had large stone pillars supporting the domed ceiling above and long windows tucked between the empty bookcases. A faded painting of a solar map adorned the ceiling, so Elliot climbed to the third floor to get a picture. After he was done, he surveyed the library from the balcony, and to his amazement, the tiles of the floor created a large mosaic of an open book. Several words crossed its pages, "as the sun grows dark, the light of the son can be found."

Elliot contacted me to let me know about his find and that he was going to continue looking around. An hour passed and I still hadn't heard from him, so I tried reaching him on his mTalk but didn't get an answer. We looked for Elliot using the e-journal's tracking application. We were directly where his beacon showed he should be, but he wasn't there. There were no upper floors at our location, so we knew he must be below us. Upon entering the library, we noticed one of the bookshelves had been moved. Behind it was an entrance to a passageway. Rand called for Elliot, but no response came.

I opened my journal and loaded the tracking program again. The signal from Elliot's mTalk was still faint and coming from somewhere ahead. Rand lit the tunnel with his mTalk, but upon stepping into the tunnel, he fell to the ground and slid away into the darkness. His yell echoed up as he descended, but faded quickly. His tracking signal rapidly spiraled away from us. Jen immediately attached a rope to a pillar right outside the opening and locked it on to her utility belt. With a brave smile, she slid away into the darkness.

Elliot later described to me what was at the bottom of the slide. He had found a stone tunnel filled waist deep with water, and after wading several hundred yards to the end, he came to a staircase that led up to an arched opening. He walked up the stairs and discovered a large domed room made of black marble.

In the center of the room stood a single pedestal with a crimson leather book set on it. The book looked to be in excellent condition. Somehow it'd been preserved after all this time. He walked over to the book and waited a moment wondering if it was booby-trapped. As he analyzed the pedestal and the room, he heard Rand and Jen coming down the tunnel behind him. He walked back down the stairs and waved for them to come.

When they entered the room, Jen used her mTalk to take a video of it.

"Let's watch it," Austin interrupted.

Tiffany located where the images and video from the expedition were stored. "Oliver, is there a way to play it on the monitor over there?" she asked, carefully matching up the video with the entry date. The streaming preview popped up on the screen.

"Sure, search the network for galley display."

"Oh, I see. That was easy. Sent."

"Monitor on," Oliver said. The screen came to life and an image appeared. They could see only the small section of wall that the mTalk's built-in light illuminated. Tiffany tapped the screen and the video began. The camera panned upward and the kids gasped as they saw nasty-looking gargoyles sitting on perches. The camera continued to move around when something white abruptly flew past. They heard a scream and watched as Jen tried to find the white blur. Then they heard their dad's voice.

"What'd you see, Jen."

"I don't know. Probably nothing."

The video panned down, and they saw their dad and Rand looking over the pedestal that held the book. The kids smiled at the sight of their dad. Jen surveyed the entire room, and they could see that it was very high, but no more than ten yards in diameter. The camera shot left again and they heard a distinct squeaking noise. Jen zoomed the camera in on one of the gargoyles. It was a large lion with wings, its mouth open in a roar. A sound that could only be described as a tornado began to echo off the walls overhead. The squeaking noise became more prevalent as well, nearly matching the tremendous drone.

"What is that?" Rand asked.

"I don't know, but I doubt it's good. Let's grab the book and get out of here," replied their dad. No sooner had the words left his mouth when a torrent of small albino bats flew from the mouths of the gargoyles.

"Run!" yelled Rand.

The camera swept down. Elliot grabbed the book from the pedestal and waved Jen toward the door. She aimed the camera backward as she ran, and the kids watched as thousands of bats filled the room. They flew in a circle, creating what looked like a snowy cyclone. The camera turned forward again and they saw Rand leading the way, water up to his waist. Jen turned back, and they watched as their dad lit a flare and threw it onto the staircase leading up to the room. It rolled to a rest under the arched opening and smoke poured from it. Several bats had already zoomed into the tunnel and were now diving at their dad, Rand, and Jen.

Suddenly the video went black.

"Is Dad okay?" asked Mason.

Austin bumped his twin. "Of course he is. That was weeks ago."

"I'm skipping to where mom describes what we just saw." Tiffany scrolled down a little ways to find the video description. Oliver went to the cabinet and grabbed a red apple.

Several of the bats flew into the tunnel as if seeking their prey. Elliot, Rand, and Jen were able to knock a few of the bats into the water, but the rest flew up the spiral tunnel. At the bottom of the tunnel Elliot, Rand, and Jen used the rope to ascend to the library. Upon reaching me at the top, they were out of breath.

I didn't know what was happening, except that several bats had flown out of the once-hidden passage and were flying in circles high above me. When Elliot appeared at the exit from the tunnel, he handed me the book and told me to run. The four of us had barely left the library when a stream of the albino bats burst from the opening. The bats filled the library and spilled out into the hall, flying erratically.

Once inside the *Phoenix*, we sealed the airlock and watched as the bats poured from the castle. There were tens of thousands of them. The castle soon disappeared behind a solid wall of white. Now that we were safely in the *Phoenix*, my thoughts turned to the leather-bound book that I held in my hands.

"And that's where the entry ends," Tiffany said. Silence blanketed the galley for a moment. Austin sat elbows on knees, hands on cheeks, while Mason stared at the wall.

Oliver set down the core of his apple. "Well, maybe we should change course for Evad. I didn't hear anything about Jahr des Eises."

"Me either, and if the Übel are taking Dad and Mom to Evad we need to be there!" Austin exclaimed, slamming his fist against the table.

Tiffany nodded. "That's true, but there has to be a reason Dad and Mom were headed to Jahr des Eises first. And whatever the reason, it may provide us with some help."

Austin shook his head. "We don't want to miss them. If they find what they're looking for, a clue or something, they might move on and leave no trace!"

"Let me do a search on Jahr des Eises first." Tiffany activated the journal's search function.

Austin sighed. "All right." He was sure that the discoveries at Dabnis Castle were the key, and just as Vedrik said, the book was the proof.

"This shouldn't take long to do."

Austin turned and whispered to Mason. "It was weird to hear Mom refer to Dad as Elliot. I couldn't figure out who she was talking about and then I realized it was Dad."

Mason smiled and sat back in his chair. "I guess Mom doesn't call Dad 'Dad.' She calls him other stuff."

Austin smirked at him. "Like snookums."

Mason made a disgusted face. "Yeah." They laughed, and for a moment things felt normal.

Oliver gritted his teeth. "That book is the key to all of this. I should have charged in there and freed Dad and Mom."

"No, you did the right thing." Tiffany looked at Oliver. "Don't doubt yourself."

Austin nodded his head. "Yeah, without you, we'd be in a dungeon somewhere."

Everyone stared at Oliver, and he smiled at their gratitude. "That might be true. But I'd give anything to know what was in that book."

"A treasure map!" Austin guessed excitedly.

Tiffany smiled at him. "Doubtful, Mom and Dad were more than treasure hunters. Whatever they found, it was likely more valuable."

"Valuable enough to make them pack enough supplies to live for a year or more," Oliver interjected.

"What do you mean?" asked Tiffany.

"Look at this." Oliver stepped to the monitor and brought up the main screen for the *Phoenix's* computer system. He touched his finger on an icon resembling a crate, and the ship's inventory log loaded to the display. The cargo manifest listed forty containers of food and forty of water, enough to last the entire family for a year or more. There were building supplies, solar panels, a wind turbine, and a wide variety of seeds and bulbs. Only two of the family's four sky scooters were listed, as the other two hadn't been checked in and were abandoned at the compound. The small submersible, *Deep Blue*, was also listed. There was enough equipment to set up a base camp for a year-long dig. "I was only supposed to be home for two months, but it appears Dad and Mom weren't planning on me returning to the Academy. The book they'd found must have given them a solid reason to go on an extensive expedition."

"They never mentioned . . ." Tiffany's voice faded.

"So really we weren't going back to school," Austin interrupted incredulously.

Oliver shook his head. "I don't think so."

"Vedrik mentioned knowing of Dad and Mom's recent discoveries." Tiffany furrowed her eyebrows. "Do you think they knew they were being tracked?"

"Dad had said they'd hoped it'd be a few more days before Vedrik arrived," Oliver said. "I'm sure they knew they were in danger."

"So how are we going to rescue them?" Mason asked.

Austin's eyes lit up. "We should wait high in the trees and ambush the soldiers when they walk under us."

Mason turned to Austin. "Yeah, I'll drop right onto their backs!"

Oliver smiled appreciatively. "Although I love your enthusiasm, I don't think a frontal assault would be very successful."

Austin's hands flew up. "No! We're going to wait and surprise them. That's why we'll be in the trees. Just like you said, 'surprise is our greatest advantage,' " he said, mimicking Oliver's voice.

Oliver laughed. "Okay, but even if we surprise them, our numbers will still matter."

Mason patted Austin's arm. "I liked the tree idea."

"I liked the idea too." Oliver smiled at the twins. "Keep sharing your ideas. The more we brainstorm the better our plan will be."

Oliver yawned, which drew yawns from his siblings. He stood up, stretching his arms. "I think it'd be good for everyone to get a couple hours' sleep while the ship cruises."

"That's a great idea," Tiffany agreed.

Austin walked over to Oliver. "Do you want me to watch the ship?"

Oliver ruffled his youngest brother's hair. "No Aus. Thanks, but the ship will be fine. If anything happens my mTalk will alert me." He noticed Austin's disappointment. "Besides, you need to be rested if we're going to take on the Übel!" Austin smiled as his excitement returned.

Tiffany rolled her eyes at Oliver, but smiled. "All right, let's all get some rest."

"I'll set the alarm for two hours. But you can sleep longer if you'd like." Oliver tapped his mTalk and the young Wikks headed for their cabins.

1.7

Sky Scooter

Tiffany sat up and stretched her arms. She looked at the clock on the wall. Six! Four hours she'd overslept. Why hadn't Oliver woken her? She scrambled out of her bed. Her feet found a pair of slippers. Maybe the others weren't awake? What if there was a problem? She pulled her long brown hair into a ponytail and ran for the bridge.

Austin was looking over the shoulder of Mason, who was sitting in the captain's chair. Oliver was seated at the NavCom, tapping the left screen. The heat shields were open. Millions of tiny lights sprinkled the deep black expanse. They'd apparently come out of hyper flight.

"Hey, Tiff," Oliver said at the sound of her footsteps.

"Why didn't you wake me?"

"You needed sleep. We all did." He turned the chair to face her. "I was checking Mom's journal and found some information about Jahr des Eises. Does the name Phelan O'Farrell mean anything to you?"

Tiffany nodded. "He practically funded all of Dad and Mom's last five digs."

"You're right, he did, and he was the one who gave them this ship. He happens to live on Jahr des Eises." Oliver tapped an icon and the small green globe with purple swirling spots appeared on the screen. Tiffany walked over and stood behind Oliver to look at the screen. "I've charted a landing spot in the woods outside Brighton. No need to draw attention to four kids flying around in a star cruiser alone," Oliver said anxiously.

"So we're not going to land at the star port?" Tiffany asked.

"Nope. I was hoping to rendezvous with Phelan near one of the moons. But then I tried contacting him—"

Tiffany interrupted. "Mr. O'Farrell, you mean?"

"Mr. O'Farrell," Oliver corrected himself with an air of annoyance. "I remembered the alert from when the *Phoenix* brushed the side of the cavern."

Tiffany frowned. Brushed indeed.

"The communication equipment is down, so I can't contact him. The radar didn't pick up any federal space stations in the near vicinity, so we shouldn't have any problems landing," Oliver said promptly. "Once we've landed, I'll try using one of the sky scooters' radios. Besides, we need to find parts to fix the *Phoenix's* communication transponders."

"How will we pay for that?" asked Tiffany.

"Dad and Mom left their credit token in their cabin. We have enough to cover the part." Oliver held out a two-inch silver card.

Reaching down, Tiffany took it. The little card had five buttons and a small screen. "345,000 credits!" she exclaimed.

Oliver nodded. "They must have known they were being watched for a long time. I think they let me go to the Academy to avoid suspicion."

"You're probably right. Not attending the Academy after being offered a full scholarship would have raised some eyebrows," Tiffany said.

"Whatever was in that book led them to believe they wouldn't be returning this time." Oliver looked out toward the approaching planet. "Hopefully, we'll have some answers soon. The NavCom says we'll be landing in twenty-three minutes."

"Do you think stopping on Jahr des Eises will keep us from finding Dad and Mom on Evad?" Austin asked.

"I don't know, but probably not," Oliver stated bluntly as he handed Tiffany their mom's journal. "It took several days to find the book; it'll likely take several more to find the next clue." Tiffany agreed. Archeology was difficult; discoveries usually came only after months on site and lots of hard research.

"Mason, I need you to go make sure that all the supplies are securely tied down in the cargo bay because they may have shifted during the flight through the canyon. The *Phoenix* wasn't properly pressurized at the time. Austin, you check and make sure that the sky scooters are fully charged. If not, hook them up for charging."

"Why does Austin get to work with the scooters? I want to," Mason whined.

"Next time you can," Oliver promised. Mason got up from the pilot's chair and gloomily walked toward the corridor. Austin followed behind him, smiling triumphantly.

Oliver got up and crossed to the pilot's chair, and Tiffany took his seat and started reading. After several notes on the establishment of the two towns and a bitter dispute with Mudo and the Federation, she came across a disturbing entry about the weather.

"We may have a slight problem. What is Jahr des Eises's current planetary order from the sun, and is it heading toward or away?"

"Why?" asked Oliver.

"I came across an entry about Jahr des Eises that could mean bad news."

"Uh, let's see." Oliver looked down at the NavCom. "It's the twelfth planet from the sun on its apogee."

Tiffany shook her head. "That's not good. Right here Mom wrote 'when Jahr des Eises passes the planet Vor Eis, becoming the thirteenth planet, an entire year of ice ensues.' How long until Jahr des Eises surpasses Vor Eis?"

"Four days!"

"Apparently Dad and Mom were almost caught in a blizzard. Some sort of atmospheric storm kicks off and the planet's temperature drops rapidly. Within days the planet is covered in ice. Sometimes the leaves don't even fall off the trees; they just freeze to the branches, like yellow, orange, and red icicles."

"Great! Does it say exactly how long it takes to freeze after it becomes the thirteenth planet?"

Tiffany shook her head. A minute passed with neither speaking. "A prior entry noted that the town of Brighton is covered by a large dome. Brighton's people are well protected, and its entrance is locked down once the temperature hits negative fifteen degrees," Tiffany said nervously. "The other city, Mudo, is not protected and is somewhat run down. Mom refers to it as an outpost."

"Does it say which city Mr. O'Farrell lives in?"

"Let me check his profile." She tapped the screen and began reading. "He lives in Brighton."

"Well, that's good."

"Yeah, that way we don't have to go to the outpost."

"Is there more information about Mr. O'Farrell?" Oliver asked.

"Yes, a few details, but not a whole lot," Tiffany sighed. "Do you think we should tell Austin and Mason about the weather?"

"No, it'll only frighten them," Oliver said. "Speaking of—" Oliver looked toward the door. "Will you go get them if they aren't back in ten minutes? I need to make final preparations. I don't want to begin landing until they're seated and strapped in."

"All right, I will."

"Meanwhile, can you see if there is anything about Evad in the journal?"

"Yeah, one second." Tiffany tapped *Evad* on the journal's screen and scanned the information that came up.

"Oliver, there's a lot of information here. It's in the Rel Krev system. It's one of seventeen small planets, but it's the only habitable one. The planet is covered in lush green tropical plants, some of which can be deadly." Her face tightened nervously. "The atmosphere is breathable, but hot and humid. There are also many wild animals. Mom wrote that she assumes the animals were at one point under the control of whomever lived there. Now they run free. She lists several animals and then at the end makes an interesting note:

> As a little girl, I had heard fantasy stories of tall spotted animals with necks that reached into the trees, but I had been told they had lived long ago on a planet far away and long forgotten. They had apparently perished with Ursprung during the Exodus. As we flew over the trees on our way home from our dig, I spotted a long neck bobbing through the tops of the trees. Although I couldn't confirm that it was indeed the animal talked about in the story, it had a long neck covered in large black-brown spots and pale orange skin. By the time Elliot had flown back around, the creature had disappeared. We didn't have time to search for the animal, but someday I hope to return to Evad to find it.

Tiffany turned to Oliver. "What do you think it is?"

Oliver shrugged and stayed focused on the screen in front of him.

Trees were flying past Austin. He leaned left to avoid a branch, and then ducked under another. "Zoom, Zoooooom!" he cried as the scooter hurled through the forest.

"Austin, quit pretending and plug the sky scooters in," Mason sneered.

Austin hadn't left the *Phoenix's* cargo bay; his imagination had. "Mind your own business. Have you finished checking all the crate straps?"

Mason tugged on a nearby tether. "All done!" Running over to the other sky scooter, he slung his leg over and straddled the small craft.

"Get off that, Mason!" Austin commanded. "I'm in charge of the sky scooters!"

Mason leaned into an imaginary turn. "I'm all done," he said as he shifted in the seat. "You, on the other hand, haven't plugged either of the scooters in." Mason smirked at his brother. "This one is definitely low." He tossed back his shaggy bangs and then leaned forward as he imagined his scooter accelerating.

Austin hopped off his scooter, clamped the charging cable into the outlet, and hurried toward Mason. "Get off; I need to plug it in." He pushed his twin in the side.

"No!"

"Get off now!"

"Just plug it in!"

Austin shoved harder. "Get—OFF!"

Mason reached out as his balance vanished. His fingers found his twin's unruly hair.

"Yeow!" shouted Austin. The twins fell hard to the floor. A second later, they were brawling. Too distracted to hear anything beyond their insults to each other, Mason and Austin didn't hear the scooter crashing to the ground. Austin had Mason's hair, and Mason had Austin's shirt collar. They rolled back and forth, until they heard Austin's collar rip. He pulled away from his twin. It was one of his favorite shirts. He pulled the torn rag over his head and tossed it to the side.

"You'll pay for that." Mason didn't have time to react as Austin dived at him and pinned him to the floor. Then he was in a headlock with one leg wedged against his chest.

"Austin, you're hurting me."

His brother only grunted and pressed harder.

"Austin!" screamed Tiffany. Shocked at her arrival, Austin fell backwards. Mason scurried away, his lip bleeding. The scene was appalling. Remnants of Austin's shirt were on the floor, his collarbone scratched. Mason's lip was bleeding, and the left knee of his pants was torn. But that wasn't the worst part.

Lying on its side, wing cracked, was one of the sky scooters. The scooter had fallen over. A long tear had nearly separated the wing from the craft's body. The rudder was also bent, and the windshield was cracked. Austin couldn't look his sister in the eye, and he didn't want to. The glimpse he caught of her was terrifying. He'd never seen her so angry.

"What are you guys thinking? Oliver gives you each one job, and you act like baboons." Her eyes burned with anger. "You two, get to the bridge right now. Austin, put your shirt on." She stormed away.

Austin didn't want to think about what awaited him and Mason on the bridge. He looked at his twin and almost felt bad about Mason's bloody lip, but Mason had started it, interfering like he did. If he'd never climbed on the scooter, it would never have fallen over.

On his feet first, Mason grabbed Austin's shirt and attempted to help his twin up.

"Yeah, right," Austin blurted.

"Whatever." Mason tossed the clothing aside, ran up the stairs, and disappeared into the corridor. Austin looked around. He crossed to the crumpled scooter. It was no use; he couldn't lift it on his own. He'd have to secure it right there. With an extra tether stretched across its body, and a chain slung around its tail, he hoped it wouldn't get damaged any further. What a mess he was in. His shirt lay crumpled on the ground. He picked it up and unfurled it. His dad had given it to him just yesterday. Across the chest was the phrase, "I am the adventure." It was perfect, and it was the last thing his dad had given him. Now it was unusable. Austin wadded it back up and angrily tossed it across the room. Twins. What a joke! He and Mason couldn't be more different. Stomping up the stairs, Austin promised to seek revenge when the time was right. He'd ruin something important to Mason.

He got a new shirt from his cabin and headed to face his punishment. As he neared the bridge, he heard something behind him. It was Mason—the coward had been waiting for him. He couldn't face Oliver and Tiffany's combined wrath alone.

"Chicken," he accused when Mason approached. Mason glared and shook his head, but said nothing. Entering the bridge, they saw their older brother standing motionless, sternly staring at them. Tiffany stood at his side; she had reported everything.

Oliver's nostrils flared. "If you were at the Academy, you'd be given cleaning detail and be sentenced to strenuous physical training." He paused, his face sad. "But since I'm about to attempt my first real landing, I can't think about your punishment right now."

Tiffany stepped forward. "You guys might be only eleven, but this is ridiculous. We all have to step up if we're going to ever see Mom and Dad again."

"Tiffany's right. She and I are still teenagers, but that can't be an excuse. For now, get in your seats. We'll be landing soon. If we survive, we'll worry about your punishment."

As his siblings got ready to land, Austin crinkled his nose and glared in their direction. Who did they think they were? They weren't his parents. They were his brother and sister. Who were they to give out punishments? He sort of wished he were on good terms with Mason, so he could get his agreement. But as he surveyed his twin, it was obvious Tiffany's words had cut him deeply. Mason's face was in his hands, and Austin could hear him sobbing. Austin shrugged it off, but his twin was just too weak. Even though he was the younger, Austin knew he was on his own.

Tiffany started talking to Oliver, and Austin tuned in on their conversation.

"Oliver, you really need to concentrate. Let go of the twins' foolish behavior. Just before we heard the crash, I read something else," Tiffany said, her voice serious.

"Like I don't know that," he snapped. The edge in his voice carried obvious stress. "What'd you read?"

Tiffany cleared her throat.

As the atmosphere gets colder on Jahr des Eises, a dangerous weather event occurs. A dense cloud layer forms near the planet's surface trapping warm air beneath, while the air above grows colder as the planet moves farther from the sun. The danger comes when a second layer of cloud forms above the lower layer. Kinetic energy builds up and discharges in the form of lighting. When the lightning strikes the lower layer, columns of warm air rocket upward at nearly a thousand miles per hour. The resulting gaps in the surface allow the trapped, warm air to escape, and the temperatures on the planet plummet. Within a matter of days, ice and snow will cover the surface.

"I thought you would want to know."

Oliver nodded. "Thanks," he said—not sarcastically this time, but sincerely. "This is going to be tough enough without surprises."

Austin felt a twinge of guilt for his behavior, but it was momentary and quickly gave way to anger. Oliver and Tiffany were acting all responsible, but he knew them better than that. Just a day after returning they'd both gotten in trouble for not getting their chores done when asked. No, Austin wasn't about to take orders, much less punishments, from the two of them.

1.8

Jahr des Eises

"It's time." Oliver tried to prepare himself for whatever they might encounter on the descent.

The computer spoke. "Commencing entry in fifteen seconds." The three protective sheets of titanium slid over the windows. "Bridge heat shields locked. Ten . . . nine . . . eight . . . seven . . ."

"Hold on!" Oliver shouted.

"Five . . . four . . . three . . . two . . . one."

The *Phoenix* shuddered, twisted violently, and dropped suddenly. The entry had been very quick.

A feeling of weightlessness took over. If not for the harnesses, the Wikks would have floated up to the ceiling. Tiffany's ponytail floated over her head. Oliver tapped the screen and the titanium heat shields slid away, revealing a purple haze. The sun glinted off the tops of radiantly glowing clouds.

Numbers indicating their altitude streamed across the bottom of the screen as they plummeted toward the surface. Oliver pulled back on the controls and adjusted the thrusters. The numbers slowed, and the *Phoenix* pulled out of its dive. They felt the effects of gravity once more, and Oliver quickly adjusted the ship's internal pressure. Tiffany exhaled and readjusted her ponytail band. Mason looked at his twin, who started undoing his harness. He put his hand on Austin's strap. "Not yet! We haven't landed." Austin pushed his brother's hand away, annoyed.

Oliver steered the *Phoenix* into the purple clouds that hid the surface of Jahr des Eises, and all went dark. Occasionally a blue flash illuminated the misty atmosphere around them, revealing wisps of purple. Soon they were underneath the top layer of clouds, and a second layer of pink clouds was revealed below. A flash of lightning flowed like blue liquid from the purple clouds to the pink ones. At the spot where the lightning struck, a plume of pinkish-purple vapor blasted upward with deadly force.

"Updrafts!" Tiffany shrieked.

Oliver frowned. "Don't worry, I've got this."

"I wish our parents were here!" said Mason.

"Me too," agreed Austin as he started to strap himself back in. But it was too late. Before he could lock his harness in place, the nose of the *Phoenix* whipped upward, throwing the ship into a somersault and Austin's body toward the ceiling.

A siren blared. Mason reached out and grabbed his twin's pant leg. Austin's body jerked and fell to the floor. He groaned in agony on impact. Turning around, Tiffany saw Mason gripping Austin, who was sprawled across the floor. Austin's body floated upward and then smashed back onto the floor with every rotation of the ship. Mason was losing his grip, his knuckles white as he tried to hold on.

"Grab the chair, Austin. I'm losing—" Mason cried.

Tiffany turned to Oliver. "Do something! Austin's not strapped in!"

"Don't let go!" Austin pleaded, as his body rose and then fell to the floor again.

Oliver gritted his teeth. "I'm trying." The controls were slick with sweat. He too was losing his grip. Several alerts suddenly flashed across the navigation console: "Artificial gravity system offline! Stability sensors offline! Internal pressure dangerously low! Ground clearance sensors offline! Oxygen level dropping!" The *Phoenix* was out of control, turning end over end and hurtling toward the planet below. There would be nothing left but an ashen crater if Oliver didn't do something soon.

Tiffany reached for Austin's leg, but he was beyond her grasp. Mason unfastened his harness, and holding tightly to his chair, he extended a leg to Austin. "Grab hold!" Austin reached, and Mason stretched to his limit while the ship continued to spin. Austin's arm was yanked away and Mason's legs flew upward. They groaned as their bodies slammed against the floor and seat. But in that moment, as their bodies remained still, Mason yelled, "Now!"

Austin extended his arm, grabbing Mason's pant leg. Struggling to pull their combined weight, Mason grunted as he wiggled himself into his seat and then pulled Austin up next to him. Mason strapped the harness across their laps and locked it in place. Relieved to be secured again, they relaxed for a moment, but the *Phoenix* was still spinning out of control and losing altitude.

Streaks of blue light rippled across the sky, and several more updrafts streamed past the silver ship. Everything became hazy again as they sunk into the layer of pink clouds. A burst of blue light flashed and thunder shook the ship. A moment later the ship burst into clear skies. Oliver watched the planet's surface rush up to meet them. They were seconds away from impact.

"Do something!" Tiffany screamed.

"I'm trying!" Oliver roared back. He kept adjusting the thrusters and shifting the flaps, hoping to find equilibrium. "Someone help me. Let us live," his mind begged. The *Phoenix's* spin slowed and the ship leveled, stopping horizontally over the treetops.

"You did it!" Austin shouted from the second row.

"Almost there." He wanted to activate the *Phoenix's* automated landing system, but a warning flashed across the screen, "improper data."

"Looks like I'll be landing this thing manually," Oliver said.

The planet's surface was blanketed by a dense, green forest spotted with orange and red, a sign that cold weather was coming. The forest stretched in every direction, except for a short range of blue mountains that reached up and disappeared into the pink clouds.

"There's an awful lot of light filtering through the holes in the clouds, and that means updrafts," Tiffany whispered to Oliver. "The forest could turn to ice overnight. We have to hurry."

He nodded in agreement. It was true, and it only heightened his anxiety. Flying low to avoid detection, Oliver guided the *Phoenix* to an area between Brighton and Mudo. As he neared the coordinates, he watched the terrain scanner for a suitable clearing. He found one area that was just large enough for the *Phoenix*. Everywhere else, the trees towered four hundred feet into the sky and were so densely grouped that he doubted any sun graced the forest floor.

He'd have to land with a perfect vertical descent to fit into the clearing, a maneuver that was difficult for even experienced pilots. A heavy gust of wind or any loss of concentration could cause him to shift right or left, and he could tear off one of the wings, which would result in a deadly spiral to the ground.

Oliver adjusted the thrusters, and the ship shook as it slowed to a standstill. The gap in the trees was almost directly below. Bingo! He was over the spot, dead center. With decreasing thrust, the ship sank lower and lower. Treetops in front of the *Phoenix* came into view. As the trunks rose around them, the ship was cast into shadow. Oliver lowered the landing gear, and the noise of the engines grew louder as their sound echoed off the trees. Only moments later and with a thud, the gear touched down on the forest floor. The *Phoenix* was safely on solid ground.

Oliver silenced the engines, and the reactors went into standby. "We're clear. You can unstrap yourselves." Taking a deep breath, he stretched his sore arms.

Mason and Tiffany cheered and praised Oliver, thankful to be safely on the ground.

"Great job, Oliver," Mason said. "I thought for a moment we were goners."

Oliver didn't want to admit it, but he'd thought so too. "Yeah, it was a bit hairy there for a moment."

"But at least you got us down safely," Tiffany added. "Those updrafts were something!"

A row of tall tree trunks stood before them so they could see little else. "So how far out in the woods are we?" Mason asked casually.

"I bet we're going to see all sorts of animals on our trip to the towns!" Austin piped up.

Oliver looked at Austin in surprise. Did he actually think he was going? After what the twins had done and how they'd acted? Besides, from what Tiffany said, the other scooter was wrecked and he certainly didn't have time to repair it. No, the twins would have to stay behind.

"Neither of you are going to town. You're staying here!" Oliver proclaimed.

"What?" cried the twins.

"What do you mean we aren't going?" Austin got to his feet. "You can't make us stay here! It's not fair!"

"Austin, sit down. You're not going," Oliver commanded. Austin glared at Oliver, but sat back down. "There isn't room on the remaining sky scooter."

"But Oliver, will they be safe?" asked Tiffany.

"They'll be fine. We'll lock the hatches and be in contact via our mTalks. If anything happens—" Oliver scowled at the twins and then nodded to Tiffany, "they can get a hold of us."

"Well, why can't I go and Tiffany stay behind?" asked Austin.

"Tiffany has better knowledge of our parents' work. Plus, she knows several languages, which may come in handy."

"I'm not sure knowing different languages will be that helpful," admitted Tiffany. "Brighton is part of the Federation. Are you sure the twins will be all right?"

"They will as long as they stay in the *Phoenix*." Oliver raised his eyebrows at the twins. "Which they are going to promise to do." Mason and Austin sunk low in their seats and remained silent. Oliver turned to Tiffany. "We need to contact Mr. O'Farrell and get the scooter ready and loaded."

"I'll help," Austin offered quietly, but when he stood, he stumbled back into his seat with a grimace. His knee had been bashed against the floor so many times that the skin had split open and blood soaked his pant leg.

Tiffany walked over to Austin and helped him up. "Let's get that bandaged." He didn't protest.

"Good, you take care of that and then meet me in the cargo bay," Oliver said. Austin hobbled along beside Tiffany as she guided him from the bridge.

1.9

Separated

As Mason and Oliver walked to the cargo bay, Mason felt an urge to explain about the broken scooter. "Oliver, I'm sorry about the scooter, but Austin pushed me."

"Enough of that," scolded Oliver. "We all need to take responsibility for ourselves." Mason looked at his feet. He wasn't expecting that, and it made him feel worse. He followed Oliver in silence thinking how unfair it was. It wasn't his fault. He'd finished his boring task while Austin had been the one goofing off. He's the one who'd messed up. Upon stepping onto the balcony over the cargo bay, Mason flinched. Oliver's expression turned grim at the sight of the crippled scooter. Mason wondered why he had volunteered to help.

Oliver said nothing and walked down the stairs to the hoist. He moved it into position over the remaining intact scooter. "Mason, open the large bay door. The code is 83, 85, 88, 89." His brother's voice was tense. Mason knew that it was taking great self-control to hold in his anger. Mason went to the control pad and selected the large cargo bay door, as opposed to the small hatch. As he typed in the numbers, he smiled, and for a moment the heavy mood in the room vanished. The numbers were the birth years of the four Wikk children from oldest to youngest. His parents liked adding little reminders of their kids to everyday situations. Mason really missed them. He wondered where they were and whether they were safe. His thoughts evaporated when the bay door slid open.

An eerie, forbidding forest lay before him. A wall of wide trunks hemmed him in on all sides and dense foliage cast black shadows over the clearing. It looked as if no human had ever ventured into these woods, and he certainly didn't want to. A siren rang, and Mason jumped. He turned to see Oliver using the hoist and winch to move the scooter out of the ship and into the clearing.

Mason shivered. He had the creepy feeling that they were being watched. He looked to Oliver to confirm his feeling, but instead his brother had already stepped back into the ship.

Oliver was rifling through one of the containers. He collected a tent, his and Tiffany's sleeping bags, several fireballs, and a few flares. Mason's throat tightened when he saw Oliver attaching a holster with a Zapp-it around his waist. This just confirmed how real the danger he felt was. "Mason, can you help me?" asked Oliver. Mason swallowed hard and ran inside. He was happy for an excuse to go back into the ship and be near his strong older brother.

They carried the supplies to the scooter and packed them into its small compartments. Whatever didn't fit was strapped to the rear of the craft.

"Mason, will you get some H_2O, soup canisters, and meal packets from the galley?"

"Sure, do you want an Energen?"

"Yeah, a couple wouldn't hurt."

Mason ran into the *Phoenix*, up the stairs, and toward the galley. He stopped at Tiffany's cabin and saw that she was still bandaging Austin's leg. He would normally feel bad, but this time Austin deserved it. He had pushed Mason off the scooter and gave him a bloody lip. Now Oliver and Tiffany were angry with Mason, and it was all Austin's fault.

"Hey! Have to be quick. I'm helping Oliver with the scooter." He watched Austin's expression go flat and was pleased. Usually he and Austin would be in step with each other, but something had changed between them. An unstated rivalry had begun.

In the galley, he quickly grabbed the needed supplies and shoved them into a cloth sack. As he ran back down the corridor, he saw Austin limping toward the stairs. He felt a twinge in his stomach. Sure, Austin could be mean and reckless sometimes, but he was his brother, his twin.

"Where's Tiffany?" Mason asked as he approached.

"She went to change out of her pajamas," Austin said dismally.

"Right. Well, I'd better hurry back."

It'd been a while since he'd heard Austin sound so sad. Mason felt weird but shook off the feeling and finished helping Oliver pack the supplies. Tiffany and Austin arrived a few minutes later.

"I really think it might be better if I stayed here," said Tiffany.

Mason smiled. "Sis, you'll be fine. Oliver will take excellent care of you. He got us here, didn't he?" He looked at Oliver. "How long will you be gone?"

"I'm not sure," admitted Oliver. "We have to rendezvous with Mr. O'Farrell and find several parts for the *Phoenix*. If we don't find the parts in Brighton we may have to go to the outpost of Mudo."

"But don't worry," consoled Tiffany. "It won't be too long."

Oliver reached into his pack and pulled out three mTalks. "I found these in one of the containers." He handed one each to Tiffany, Mason, and then Austin.

"Wow? You mean we each get one?" Mason asked.

"Mom and Dad were already planning to give them to you. They gave me mine early, so I could communicate with them as I finished prepping the ship while they went back to the compound," Oliver explained.

"A lot of good that did," Austin said.

"Austin, stop!" warned Tiffany. "Can you just quit it with the negativity for a minute?" Austin grunted and kicked a large acorn that sat on the forest floor.

"Put your mTalks on and don't take them off." He glared at the twins. "Tiffany and I will always have our mTalks on. You can track us from the computer on the bridge," Oliver explained. "Now if for some reason we can't find Mr. O'Farrell or get the parts in Brighton, we'll head for Mudo. In that case, it could be a day before we return. And . . ." Oliver hesitated. "If for some reason we don't return in four days, or our tracking signals stop, I want you to contact Archeos immediately."

Mason frowned. "Even though they might have a mole?"

"Yes. There are worse things out here," Oliver said. He smiled awkwardly at the twins, making it obvious he hadn't wanted to admit to the dangers of the forest. Oliver cleared his throat. "Lock the airlock behind us. The pass code is simple, 83, 85—"

"88, 89," finished Mason.

"Just stay in the ship," Oliver ordered.

Austin smiled at Mason mischievously. It took Mason by surprise because they were at odds, and he looked so glum just minutes ago.

Oliver reacted to Austin's smirk. "No, I mean it! Stay in the ship! The last thing we need is to come back and find you two gone, lost in the woods somewhere!" Oliver said fiercely. "I haven't forgotten about the scooter either, and when we get back we'll deal with your punishment."

Austin grunted. His face was red with fury. "That's it. You think you're some hotshot, well you're not!" Austin stormed back into the ship and out of sight. Tiffany and Mason looked at Oliver, waiting for him to go angrily after Austin. But instead he remained still and silent.

"I'll try to talk to him," Mason offered. "Even though we aren't on the best of terms."

"Thanks," said Oliver. "All right, Tiff, are you ready?"

"Yep."

Mason watched as they climbed onto the sky scooter and strapped in. "Got everything you need?" Mason asked.

"Yep, I think so," Tiffany said. "When are we going to contact Mr. O'Farrell?"

"I'm not getting a very strong signal. We'll try when we get a little closer to Brighton." Oliver looked up. "It's the trees."

Flipping a switch, Oliver brought the scooter to life. The small craft rose and leveled off a few feet in the air. The only sound was the low hum of the thrusters.

"Is there a path?" asked Mason as he looked around at the thick dark tree line.

"No, we'll have to take it slow until we come to either a road or a stream."

"Can't we go over the trees?" asked Tiffany.

"No, these scooters can't go more than twenty feet off the ground. They get very hard to control because of crosswinds." Oliver pointed up at the trees. They were so tall that only a sliver of clouds could be seen high above.

Tiffany gasped. "You see that? We're running out of time."

"Why are we running out of time?" Mason asked suspiciously. He looked up; the purple clouds seemed to be mixing with the pink clouds, but there wasn't anything particularly terrifying about that.

"Nothing for you to worry about. Just keep your brother inside." A shiver ran through her words.

Mason squinted curiously. What were they trying to cover up? First his parents had been hiding things, and now Oliver and Tiffany.

"Tiffany, do you have mom's journal?" interrupted Oliver.

"Yep. Right here." Tiffany patted the side of her shoulder bag.

"All right, let's go." Oliver turned his wrist, the scooter surged forward, and they disappeared into the dark woods, leaving Mason standing alone next to the open door of the *Phoenix*.

Now, to deal with Austin.

Reflection

ustin was sitting in the galley when Mason entered. An open box of sweet cherry pies sat on the table, and Austin was messing with his new mTalk.

Mason sat across from him. "Yum, I like these things. Where'd you find them?"

Austin sighed. "In the cabinet."

"Can I have one?"

"Yeah, I've already had two."

"Thanks."

The twins sat in silence while Mason ate. Once finished with his second pie, he stood up and brushed himself off. "Want to play chess?"

Austin shrugged. "Sure. I'll go get it." He slunk from the cabin, but when he returned he seemed to be in better spirits. He had the board, and also wore his canvas inventor's pouch. Mason smiled at his twin's love for tinkering. Maybe this meant his younger brother would be in a better mood. Or maybe it meant he was going to mess with things that he shouldn't, like the broken scooter.

Austin set the board on the table. "On," he said, and with that word virtual chess pieces glowed above the surface, each in its place. "Pirates," Austin added, and the figures changed from standard chess pieces to Federal Soldiers and Space Pirates. Each figure moved as it stood there, cleaning its weapon or surveying the enemy ahead. Austin looked up at Mason. "You go first!" Mason smiled again. That was a good sign, even if he did have to be the pirates.

The twins sat quietly for several minutes making their initial moves and taking each other's pawns. Occasionally a rook or bishop was lost in the fray. The board was balanced until Mason captured Austin's queen. He thrust his arms into the air and declared victory, "It's over!"

"I don't need her," argued Austin.

"Whatever—your move."

The mood grew increasingly tense. The twins continued to battle it out on the chessboard. Austin's soldiers dwindled. Soon only his king and two pawns remained.

"I told you the game was over," sneered Mason, leaning back in his chair. Austin's eyes narrowed, and he smiled mockingly. Suddenly, Austin turned off the virtual display, and the three-dimensional images vanished. Mason couldn't believe it! The game was over and he hadn't made his final strike. He sprang from his chair and plowed into Austin, knocking him to the floor. Pinning his twin, he glared down at him, breathing heavily. Mason felt a sharp pain in his side as Austin's knee struck his ribs and knocked him onto his back. Austin scrambled to his feet and ran for the corridor. Mason clambered up and went after him furiously. When he reached the stairs to the cargo bay, he saw Austin opening the airlock hatch leading outside.

"What are you doing?" squawked Mason.

Austin entered the code to the door, it opened, and he stepped outside. Reaching his arm inside, he pressed the keypad. A yellow warning light flashed and the titanium door slid shut, sealing Mason inside. Mason slid down the railing and ran for the airlock. He dashed the code in, opening the forbidden door. The shadowy forest filled the space before him.

The oaks towered highest, their branches covered in orange and brown leaves and laden with giant acorns. The firs shot upward like fuzzy green cones on large red pillars. The long willow branches stretched to the ground, swaying and twisting in the wind like long green snakes. A particularly close call with a serpent at the age of five came to mind and he shivered. An eerie howl whistled through the firs, making the fuzzy branches shake. Mason stepped back toward the airlock. A laugh came from behind him. He turned around only to see his own reflection on the side of the ship. The laugh erupted again, coming from above.

Austin stood on top of the ship, smiling. "You look a little scared, Mason."

"Am not."

"Suuure you aren't." The wind howled and stopped their banter, as both boys stared fearfully into the woods.

"How bout we call a—a truce?" Austin asked anxiously.

Mason nodded. "Fair enough."

Austin's nostrils flared. "Smell the fresh air, Mason." Mason breathed in through his nose. The air was cold and crisp and smelled of wet leaves and pine.

Austin stretched his arms. "We've been stuck in the ship since early this morning. Let's enjoy the outdoors."

It was true. Mason could use some fresh air and the feel of the wind on his skin. "Sure, but how'd you get up there?"

Austin pointed toward the rear of the ship. "There's a service ladder on the back. Hurry, I'll help you up."

Mason noticed the reflection of the woods on the *Phoenix's* silver skin. His own reflection was clear too, tempting him to make funny faces at himself. He raised his eyebrows and stuck out his tongue, then flipped his hands over to create glasses around his eyes with his fingers.

"Whoa!" he screamed and stumbled backward. He spun around as he realized what he saw reflected was behind him, not in front of him. Something blue had run from one tree to the next. He scanned the shadowy forest. The wind howled again and something cracked in the distance. He backed into the side of the *Phoenix*, his palms against the smooth metal. Mason ran for the ladder, but kept watch on the mirrored surface of the ship. He gasped as he saw the blue thing run behind another tree. He could see its glowing eyes following his movement.

"Austin, did you see that?"

"No, what?" Austin peered over the back of the ship, while Mason was scurrying up the ladder.

"That blue thing—in the woods. It was right over there." Mason's arm shook as he pointed.

Austin brushed his bangs from his eyes and stared into the woods, but dark shadows concealed anything beyond a few feet into the trees. "I don't see anything, Mason. Is this a joke?"

The wind picked up again and the long branches of the willows swirled. Mason scoured the tree line. It was somewhere out there. "I saw something, I know I did."

"It was probably just an animal," Austin's voice cracked. "It's probably more scared of us than we are of it." Austin hadn't looked away from the woods. He began sidestepping toward the ladder. Mason followed. Suddenly, Austin jumped backward and bumped into Mason, knocking him down. They both fell with a loud, metallic thump that echoed across the clearing.

"What—what did you see?" Mason asked, looking wide-eyed at his brother.

Austin shook his head and pushed himself up on his elbows. "I don't know—it was blue—it looked human."

"Human?" Mason asked. The two sat for a second, huddled nervously on the roof of the *Phoenix*. The wind howled again menacingly.

"What should we do?"

"I don't know!"

Asterisk

Tiffany sat behind Oliver on the sky scooter. She was starting to feel motion sick from all the starting and stopping. There was no clear way through the forest. Oliver
apologized repeatedly, but Tiffany assured him that she was
all right and that he should continue. She took out her mom's
journal to pass the time. She flipped it open and it glowed
to life—she'd not put the security lock back in place. As she
scanned the entries of the last month, she decided to reread
the entries from Dabnis Castle.

As she read the last day, she noticed something she had
overlooked before. There was an asterisk behind the word *Academy*. As she stared at the small star symbol, it flashed. She took
the stylus and tapped it. The screen went blank and then came
back on. Four small boxes appeared, and a word above them
said *pin*. She thought for a moment.

"Oliver, what was that code Mom and Dad used to secure
the airlocks on the *Phoenix*?"

The scooter jolted to a stop. Tiffany felt her stomach lurch
forward. She was going to be sick. She took a deep breath and
closed her eyes.

Oliver cracked his neck. "It was 83, 85, 88, 89. Why?"

"I'm not sure, but I am hoping that's the pin that the journal is asking for."

"What do you mean? I thought you didn't need a pin," Oliver said.

"Well, up until now all I've needed is the tapping sequence, but I found something interesting on one of the words in Mom's entry and I clicked it," she explained. "I'll give those numbers a try. Keep going, and I'll let you know if I find anything interesting."

"Yeah. We're running out of time. According to my mTalk, the temperatures are already dropping."

"Then let's hurry!" Tiffany exclaimed. She reached around his waist in anticipation, and as she expected, the scooter jerked forward and they were off again.

She tapped in the airlock code but nothing happened. What could it be? Tiffany put her hand over her mouth as she thought. She closed her eyes. Had her mom ever told her the pin? Was she just not remembering? The scooter twisted to the right.

"Whoa, that was close," Oliver admitted. "This is ridiculous. There's no clear way."

The scooter surged forward again. What could it be? She had to get into this locked part of the journal. It might provide clarity for their situation. Maybe there was something in their dad and mom's cabin that could help. She lifted her mTalk, but the reception was very low. If she could get in touch with Mason, maybe he could search the cabin for her. It took her a moment, but she figured out how to call him. She certainly didn't want to interrupt Oliver again. It was getting colder, and every moment he wasted by not driving was a moment closer to them freezing.

A cute picture of Mason appeared—sandy-colored, shaggy hair and deep blue eyes. She recognized the picture as one his mom had taken the day Tiffany and the twins were dropped off at their school, Bewaldeter. A moment passed, and Mason didn't answer. Maybe his mTalk wasn't getting a good signal either.

She found Austin and tried to connect. His picture appeared too, which was identical to Mason's except for his bright green eyes. The twins looked exactly the same, with that one difference. Again, no answer. Maybe he hadn't figured out how to turn it on. No, of course not, Austin was really good with gadgets. She wondered for a moment whether something had gone wrong. She looked at the screen on her mTalk, and the signal was still very low. Oh well, they're probably fine, just out of range, she reassured herself.

Not a second later, it came to her. Of course! She typed in the numbers: 10, 25, 15, 80.

The pin was accepted and the entry screen disappeared. A new one appeared that displayed several icons. She quickly scanned them and froze on one with this label: "Oliver's Scholarship—Man in Black."

Obbin

Orange and brown leaves flittered through the air. The twins sat huddled together, frozen with fear. They were outside the safety of the ship, and a blue creature lurked in the shadows, stalking them. The sky was growing dark with clouds. A storm was coming.

An acorn bounced off the top of the *Phoenix*, with an ear-piercing zing. The nut split in two and rolled off the ship. Mason shivered and looked at Austin. "Do you see anything?"

"No," Austin said. They sat for another minute. Then they heard a creak near the back of the ship. Something was climbing the ladder. The twins' bodies jerked back involuntarily at the sight of a blue face popping into view. Green spiky hair crowned the thing's head. Wild turquoise eyes peered at the twins. A smile crossed its lips, revealing bright white teeth.

The creature spoke, "Hello." The twins looked at each other in surprise.

"It . . . he spoke," Mason whispered out of the corner of his mouth.

"And in our language," Austin added.

"My name's Obbin," the blue creature said, extending his hand toward the twins. Mason counted to himself four fingers and a thumb, each of which was adorned with a brown leather ring. He also noted a white bone or fang pierced through each of the creature's ears.

Austin nodded his head nervously and whispered through a forced smile. "Mason, say something."

"He-hello," Mason stammered hesitantly as he got to his feet.

Obbin shook his head, his spiky green hair so stiff it didn't move. "Are you guys all right?"

"Yeah, ummm, I'm Mason and this . . . this is Austin, my twin." Mason motioned for Austin to stand next to him. The creature pushed himself up onto the ship. He wore only a pair of shorts, made of grey and black striped fur. Mason sized him up. He was maybe five feet tall, just a bit shorter than he and his brother.

"He looks like a boy. Like a human boy, I mean," Mason whispered.

"But he's blue!"

"I know."

Obbin smiled and walked toward the twins. "Nice to meet you, but I can't stay long. I was out in the woods when I saw your ship land."

Mason scratched his head. "You saw us?"

"Yeah. Lots of ships fly over the forest, but very few try to land in it. I figured you guys may have crashed," Obbin said.

"We almost did," admitted Austin.

Obbin looked around at the woods. "Well, I can't stay long. There's a storm moving in." Mason looked up at the hole in the cloud canopy. "I knocked on the door earlier, but you never answered. I've been out here for a while," explained Obbin. "I was about to leave when you"—he pointed to Austin—"came rushing out the door."

"I didn't see you," Austin said.

"You only see me if I want you to see me," Obbin proclaimed, a cocky air to his voice. "It's too bad you didn't come earlier. I wanted to show you something."

Austin looked at Mason and then Obbin. "What?"

"I guess there's still time." Obbin reached into his pocket and pulled out the largest blue crystal the twins had ever seen. Their mouths dropped open simultaneously. It was a good few inches in diameter and a third as thick as it was around. Obbin held out the crystal to the twins. "Here, look at this." Mason greedily accepted the precious stone. He pulled it close to his body, and began rolling it in his hands, tracing his fingers over its straight crisp edges.

Austin peered over his twin's shoulder. "Wow!"

Obbin moved closer to the twins, eyes twinkling. "You like it? Then let's trade." Mason looked at him, but wasn't listening; he was too interested in the crystal. "Do you want to trade?" Obbin asked impatiently. The blue boy looked up at the darkening sky, as a peal of thunder rumbled far in the distance.

"Sure. Have whatever you want," Mason said softly and turned his eyes back to the cobalt jewel. Obbin smiled and walked back toward the *Phoenix's* double tailfin where the ladder was.

Austin glanced up at Obbin and then back to the crystal. "Can I hold it?"

Mason cradled the jewel closer. "In a minute."

Austin's eyebrows narrowed. "Give it to me!"

"No!"

"It's my turn." Austin grabbed for the crystal.

Mason used an arm to hold his brother back. "It's mine!" Austin lunged for the precious stone but missed, instead tripping on Mason's leg. His body slid across the silver surface toward the edge of the ship. Austin reached for something to stop himself, but found nothing and slipped over the side with a piercing scream.

Mason looked up to see his twin vanish over the edge. Stuffing the crystal into his pants pocket, he ran to the side of the ship, afraid of what he might find. Austin was sprawled out on the wing, not moving. Mason lowered himself onto the wing and ran to his brother. He shook Austin's shoulder. "Austin, Austin, are you all right?" Austin groaned and turned over. "Aus, I'm so sorry," Mason apologized as he hovered over his twin. "I didn't mean to. I don't know what got into me. Are you all right?"

Austin groaned again. "I . . . I think so."

Mason stretched out his hand and pulled his brother to his feet. "I'm really sorry."

Austin took a deep breath. "It's all right. I'm the one that lunged at you."

Mason nodded his head. "Still, I'm sorry."

"Me too." Austin said, but then looked around. "Where's the blue kid?"

"I don't know." Mason scoured the tree line. "He's gone." Then the twins heard a noise inside the cargo bay of the *Phoenix*.

"He's in the ship!" Austin exclaimed.

The wing was too high for them to jump, so Mason hoisted Austin back on top of the *Phoenix*. Austin then pulled Mason up, and together they descended the ladder. They ran to the airlock, and upon stepping inside, saw Obbin looking around at the crates and electronics. Obbin waved his hand at the cargo bay. "Nice ship." He had a crate open and was looking through its contents.

Austin rushed over to him. "No, no, don't touch anything."

Ignoring him, Obbin continued digging. He pulled out a silky orange pressure suit, held it against his body, and smiled. "I think this will fit."

Mason knew it was either his or Austin's. "Put that back."

"You took the crystal, I take the suit. It's only fair." Looking down at his pocket, Mason pulled out the jewel and looked it over. Smiling, Obbin started for the airlock with the orange pressure suit in his grasp. He looked at Mason holding the crystal, and with a wave, he darted through the airlock.

"Mason, he has a space suit! We've got to stop him." As they moved into action, the twins watched Obbin disappear into the woods.

"Quick! If Oliver comes back and he finds out we lost one of those suits, he'll never forgive us," Mason whimpered.

"Forget forgiveness—we're dead if he finds out!" Austin added.

Ploy

The air was frigid now, and Tiffany pulled a jacket from one of the scooter's compartments. She was just about to read the new entry she'd discovered when Oliver stopped for a rest.

"So Oliver, I cracked the pin. It was Dad and Mom's anniversary date."

He took a swig of his Energen. "Good job. Anything interesting?"

"Well, I don't know yet, but I think so."

Oliver seemed a bit preoccupied. He was looking over the engines on the scooter. He opened one of the side hatches and inspected something. "Cool." He closed the hatch. "We should keep going."

"Yeah, we should. I tried to reach the twins, but they didn't answer."

Oliver shrugged. "Probably the reception. I'm showing minimal coverage. The storm is not helping, I'm sure." Tiffany nodded. If anyone knew about these gadget things, it was Oliver.

They climbed back on the scooter and continued toward their destination. It wasn't long before the scooter was twisting and jerking again as Oliver tried to navigate the dense forest. It was time to read the entry. Tiffany opened the journal and reentered the pin. The entry about Oliver's scholarship was open.

April 15th, 1599.

It seems we have received a riddle today. Oliver has been given early admittance to the Federal Star Fleet Academy. While this is certainly a prestigious honor, and we, as parents, have no doubt that Oliver deserves it, we are skeptical of its authenticity. In light of our recent engagements with the man in black, we are concerned that there may be more to this invitation than it claims.

Oliver, of course, does not understand. The moment he received the message, he was ecstatic. His bags were packed before Elliot or I were aware he had received it. We told him we needed some time to discuss the opportunity.

If indeed Oliver did earn this on his own merit, and there are no strings attached, then it would make sense for him to attend. His attendance at sixteen would allow him to complete his required service earlier, and we hope, allow him to pursue his career aspirations sooner. The Academy also provides one of the best educations in the Federation, albeit militaristic in nature.

This aside, we are concerned that at this young age, Oliver may be too impressionable and may succumb to unbalanced pressure to choose the military as a career. If he enters at the required service age of eighteen, we believe he will be more mature to make his future decisions.

There is one more concern. We believe it is possible that the man in black is behind this. He seems to be lurking in the shadows, monitoring our every move. We still don't know who he is. We fear that declining this offer, would reveal our plans to begin our quest for Ursprung with our family. Without knowing this man's influence, or even who he is working for, it will be best for us to lead as normal a life as possible. This seems to mean sending Tiffany, Mason, and Austin to Bewaldeter, and allowing Oliver to go to the Academy.

So that *was* it? They had a hunch that not allowing Oliver to go might trigger some suspicion. She was about to tap Oliver on the shoulder, when she realized there was a second entry.

May 1st, 1599.

Our benefactor, Phelan O'Farrell, informed us that one of his sources has proof that Captain Vedrik, of the Übel, arranged Oliver's admittance.

Tiffany stopped reading. Captain Vedrik? He's the man in black? She felt dizzy from the impact of this sudden revelation. First, Oliver's acceptance was a scam and tied to their parents' captors, not something he earned. Second, there had to be some entries between April fifteenth and May first. Somewhere, the man in black had been identified as Captain Vedrik of the Übel. She kept reading.

The Übel may have paid off someone in the Federal Star Fleet to ensure that Oliver was one of the finalists. There is reason to believe they wanted to use the Academy to either influence Oliver or use him to gain insight into our research. We have considered not allowing him to go, but Phelan agrees that this will raise too much suspicion. We have seven months.

The entry ended, and this time there was nothing more. Seven months until what? Seven months until school started. That made sense. But what were they planning on doing in those seven months? Tiffany looked at the back of her brother's head. His arms were tense as he held tightly to the scooter. She couldn't tell him that it was all a setup; it would crush him. She couldn't lie, but she couldn't tell him now. He needed to have confidence in his abilities. Tiffany was sure their mission would fail if he didn't.

1.14

Chase

The temperature had gotten noticeably colder and the twins considered going back for jackets, but they reasoned that if the chase went quickly, they'd be back to the safety of the *Phoenix* in no time. The twins stopped at the edge of the mysterious woods. The purple storm clouds had closed over the forest, blocking most of the remaining light. The twins exchanged uneasy expressions.

"You first," encouraged Mason.

"Uh, no, how about you," countered Austin.

"Uh, I would, but I—," Mason stuttered.

"You're older," Austin interrupted.

"By thirteen minutes. And you're the one that opened the door," Mason said decidedly.

Austin sighed. "Right." He fiddled with his mTalk. "It looks like there's a light on this thing." In the midst of his tinkering the light came on, blasting him in the eyes. He stumbled backwards and fell over a branch. "Wow, that's bright." He blinked and aimed the light at the woods, but could still only see spots in the darkness.

"Hurry—" Mason said, pulling Austin to his feet. "We don't want to lose him." A few hundred feet into the woods, the twins found a narrow dirt path. It was slightly overgrown by large, green star-shaped leaves, and they couldn't see very far down it. As they proceeded, slopes formed on either side of the trail, and soon the leaves were at waist level. The forest was alive with activity. The many calls, shrieks, squawks, growls, and chirps of birds, insects, lizards, and small mammals echoed all around. Each creature was frantically preparing for the twins' arrival as if its life depended on it.

Austin looked back at his brother. "We'll never catch him by walking." The twins broke into a sprint. Their breathing grew heavy, and they quickly dropped to a jog. The air on this planet seemed thinner. The path dropped lower as they went, and soon the star-shaped leaves were as high as their chest. It was so dark. Good thing for the mTalk.

Eventually, the star leaves formed a roof over the trail, creating a tunnel. As they came around a bend in the path, the light from Austin's mTalk shone on something blue for just a moment.

"There he is!" Austin broke into a sprint again. He had to get that suit back. Mason followed close behind. The path curved several more times, and with each bend they briefly saw Obbin, each time a little closer than before. The wind howled loudly through the branches.

"We've got him now!" Austin cried triumphantly. The leaf roof disappeared as the tunnel intersected with a wide dirt road. Austin halted abruptly.

Mason bumped into Austin. "Why'd you stop?"

"He could have gone either way!"

"My guess is he stayed on this path." Austin shrugged. He wasn't sure, but there was no reason to think otherwise. "Go! We don't want to lose him." Austin nodded and ducked back into the tunnel. Now there was a strange swampy glow in the tunnel. Was it his light reflecting off the star leaves or were the leaves glowing? The path turned sharply and slanted down. The twins stumbled into a rocky clearing.

"Look! There he is!" Austin cried. Obbin had crossed the rocky expanse and was nearing a thick blue fog that looked more like a rising cloud. Obbin disappeared into it.

Tired and out of breath, the twins hobbled to the edge of the fog. Mason threw up his hands. "Hold on! Do you hear that?" he asked, nearly breathless.

Austin listened. He heard a rumbling, not like thunder, but maybe water. Breathing heavily, hand on his side, Mason spoke, "We can't . . . just run into . . . that cloud . . . we have no idea . . . what or who . . . is behind it."

"Yeah . . . but he's . . . getting away!" Austin took a deep breath, hands on knees. Wiping away his sweaty locks of hair, Mason shook his head. A few steps forward and Mason stuck his hand into the fog.

"It's warm." Austin stepped forward. It was indeed warm; fog was usually colder. "It's steam," Mason concluded. He'd finally caught his breath.

"Steam?"

"Yeah, it's really warm and if you look, it's flowing upward. Steam is water in a gaseous state," Mason explained.

"That's not what I was asking." Austin looked at his twin, the encyclopedia. "Where do you think that steam is coming from?"

"There must be a crevice or a geyser hole ahead of us," Mason suggested.

"What's making the noise?"

"I'm not sure—it's too constant to be a geyser."

"It sounds like a waterfall." Austin looked back at the forest. It spanned left to right, ending at rock cliffs on either side of the clearing. "There must be a cliff behind that mist." Shivers ran up Austin's spine as a terrible possibility crossed his mind. He looked around for something long and sturdy. He spotted a dead branch and ran to get it.

"Where are you going?"

"Getting a stick," Austin shouted over his shoulder.

"Why?"

"Just wait. I think we almost made a big mistake." Austin dragged the dead wood to the blue steam cloud. It enveloped him as he walked forward, tapping the rocky ground before him. His clothing became heavier and wetter with every step. He couldn't see anything; even the stick in his hands was invisible. Suddenly, the branch plunged into emptiness. Several more jabs and his theory was confirmed; they were at the edge of a cliff. Austin turned to walk back to his brother, but hesitated when he realized he was completely disoriented. "Mason, yell something so I know where you are."

"I'm over here Austin!" Austin zeroed in on his brother's voice, tapping the stick ahead of him as he made his way out. "Do you need me? Are you all right?" called Mason.

"Yes, I'm fine. It's just we're at the edge of a huge chasm; that's where the steam is coming from." Austin appeared out of the cloud, his clothes soaked and sticking to his body.

"That means . . ." Mason frowned.

Austin nodded. "Obbin."

"Is there anything we can do?"

"I don't think so." Standing solemnly, the twins stared silently into the mist, mourning the blue boy. They were sure he had fallen into the deep canyon ahead.

"If only . . ." Mason began.

"Yes, and we could have . . ." Austin added and then remained silent. He'd been the one who ruined the chess game. The one who opened the door. The one who wanted to stay outdoors. The one who had commanded the pursuit. This was his fault.

A loud rumble echoed in the clouds overhead, breaking the melancholy silence. This time it was thunder. "I think it's going to storm." Mason looked toward the clouds swirling above.

"That's what . . . Obbin said," stammered Austin. He tossed the stick aside.

"I don't think there's anything we can do. We need to get back." Mason scowled at the forbidding woods behind. "Do you know how to get back?"

Austin looked up in disbelief. "No!" This was just another example of his carelessness. Again the thunder warned of the coming onslaught of wind, rain, and lightning.

Mason started toward the tree line. "We'll just follow the path we came on. It only broke off once, where it crossed that road." Austin followed toward the forest, but before entering the woods, he looked back to the mist mournfully. Mason did as well and folded his hands, looking at the ground. "We're sorry."

"Yes, we are."

Prisoners

The woods had grown darker since their brush with death. Austin was covered in goose bumps from both fear and cold. On the way in, birds chirped, bugs buzzed, and an occasional animal would howl. But now it was oddly silent. He wondered if something was out there stalking them and causing the smaller beasts to go quiet. Mason jumped as a roll of thunder rumbled overhead. "We really should get going," said Mason.

A bright flash lit the underside of the forest canopy as a bolt of lightning pierced the trunk of a nearby oak tree. Austin threw himself to the ground, pulling Mason down with him. The earth shook and it sounded as if the sky were being torn apart. Austin lifted his head and looked around, then slid his arm from his brother's back. "This is bad, Mason."

The rain pounded against the leaves overhead. Lightning flashed again followed by roaring thunder. The stricken oak had burst into flame. Loud pops resounded as its sap boiled to the surface in bubbles and bursts, and a burning branch crashed to the ground. "We've got to go. We're in a field of lighting rods." Austin turned on the light on his mTalk. "On the count of three we go. One! Two! Three!" The twins scrambled to their feet and ran. Large, cold drops of rain pelted the canopy above, pouring to the undergrowth below in waterfalls, and sparkling like chains of diamonds each time the lightning flashed.

Austin could feel his heart beating as adrenaline surged through his body. With each new flash and thunderclap, he ran quicker. The weariness he'd felt before hadn't returned. Austin looked back; Mason was lagging behind. "Come on!" They were deep in the leafy trench now. The leaves glowed when his light struck them as before. Trickles of water ran down the sides of the tunnel. The path was soggy and a shallow stream flowed at their feet.

A few minutes later the boys arrived back at the road. Austin pointed up the wide dirt path. "Let's take the road instead."

"We don't know where it goes."

Austin shivered. "But it's not flooding. It looks easier."

"Easier isn't always better. Let's go back the way we came." Mason insisted. He wrapped his arms around his sides. "I'm soaking wet and it's getting colder. We'll just get more lost if we take a different path." A bright flash illuminated the road. He'd never heard thunder sound like this, as if a sheet of metal was being torn in two. A tree trunk, marred with black ash, split down the middle, each side crashing into neighboring trees.

Austin darted for the opening to the tunnel. "Fine! I just want to get out of here!" Within seconds the mud was caked so thickly on Austin's ankles and shoes that it felt like he'd gained twenty pounds.

"Yuck!" shouted Mason as a large glob of mud splattered his face and went into his mouth. "Stop! You're kicking up mud!"

"Sorry! I'm not doing it on purpose. I can't move."

Mason slowed to wipe the muck from his lips, spitting a couple of times, then he froze. "Do you hear that?"

"What?" Austin continued to trudge forward.

"That noise, it's growing louder."

Austin listened but pushed forward. He looked back at his twin. "It's just the thunder in the distance."

Mason listened again and then frowned. "It sounds like the engines of the *Phoenix*."

Austin looked up the path ahead. "It can't be. They wouldn't leave us." A cool wind blew down the path, giving the twins a deep chill. He looked curiously at Mason.

"Do you feel that?" Mason asked.

"Yeah, what is—?" Before Austin could finish his sentence, a torrent of water crashed around the bend in the path.

"Run!" Mason yelled, turning from the surging water.

Austin spun around and tried to follow, but the mud would not release him. Mason wasn't much farther ahead. Within seconds of the ill-fated attempt to escape, the water knocked them off their feet and swallowed them. Taking a deep breath as the torrent pulled him under, Austin fought to get his head above the water. For a brief moment, he sucked fresh air into his lungs. His left foot snagged a root, which pulled him back under the muddy liquid. He flailed his arms, jerked his leg, but his shoe was stuck. His lungs burned and his air supply quickly became stale. The current was pulling his upper body away from his caught leg, making it impossible for him to use his hands. He twisted his ankle to the left and right, and finally his foot popped out of his shoe. He gasped as his head bobbed above the water again.

"Austin!" Mason shouted. The water was pulling him toward the voice.

"Mas—!" Water flooded Austin's mouth as his body flipped over. His head broke into air again. "Ma—!" Another swallow of water. "—son!"

"Reach up! Quick!" Mason was on his stomach reaching down from a branch. Austin stretched out his hand, but the current pulled him beyond Mason's reach. For several minutes, Austin thrashed his arms. He was tired and he was short of breath. He couldn't take much more.

Suddenly, his body was thrown into a somersault onto the ground. He'd reached the crossroads, and the water poured out into the wide path. For several minutes the brown liquid streamed out of the tunnel. He couldn't get to his feet, but at least he could breathe. Slowly the water spread out and disappeared into the forest floor. Austin lay sprawled out on the road, soaked and muddied.

Sitting up, he looked around. It seemed that the storm had stopped. A spray of water droplets released from his hair as he shook his head to relieve his clogged ears. Wet hair and mud stuck to his face.

"Austin, come here. Quickly!" His twin was crouching in the leaves high on the embankment. "Come on! Hurry!"

"What?" Austin shouted, pushing himself up. Mason put a finger to his lips and motioned for Austin to join him in the foliage. "What's going on?" Austin asked, as he climbed the embankment.

Mason was soaked and covered in bits of dried leaves and dirt. He nodded toward the road. "Listen." The torrential downpour of rain had ceased and only a light drizzle filtered down through the leaves, casting the road in an eerie fog. He still couldn't hear very well, but he closed his eyes to concentrate. Then he heard it. A soft rhythmic beat. The noise grew louder, or perhaps nearer. He opened his eyes and saw a flickering blue glow illuminating the rainy mist.

What Austin saw next would have terrified him, had he not already met Obbin. Two blue men with long green hair marched into view, each carrying torches burning brightly with blue flames. The men wore furry shorts like Obbin, but also leather sashes across their bare chests.

"Obbin," Austin whispered to Mason, who nodded in agreement. Two men beating large drums marched into view, followed by four more men. They carried long spears and looked ready to skewer anything that crossed their path.

"Soldiers," Mason observed. "Do you think they're looking for us?"

Austin looked at Mason and shrugged his shoulders. As he watched the caravan, the most peculiar things emerged. "Are those oxen?"

"They look like oxen, but they're blue," Mason answered quietly.

"And huge," added Austin.

Sitting in a saddle on the middle ox, a blue man with dark blue-black hair held three sets of reins. The oxen pulled a large wagon, accented on every corner by glowing torches. The procession was almost directly in front of the twins. Austin signaled to fall back, and the twins quietly edged themselves deeper into the dense green foliage. Two more rows of four soldiers with spears and two more torchbearers followed the wagon. Animal hides had been draped over the wagon's contents. As it passed, Austin's eyes widened. An orange sleeve hung out of a large silver crate that looked similar to the ones in the *Phoenix*.

"Mason do you see that? That . . . that's our stuff," Austin pointed wildly at the wagon, his hand slightly exposed through the bushes.

"What? Impossible!" Mason looked at the opening under the animal hides. Clearly printed on the silver crates was the proof: "E4:32 Phoenix."

"We left the door open!" Austin shouted. Mason stared at Austin, his blue eyes wide with horror. Austin realized his mistake, but it was too late.

A soldier glared at the embankment. "Halt!" he shouted to the caravan. The wagon driver pulled hard on the reins and the oxen stopped. The soldier stepped out of formation and toward the embankment. "Silence!" he shouted. The drums stopped.

Austin felt his heart in his throat, and his stomach in his feet. He crouched lower, his chin nearly touching the moist earth, and started to shift backwards. He tapped Mason to signal a retreat. A small branch cracked under Austin's remaining shoe and a loud snap seemed to echo in the silent forest. Several other soldiers looked toward the sound.

"Alsi, Gizzee, come with me," the soldier ordered. Two more soldiers joined him as he approached the embankment.

Mason mouthed, "Run," and began counting down on his fingers: five, four, three, two. At one, the twins sprang to their feet and ran. Austin stumbled immediately; his left foot was shoeless and struck a sharp rock. His left knee involuntarily bent in reaction, pulling his foot away from the offending stone. The forward motion of his body brought him tumbling to the muddy earth. He rolled to his back, panting.

One of the soldiers cried out, "Find them!" If he didn't run now, he'd be captured. Austin stood and took off, ignoring the uncomfortable footfalls. "Halt!" cried the soldier. A spear flew past Austin and lodged in a nearby tree trunk. These guys meant business. For the second time in as many seconds, Austin headed to the ground, this time by choice. His hands covered his head in protection.

Footsteps crunched the leaves that littered the ground. Austin was pulled to his feet by the collar of his shirt and spun around to see a blue face with steel grey eyes. Frowning, the soldier lifted Austin off the ground and heaved him over his shoulder. "A kid," the soldier mumbled.

Another soldier had found Mason, who was also lying on the ground, and heaved him over his shoulder. Austin's captor pointed to a spear lodged in a nearby willow and commanded, "Get the spears."

The twins were taken back to the wagon and patted down. Austin's soldier stopped when he felt the inventor's pouch. "Give me that." Austin reluctantly removed the pouch. His grandpa had given it to him, one of the last presents he'd received from him.

"Captain Feng, what shall we do with these?" Mason's guard pointed to the mTalk on his wrist.

"Remove them and set them in the wagon." Austin's conqueror, Captain Feng, reached down and undid his mTalk. "Do you have any more items of interest?" Austin shook his head. The captain pointed to Mason. "All right, go stand by him." Captain Feng grabbed some rope off the wagon and tossed it to Mason's soldier. "Alsi, tie them up." Alsi tied the twins back to back and effortlessly heaved them onto the tailgate of the wagon. Gizzee walked over with a muddy shoe. It was Austin's. The soldier tossed it carelessly into the back of the wagon instead of giving it back to Austin.

"Onward!" shouted the captain. The twins felt the wagon jerk as it began moving again. The drummers restarted their beat. Austin strained to hear the conversation that started between the captain and Alsi, but the thumping of the drums was too much. What could they do now? Not only had they left the ship, killed Obbin, and lost their supplies, they were now prisoners of a group of blue savages.

Austin tried to squirm out of the ropes, but it was no use; they were tied too tight. If only he had listened to his brother. But then something else crossed his mind. If only his brother had freed his parents, he and Mason wouldn't be tied up on the back of a wagon. Like the roots of a weed growing deep in the cracks of concrete, Austin remembered what was really to blame: Oliver's cowardice. Now he would have to be the hero. It was up to him to set things right. When he and Mason got back to the *Phoenix* he would take control of the mission.

First things first, they had to get away from the soldiers. "Mason, can you get your hands free?"

Mason wiggled his wrists. "The ropes are tied so tight it hurts. Where are we going?"

"How should I know?" Austin retorted.

"Sorry."

Austin sighed. "They're probably from wherever the boy was from."

"Do you think they know what happened to Obbin?"

"I doubt they could yet." He remembered the smiling kid with the jewel. A simple trade was all that had been meant. Austin's thoughts were interrupted when he heard a familiar voice. It was coming from under the animal hides. "That's Tiffany," he whispered to Mason.

"Halt!" shouted one of the soldiers involved in the twins' capture. The procession stopped and the soldier walked up to the front of the wagon. He pulled the offending mTalk from the wagon.

"Mason, are you there?" came Tiffany's voice clearly over the speaker. The blue man fumbled with the mTalk, trying to shut it off. Tiffany repeated her question several more times.

"Shut it off!" Captain Feng commanded as he approached the soldier. "They may be trying to track the boys." Unable to shut the mTalk off and under pressure from his commander, the man slammed the device onto the ground and stepped on it. The mTalk's speaker screeched and went silent. The soldier picked up the broken device and threw it into the wagon, a pleased smile on his face. The captain shook his head and frowned. "Get back in formation! Next time give it to me if you can't figure it out!" The reprimanded soldier walked back to his place, head hung low.

"Proceed!" shouted Captain Feng. The drummers struck up their beat and the caravan continued its march to a destination unbeknownst to the twins.

Only a few seconds passed when Austin heard Tiffany's voice again. He nudged Mason. "Quick, sing loudly. We can't let them hear the other mTalk. If they break it, we can't be tracked or communicate with Oliver and Tiffany." They began singing a song they'd learned at school about a lizard who wanted to fly. As the twins sang, the soldiers behind them looked puzzled.

After three verses of the song, the twins stopped and listened. To their relief, the mTalk had gone silent.

"Good job," Austin whispered to Mason. "We did it."

"Sure did."

Austin yawned. "Boy, am I tired," he admitted.

"Me, too. I only slept a couple of hours." Mason looked at the blue soldiers marching beside them. "Do you think it's safe to sleep?"

"It can't get much worse than this," Austin posed. "What do we have to lose?" Austin wiggled his wrists. "We certainly aren't getting free at the moment."

"Okay," Mason agreed.

Austin laid his head back on Mason's shoulder, and Mason did the same on Austin. It only took a moment and they were out.

Maglev

Navigating the forest was far more difficult than Oliver had expected. He'd hoped they'd have run across an animal trail or creek by now. Instead, he had to slowly steer the scooter around tree trunk after tree trunk while avoiding low branches and vines. The muscles in his arms were sore and night was approaching. It was time to set up camp. If he didn't get some sleep, tomorrow would be really bad. He already dreaded putting his aching arms through another day of strenuous flying.

Making the situation worse, a rainstorm had passed over and soaked Oliver and his sister, further slowing them down. *Miserable* was the only word to describe the last few hours. Twice, Oliver considered turning back, but the thought of his parents being held captive renewed his vigor each time. Every second was valuable. He also kept in mind that if the ride was rough on him, then it was equally hard on his sister. He had to be strong for her.

Tiffany pondered the truth she'd learned of Oliver's scholarship. If she told him, it might give him doubts in his abilities. But she wondered whether she was lying if she didn't. She knew that beneath Oliver's newly acquired haughty persona was the same brother she knew last year, a much less confident boy. Oliver was the only one who could get them off the planet. The only one who could save her parents. The only one she truly could trust. For these reasons, she would wait for the right moment. Being wet, tired, and only just beginning their adventure made it clear that now was not that time.

Internally, another battle raged. Tiffany was angry that her parents had not shared their plans with her, but also felt guilty for feeling that way. After all, they were being held prisoner. There was a lump in her throat, and a tear rolled down her cheek.

She quickly wiped it away. She had to be strong and remain optimistic. The glass is always half full, she reminded herself. They were on their way to meet a man who knew their parents and funded their expeditions. He could—no, he *would*—save their parents.

She forced a smile. "Oliver, how far from the city are we?" She crossed her fingers. Please say a few minutes, she hoped.

Oliver looked at the sky scooter's navigation screen. "We haven't made much ground. We're still around thirty miles away."

Tiffany patted him on the back. "I'm sorry." Oliver shrugged and sighed. "We'll get there."

"It's getting darker, and I'm not sure we should keep going," Oliver admitted, to Tiffany's surprise. "Maybe we should camp for the night."

"I could use some sleep." Tiffany leaned her head to the side to look at Oliver. "I just hope the boys are all right."

"I know. I'm a little concerned about them," Oliver said. "Not because I think they're in any danger from something outside the ship, but because I think they're a danger to each other." He grimaced as he steered the scooter around another large oak tree. His muscles burned.

Tiffany tapped Oliver's shoulder. "Hey, it looks lighter up ahead." The number of trees thinned out, and a gap appeared in the forest. Oliver turned and smiled at Tiffany. She saw him reenergize. This was the break they needed. As they emerged from the suffocating tangle of trees, they saw a single metallic rail stretch out in both directions. The path was for a maglev train. The dull thrum of energy zipping through the magnetized rail resounded the closer they got.

"Awesome!" Oliver shouted and, in his excitement, let go of the handles. The scooter swung left, and he let out an embarrassed laugh as he quickly maneuvered the scooter back onto the path. Tiffany giggled uneasily behind him and held on a little tighter. He looked at the navigation screen and pointed to the right. "All right, I think if we follow the rail that way, we'll run directly into Brighton."

"Are you sure you're not too tired?"

"No, I'm fine if you are."

"I'm fine," Tiffany said with a yawn. "I'm just glad we finally have a clear path."

"Me too." Oliver gave a hard twist on the throttle and the scooter surged forward.

Tiffany sat back in her seat and placed the journal into her mom's pack. "I think I'm going to take a break from reading."

"Good idea. Just relax and enjoy the scenery."

The forest looked as though it was ready to reclaim the maglev path at any moment; the tree trunks loomed high above, leaving just a sliver of sky. Pink and purple clouds swirled high above. The purple ones grew more prevalent every moment. Occasionally, blue streaks sizzled through the sky, followed by the low growl of thunder. The storm was still clashing overhead.

Oliver and Tiffany covered several miles very quickly. There were no longer any obstacles, just a wide trench through the forest. They crossed bridges spanning deep canyons and flew through dark tunnels dug roughly through hills. It had been ten minutes since they'd found the maglev track, when Tiffany looked up quickly.

"What was that?" She looked around at the forest curiously.

"What?" Oliver asked casually.

"That noise. Listen."

All Oliver could hear was the buzzing noise of the scooter. "I don't hear—" The sound of a loud horn stopped him in mid-sentence. He looked down and saw a small blip flashing on the short-range radar. Looking up quickly, Oliver saw the engine of a maglev train coming around the bend. "Whoa!" He swung the scooter to the left of the track.

Pain shot through his left arm as it clipped a branch. The sticks tore his shirtsleeve and dug into his flesh. His left hand lost its grip, and his right arm overpowered the scooter, jerking the small craft back across the track. Tiffany squeezed Oliver's waist tightly, in an attempt not to fall off.

Oliver swung the scooter back to the side, and pain shot through his wounded elbow. He swallowed the lump in his throat. Only yards remained, and there wasn't enough room between the woods and train. They'd be smashed thinner than butter on toast.

A clearing! It had been only a little ways back. There might be enough room. If he could just get turned around.

The train closed in as Oliver swung the scooter's nose around. The hair on the back of his neck stood on end, and his whole body tingled. His heart was about to leap from his chest. There wasn't enough time to turn. Tiffany let out a terrified scream.

Oliver pulled back on the handles as hard as he could. The front of the scooter rose into the air. He hammered the throttle. The scooter shot forward. Oliver leaned back, forcing the scooter to slide up and away from the train. A second passed as vertigo set in. He held on, keeping his eyes closed, Tiffany's grip like a steel vise around his waist.

The maglev's deafening horn blew. Oliver looked down and watched the maglev cruising by beneath them. "Woohoo!" shouted Oliver, overcome with sheer thankfulness to be alive. His sister's arms still clung around his midsection. She was shaking, and her head pressed into Oliver's shoulder. Tears soaked the fabric of his shirt. Oliver hovered the scooter above the train until it had passed and then brought it down next to the forest.

He dismounted and hugged his sister. "I'm sorry." Tiffany didn't lift her head from his shoulder. For several minutes she shook with intense sobs.

"Don't . . . be sorry," Tiffany said between breaths, lifting her head, tears streaming from her brown eyes.

"I should have been more careful," Oliver admitted. "I got ahead of myself once we were free of the woods and forgot to switch the radar over to mid-range."

"You saved us again," Tiffany said with a meager smile as she got off the scooter. Feeling guilty, Oliver blushed. In his mind, they should be dead. What he'd done had been beyond his control. An extra strength he didn't understand had overtaken him. A chill air swept down the tracks and rustled Oliver's hair. A few orange and yellow leaves flittered to the ground.

Wiping her eyes, Tiffany sniffled. "I've been trying to be strong for Austin, and Mason, and . . ." her voice quivered, ". . . and you. I don't know if I can do it anymore." She looked at the ground. "Can we do this? Can we get to Evad and rescue our parents, or is this out of our hands?" Oliver turned away. He didn't know anymore. "Maybe we should have gone to Archeos headquarters," she said, wiping her eyes again.

Oliver took a deep breath. If he opened up about his fears he would only frighten her more. He took another long breath. "Hey, we can do it. We have to."

Neither he nor Tiffany spoke. It seemed like hours had passed when Oliver grasped Tiffany's shoulder. "Together we can do this. Think about what we've already done over this past day."

"But that was all you," she started.

"No, you uncovered the clues."

Tiffany nodded weakly.

"And Mason suggested that the Übel knew too much of our parents' discoveries and must have a mole within Archeos," Oliver reminded her.

"You're right. He—" but she caught herself. "Judging by what Captain Vedrik knew about the book and Dabnis Castle, only someone from the inside could have tipped him off."

Oliver smiled. It had worked. Tiffany's mind was onto the bigger picture. "Do you think it was Rand or Jen?" Oliver asked. "They were there."

"I thought about that. But they've been Mom and Dad's friends forever."

"Yeah, but remember how the Übel offered our parents money? Maybe they made an offer that the McGregors couldn't resist," Oliver accused. He remembered the captain's words about everybody having a price.

"Maybe, but let's not jump to any conclusions," Tiffany warned.

"You're right." Oliver looked up the track from where the maglev had come. The sky was dark, and the air was frigid. Oliver looked at his mTalk. "Wow, it's nearly midnight." He frowned. Last night at this time he was getting angry at his parents for leaving him to finish all the loading work. A wave of guilt crashed over him for being so impatient with them. "Do you think we should try to make it to the city, or should we just camp here?"

Tiffany yawned. "I think we should sleep for the night. It might be suspicious for two kids to come flying out of the woods on a scooter this late."

"All right, I'll park the scooter a little ways into the woods. Then we can set up camp." Oliver stretched his arms. He wasn't sure who or what lurked here at night and he didn't want to remain exposed. Riding the scooter into the woods, they found a small clearing.

"Tiffany, are you hungry?"

"Yeah. I know it's late, but for some reason, I really am."

"Well, if you get some food started, I'll make a fire and build the tent."

"Sounds good."

Oliver stretched. The adrenaline had dissipated, and his limbs revealed how sore they were.

Tiffany smiled. "I should try to reach the twins again. I'll do that while you build the fire."

Oliver walked around the little clearing, collecting sticks for firewood. There were many branches, but most were wet from the storm. As he searched for sticks, he came across a large track in the wet dirt. He stooped down to examine it. The rain had washed most if it away, but it looked like a human foot—larger than his own, but human. He tried to imagine why someone would be barefoot in the woods. The track looked fresh, too. Whoever made it might be close and possibly hostile. He'd better not mention it to Tiffany, not right before bed.

Oliver continued his exploration for firewood. He wandered a bit farther from the camp, hoping to find more tracks and possibly discover where they had come from. Several minutes of searching turned up nothing. He did, however, find several pieces of dry wood protected by the freshly fallen leaves. He gathered a bundle in his arms and headed back to the campsite.

Oliver piled the wood several feet away from the scooter. He made a small pile of dry leaves, then a larger pile of twigs. He took the biggest branches he could find and leaned them against each other, creating a teepee over the kindling.

Digging in his pack, Oliver pulled out a little orange ball. He rolled it between his fingers and remembered that his parents had once told him that humans, thousands and thousands of years ago, didn't have an easy way to create fire. They used sticks and stones! That had seemed ridiculous when he was younger, but in the first week of survival training at the Academy he learned some basic fire-building techniques. Oliver smiled and threw the ball against the woodpile. The ball exploded and instantly a fire was crackling. "I love fireballs!" Oliver brushed his hands together in satisfaction for a job well done.

Reaching into his pack again, Oliver pulled out a one-foot camouflage square. He used his foot to scatter some stray leaves and an especially large acorn. He set the camo square on the ground and pulled a small grey wire. The square unfolded, forming a small dome tent.

"Perfect," he said at his second completed task.

Tiffany tried to contact the twins, but didn't get a response. She tapped off the mTalk. "Oliver, neither of them are responding, and they didn't answer when I tried them earlier either."

"Don't worry. They're probably playing a game or chasing after each other. We shut the airlock. I'm sure they'd be too scared to go outside, especially at night and after that storm," Oliver said as he unzipped the opening to the tent. "Maybe they're taking showers."

"They must be playing games!" Tiffany laughed. "I've heard the millions of excuses they give Mom for not showering. Besides, you're right—they wouldn't go outside; they'd be too frightened. Even I am now, a little." Tiffany shivered as she surveyed the dark forest.

Oliver turned on his mTalk's light and swept the perimeter. "The trees are probably causing interference. It's the reason I haven't tried contacting Mr. O'Farrell yet. I can't get a good signal."

"You're probably right. I'll try them again in the morning, maybe once we get to Brighton."

Tiffany opened the food compartment and pulled out two bottles of soup. She unscrewed the caps, which activated the cooking mechanism in the bottles, and steam poured from the openings. Tiffany handed a bottle to Oliver. "What kind did you get? I got potato," Tiffany said.

He didn't even look at the label. Oliver took a sip of the hot soup. The liquid took away the chill of the wind as it coursed through his body. "Wild mushroom."

"Yuck!"

The next few minutes, Oliver and Tiffany ate their soup and discussed the weird types of food they each liked. Once finished, they closed up their packs and secured everything inside compartments on the scooter.

Oliver closed the hatch with a snap. "This way, no animals will get into our stuff."

"Are there any?" Tiffany asked anxiously.

"I don't know, but if there are, I'll have the Zapp-It with me all night." He showed her the small black device with the two silver prongs at the end. "It's set at five thousand volts." Tiffany frowned. "It's just enough to stun something; it's not lethal." His sister's frown turned to a smile. "It's a little disappointing that I won't be heading back to the Academy. There were a lot of really cool things I was going to learn over the next couple of years. I was hoping to become a pilot, maybe even an admiral someday."

Tiffany laughed, and Oliver looked at her, hurt. She quickly clarified why she'd laughed. "You already are a pilot! You just flew the *Phoenix* through a canyon, in hyper flight, and landed in a storm."

Oliver nodded. "That's true."

"I was looking forward to my next semester as well." Tiffany looked at her brother with a half smile. "I missed you at Bewaldeter though. It was weird not watching you play any of your sports."

"I'm sorry. I did miss playing," he cracked a smile. "And I'll admit, I missed you . . . and the twins too."

"Wherever this adventure leads, I don't think our lives will ever be the same."

"I just hope I—we know what to do when the time comes."

"We'll figure it out. Good will prevail over evil. Whoever these men are, the Übel, they don't stand a chance against the Wikk family," Tiffany said firmly.

"You're right." Oliver bowed his head. "Let's get some sleep. We'll need to get up early tomorrow. Every second counts if we're going to rescue our parents on Evad."

Tiffany stood up, stretched her arms, and walked over to the scooter to grab her sleeping bag. With a smile, she climbed into the tent. Oliver grabbed a small lantern out of his bag and turned it on. The light illuminated the clearing. He dimmed it and hung it on a nearby branch. Oliver reached into his pack, pulled out a small black ball, and threw it into the fire. Instantly, the fire vanished, and not even a glowing ember remained.

He thought back to the footprint. Was someone or something out there now? He patted his pocket where the Zapp-It was stored. He'd be ready. Oliver grabbed his sleeping bag from the scooter and climbed into a warm tent, zipping the flap shut.

"I hope the twins are safe," Tiffany said sleepily as she yawned.

"They are." Oliver climbed into his sleeping bag and zipped it up. "Good night, sis."

"Night, Oliver."

Mist

Mason awoke to the trumpeting of a loud horn. He bumped against Austin with his back. "Wake up!"

"Mmm—what?" Austin grumbled, opening his eyes.

"Wake up; something is happening." Mason craned his neck to see over the crates, but couldn't. A moment later, somewhere in the distance, a horn replied. The forest disappeared as they passed into the open. A large blue-grey cliff sat snug against the tall, dark tree line. There was no gap between the two. The rock face towered high over them, disappearing into the clouds.

"Do you hear that?" Austin asked. "Is that—?"

"The water sound," Mason finished. "I think this is the same place we were before."

"They must know," Austin said. "They're going to throw us over the edge. They want justice for the boy." His voice was panicked.

Mason shook his head. "It's not possible. They can't know." A loud horn sounded from within the mist. The caravan's trumpeter answered a reply of several short bugles. The caravan halted and the soldiers approached the twins. Mason frowned. Austin was right. They were going to be thrown over the edge and into the steamy chasm below. His stomach was in knots.

Captain Feng and Alsi untied the boys from each other and helped them off the back of the wagon. The twins were led to opposite sides of the wagon. Austin stumbled forward awkwardly, and Mason realized his twin was missing his left shoe. The blue steam rose up before them like a ferocious torrent swirling and spinning, ready to consume him and his brother. Mason swallowed, but the lump in his throat remained.

Then something broke through the mist. The snout of a huge monster appeared as its lower jaw slammed into the ground before them. Blue steam poured from its mouth. But it wasn't a monster. It was a covered bridge. What had appeared to be a mouth was actually wooden planks and a roof. The wagon driver shook the reins and the three oxen trotted forward. The wagon disappeared into the dense cloud of blue mist. Mason could hear only the sound of the beasts' hooves on wood.

"Let's go." Feng motioned Mason forward. Mason took a deep breath and walked toward the dark mist. Although he was relieved that he wasn't being tossed off a cliff or fed to a monster, he still felt that he was marching to his doom. He glanced at Austin, who returned an uneasy look. Mason moved slowly. Unable to see his own feet, he felt for the wooden planks of the bridge before stepping onto them. The blue mist quickly consumed him, and he lost sight of his brother.

"Mason, are you there?" he heard Austin whisper.

"I'm next to you, I think."

"All right," Austin replied nervously.

The bridge rocked left and right as the warm air rose around them. The faint sound of the oxen's hooves against the wood meant they had some distance to go before they'd be across the ravine. An odd blue glow flickered ahead, infiltrating the mist and eerily electrifying the cloud. A moment later the mist thinned and the flickering became brighter.

Mason's foot struck stone and he tripped, falling free of the blue cloud. He could see everything. They were at the entrance to a fort. Two large ropes made from vines angled down from watchtowers on either side of the bridge. High on the roof of each tower, blue bonfires burned in large stone bowls. Soldiers armed with bows were stationed in the towers.

"Do you see them?" Mason whispered to Austin, pointing his bound hands at one of the towers. Every bow was trained on the twins.

"What are they afraid of?" Austin asked.

Mason shrugged. "I don't know."

Feng looked at the frightened twins and laughed. "Lower your weapons!" he called to each of the towers. "They're just kids."

The twins were standing on a small strip of rock bounded on either side by rivers of the brightest blue Mason had ever seen. The water roared past and poured into the crevice they'd just crossed, creating twin waterfalls. There had to be something really hot deep in that crevice to create all the steam.

A set of large wooden doors was tucked into the cliff ahead. The drawbridge, towers, and archers were there at its defense. The doors stood twenty feet wide and twice as tall. Metal grates allowed only the two rivers to pass through the door unchecked. Mason shivered. Something was being held behind those doors, probably a monstrous beast of some sort. Two men lowered a large wooden wheel into one of the rivers. The wheel slowly began to spin and picked up speed. The ropes attached to the bridge tightened, and the long wooden crossing rose into the air with a painful creaking. The only known escape route vanished before them. A chill crawled over Mason's body.

The twins' captors untied their bound hands. Mason rubbed his wrists and felt small indentations from the rope. Mason's guard, Feng, bowed to the twins. "I am Feng, Captain of the Royal Guard. What are your names?"

"I'm Mason, and this is Austin."

Feng nodded. He pointed to Austin's guard. "This is Alsi. He is my second in command."

"Mr. Feng . . . ummm . . . sir," Austin started. "I think that's our stuff you have in that wagon and—" Austin stopped. He looked at Mason, who shrugged. "—And, well, I lost my shoe. Do you think I could look for a new pair?"

The captain frowned, and then a smile cracked across his face. "Of course you can, but don't take anything but shoes. And don't try anything," Captain Feng warned. Austin nodded and went to the back of the wagon.

Mason looked around at the towers and the fortress that guarded the doors. The position on this side of the chasm was tactically superior to anything that might attempt to breech the rift between the woods and waterfall. A moment later Austin came back wearing a pair of water shoes, but Mason noticed they were actually his. "Hey, those are mine!"

"Yeah, well, I didn't see any of my extra shoes and I didn't have a lot of time," Austin said. "I found my lost shoe that they'd tossed into the wagon, but it was torn across the front."

Mason grunted. "Whatever."

"But I found something useful," Austin whispered.

"What?"

"Well I—," Austin started, but a low horn interrupted their conversation. A rush of cold air swept around the twins, ruffling their hair. They looked toward its source and saw that the large wooden doors were slowly opening. Two soldiers carrying torches stepped forward and lit the torches on either side of the wagon. The wagon rolled forward, its torches now flickering, followed by several soldiers. Feng motioned for the twins to follow. The remaining soldiers from the raiding party followed some distance behind, talking and laughing casually.

"What do you think is in here?" Austin whispered.

"Don't know. Could be all sorts of things—maybe it's a dragon!"

"You're not serious; there are no such things as dragons," Austin replied smugly.

Mason looked at his twin and shrugged his shoulders. "Who says? Did you think there were blue people?"

Austin looked slightly stumped. "Good point. So if there are dragons, don't you think that's bad news for us?"

Mason swallowed. That was true. If they were headed for a dragon, that was extremely bad news. Everything he'd ever read about them said "barbeque."

The twins walked for what felt like miles, with no end in sight. The tunnel curved and branched off so often that Mason lost track of how to get back. Without the mTalk on his wrist, he couldn't rely on his technology to show him where they had been, were now, or would end up. He had noticed that the path they were following was flanked on either side by the same two rivers that had dumped into the chasm at the entrance to the cave. No other rivers existed in the tunnel or flowed out from any of the linking passages. These waterways were the only clear marker of their trail.

The walls of the caves glittered from the flickering blue light of the torches. There was some mineral embedded in the walls that sparkled in the firelight. Perhaps the stone Obbin had tried to trade was native to this cave.

The air was frigid, and Mason was still damp from the rainstorm. He tried rubbing his arms, but it didn't do much good. Goosebumps covered his body. He looked at Austin, who was holding back the shivers as best he could. "We've been walking for at least an hour and I'm so cold."

"I know—it's frrr—eeezing in this cave," Austin answered with a shiver.

"I bet that water is freezing too," Mason said, pointing at one of the rivers flowing next to them. His throat suddenly felt dry. He couldn't remember the last time he had drunk anything. "Boy, I could use a drink."

"Then ask Feng." The captain had walked up to the soldiers guarding the wagon and was talking with them.

Mason shook his head. "No, I don't think so."

"Why not? He was nice when I asked him for the shoes."

Mason sighed. "Sir?" he whispered.

Austin elbowed Mason in the side. "You'll have to speak louder than that."

Mason cleared his throat. "Sir, Captain Feng?" he nearly shouted.

Feng turned around to look at Mason. "Yes, lad?"

"Could I get a drink?"

"Why of course, the water in the river is clean." Feng called for the wagon to stop. "You may get a drink," the captain said as he pointed at one of the rivers. "Do either of you need something to eat?"

Mason nodded. "I could eat something."

"I'll get something from our supplies. Meet me back at the wagon when you're finished."

The twins made their way to the side of the river a short distance from the wagon, but far enough that they had a bit of privacy.

"Now that we're alone I can share my plan with you," Austin said as he crouched down next to the stream.

"What's that?"

Austin stuck his face against the surface of the river and sucked up some water. "Cold!" Austin wiped his mouth with his sleeve. "Look what I took from the wagon." Mason watched as Austin pulled something from his pants: a small silver disc with a screen embedded in its top.

"A LOCA-drone!" Mason exclaimed almost too loudly. The twins looked around to see whether the guards had noticed Mason's outburst, but they didn't seem to be paying attention.

"Yes, but it'll only do us any good if we get out of this cave," Austin admitted.

Mason nodded. "And if Oliver and Tiffany make it back and think to turn on the LOCATOR."

"If we're missing, they'll try everything," Austin assured Mason. "But it won't come to that, because we're escaping."

"How?" Mason asked. "Did you see how heavily guarded the entrance was?"

Austin nodded. "Yes, but the tunnel broke off several times. One of the side tunnels has to lead out."

"You really think so?"

"Sure. First, we have to get away from the soldiers."

"What about now?" Mason asked as he tipped a handful of water into his mouth.

Austin shook his head; only one side of his face could be seen in the flickering blue torchlight. "No, too risky. That captain is watching us, and there are more soldiers behind." Austin bent over to take another draft from the blue water.

"Good point." Mason looked toward the wagon and saw Feng talking to Alsi, who nodded and started toward the twins.

"I think it's time to go; one of them is coming."

Austin stood and looked at Mason. "Try to act normal." Mason nodded and the twins were silent again. Alsi approached and motioned for the boys to come back.

"Are you done?" the soldier asked.

"Yep," replied Austin. The twins rejoined Feng, who handed them each a small blue ball.

"Peel it first, and then you can eat it." Feng pulled out a small blade and slid it across the peel.

"What is it?" Austin asked.

"It's fruit." Mason used his fingers to separate the peel from the inside flesh. He held it to his lips and looked at Austin, who nodded curiously.

He took a bite. The fruit was sweet and juicy. "Orange?"

"It's blue," Austin clarified.

"I know, but it's an orange."

"Weird." Austin bit down and juice trickled down his chin. "Yum."

"Do you like it?" the captain asked. The twins nodded. "You can toss the peel off to the side. One of the cave rodents will enjoy it later."

"Cave rodents?" asked Austin.

"Don't worry, the light from our torches keeps them away."

Austin looked at Mason. "Those things might be a problem," he whispered.

Mason nodded.

"It's time to continue our journey," Feng said, motioning them forward. They walked for several more minutes and around another curve in the tunnel. As they did, the tunnel grew bright with blue light. Several large silver bowls, each lit with blue bonfires, lined either side of the path, like beacons bringing a spaceship in for landing. Two short waterfalls flowed from metal grates set into the rock wall ahead, feeding the parallel rivers. There, between the falls, stood another set of doors.

Blue

One of the oxen made a low humming noise as the driver pulled back on the reins, bringing the wagon to a halt. Feng and Alsi walked past the wagon, picked up two large vines, and began to pull them. A sliver of blue light flickered through the space between the two large doors as they opened. Feng motioned the twins forward, and Austin and Mason stepped through the opening of the cave.

The ground sloped upward, and after a few steps they found themselves between two bridges, one leading to the right and one to the left. The two rivers that had flowed through the cave now merged into a single, wider river that ran down the center of a deep gorge. The bridges led to cobblestone roads running along each side of the river.

Ornate buildings made of blue stucco protruded directly out from the sloping sides of the gorge, almost touching each other. A few narrow alleyways lead to other levels of buildings perched higher on the slope. The structures varied in shades of blue and had exposed wooden frames. Some of the buildings were several stories tall with balconies overlooking the road, while others were only one story with little courtyards and fountains.

"Is this where they live?" Mason wondered in awe.

"Yeah, I think it is." Austin looked around the gorge. "There are hundreds if not thousands of buildings."

"I wonder how long they've been here."

Austin glanced around them and then lowered his voice. "Longer than we'll ever be; we're getting out of here."

Mason pointed at the sides of the gorge. "I don't think we'll be climbing out." Covered by blue-green ferns and tall palms, the rocky walls stretched upward and disappeared into a blue cloud that extended over the entire length of the city. Austin strained his eyes to see the end of the gorge, but it stretched out of view. About every half mile, a tall five-sided tower had been built, and at the top of each, beams protruded with bowls of blue flames hanging from them. The towers lit the nearby hill and street below. The fires burned so brightly that their flicker reflected off the underside of the clouds high above.

Feng walked up beside the twins and pointed them toward the bridge to their left. Austin watched as the wagon crossed the bridge to their right. Getting the supplies would be a lot harder now. Austin kept his eyes on the wagon as they walked. The streets were empty. With his mTalk in the wagon across the sparkling aqua river, Austin had no way to tell the time. His stomach grumbled. The only thing he'd had to eat in a long time was that orange.

"Do you smell that?" Austin asked, sniffing the air. His stomach grumbled again. The smell was increasing his hunger.

Mason sniffed several times. "Yeah." The twins looked around and Mason pointed across the river. Several tables sat under the awning of a two-story building.

"Is that a bakery?" Mason asked.

Austin sniffed again and rubbed his stomach. "Sure smells like fresh bread. It must be morning or something."

Feng looked at them. "Are you still hungry?"

Austin nodded. "Yeah, Mom always says I'm a growing boy." Mason looked at him sadly at the mention of their mom. But

Austin's hungry stomach left him no opportunity for sadness. He had a mission. There was no time to feel emotion.

Feng walked across a high arching bridge to the other side of the river and picked up two small blue bricks. He pointed to the twins and said something to the blue man standing by the tables. The baker nodded and smiled at the twins. Feng brought back the blue bricks and handed one to each of the boys. "You'll like this. Yommus makes the best sweet bread."

Austin smiled nervously, staring at the blue loaf in his hands. It was soft and warm like the bread his mom had made at their compound on Tragiws. He lifted the loaf to his mouth and bit down. The outer layer was crisp and the inside soft and fluffy. His mouth began to water for another bite. It may have been blue, but it was the best bread he had ever eaten. "Thank you," he said with his mouth full. "It's very good." Since Austin was enjoying the bread, Mason took a taste too.

Feng smiled. "You like it?"

"Yes, it's wonderful," Mason said before taking another bite.

Feng nodded and motioned for the twins to follow. "Good, I'm glad." The twins ate as they walked. They admired the grand architecture of the buildings and the ornate sculptures that adorned the courtyards and gardens. Austin had once wanted to be an architect, but that had passed. He'd settled on being an inventor like his grandpa.

They crossed over a small stream. Austin's eyes followed the stream to a waterfall and then up the gorge until it disappeared into the clouds. Mason had already rejected it as an escape option, but how high could the gorge actually stretch? Surely there were hand- and footholds. But, of course, there would be no way to get the supplies out that way. Then his mind jumped to something more daring. He could fly the *Phoenix* into the gorge, land it, repossess the supplies, and escape again. After all, Oliver had no *real* flight time and Austin had probably spent as much time playing flight simulation games as Oliver had in the actual simulator. He was brought back to reality by a tap on his shoulder.

"Do you see that?" Mason asked. He pointed out a small trench branching from the river and pouring into a drain of sorts. Nearby, blue mist poured from several vents. "Maybe that's how they keep it so warm in here. They channel the water to whatever is so hot below, and create steam."

"It's certainly humid in here." Austin started to admire the city. These people had been here awhile, but they lacked the technology that the Wikks were accustomed to. So they had invented machines to meet their needs. A set of waterwheels spinning in the river turned long axles that disappeared into the sides of a building perched on the riverbank. "Some sort of pumping device?" Austin asked.

"Maybe, or maybe it's producing energy." Austin nodded. There was a lot to discover here. Maybe it wasn't urgent to leave immediately. Maybe they'd have a chance to explore a little.

After another mile, they entered a tunnel covered by lush green plants and lit by torches. The flickering blue light reflected off the waxy leaves, giving the tunnel an eerie swamp-like glow. The tunnel walls obstructed the twins' view of the end of the gorge, and when they crossed into the open, they were amazed at what they saw.

The wispy figure of a waterfall laced the face of a tall cliff, its water gracefully weaving among rock and air. The cliff was the end to the city and melded the sides of the gorge together. As they got closer, the thundering noise of the waterfall filled the air. They eventually entered a large, empty cobblestone courtyard. The river they'd been walking beside streamed through the center of the courtyard from where it was born at the base of the waterfall. Louder and louder, the noise of the crashing water grew. A cold wind blew around Austin, ruffling his hair. He could feel the spray of water on his face and bare arms. He gazed up and watched as the water danced along the rocks and on the updrafts of air.

"Do you see that?" asked Mason. Austin brushed his bangs from his eyes and looked at the spot where Mason was pointing. Shrouded behind mist and perched high on the edge of the cliff, sat a cluster of buildings. "Are we going up there?" Mason asked Feng.

Feng turned to look at Mason. "Yes, we're heading to the palace."

Mason looked at his twin and cocked an eyebrow. "Palace?"

The twins followed Feng across the courtyard, toward a tall stone wall. The cliff seemed to grow taller and taller, and they soon lost sight of the palace on top. They stopped at an ornate metal gate, guarded by several soldiers. The one standing nearest to the gate made a slight bow to Feng and opened the door. As they passed through, Austin noticed the wagon on the other side of the river. It sat on a large wooden platform, to which men were attaching large ropes.

Austin nudged Mason and pointed across the river. "The wagon! I almost forgot about it."

Mason frowned, but nodded toward a large wooden platform in front of them. "We're taking the elevator too." Feng guided them onto the platform, and the twins took places in the center. Soldiers attached ropes to the four corners and Feng waved his hand at one of them, who blew four quick notes on a horn. A moment later, the cables tightened and the twins felt a jolt as the elevator lifted from the ground. As they glided upward, Mason grabbed his stomach and bent over.

Austin moved close to his brother and put his arm around him. "You'll be okay."

"I don't like how high up we are," Mason mumbled nervously and then took a seat. "Couldn't there at least be rails or something?" For Mason, the next ten minutes were agonizing, but for Austin they were exciting. He could see the whole gorge, including the entrance to the cave. The city looked even larger from this high up and he could clearly see the different terraces of buildings and gardens. Bright blue waterfalls flowed intermittently between the buildings, eventually feeding into the river below. Suddenly Austin felt small and alone. How could they ever find their way back to the ship? Oliver? Tiffany? They were supposed to be searching for their parents; instead, he and Mason had gotten lost, threatening the success of their quest.

Mason let out a loud groan. Austin looked down and patted his back. "We're almost there."

Less than a minute passed and the platform came level with the top of the cliff. Austin helped Mason to his feet and then onto solid ground. Mason turned and heaved into a bush. Austin turned away, but kept one hand on his twin's shoulder.

Mason recovered, wiped the bile from his mouth, and smiled. "I feel better now."

Austin nodded. "Sure thing." He looked around. They were in a beautiful garden. A large, colorful bird waddled out from under a palm tree.

"What is it?" Mason asked.

Feng smiled. "It's a peacock," he said, and waved them onto a stone path. "There are many roaming the gardens. They were brought here when the gorge was founded many centuries ago." Centuries? This city *was* old, the twins thought.

The twins followed Feng along the garden path as it curved past statues and fountains. Each intricately carved statue was life-sized and made of glossy white stone, the detail so minute that the images looked alive. The fountains were made of multiple tiers; some had jewels inlaid in their stone, while others had carvings of large wild animals spouting water from their mouths or trunks.

It was a serene setting; however, the twins soon came to the end of the stone path where they found themselves staring at yet another door.

Squirrel

Fear awoke Tiffany. She sat up and looked around, listening closely. She heard it again.

"Oliver, Oliver, wake up," she whispered, shaking her sleeping brother. "Wake up! Did you hear that?" His body stirred a little, and he groaned. "Oliver!" she whispered again.

"No, I'm asleep," he mumbled, still lying on his stomach, his eyes closed. He turned his head away from her.

"I heard something outside the tent."

"It's nothing. Go back to sleep." Oliver sat up quickly as an eerie growl came from somewhere outside the tent.

Tiffany stared at the tent flap, wide-eyed. "You had to have heard that!" She leaned closer to her brother.

"Yeah—I heard that."

Her voice quivered. "What was it?"

"How should I know?"

"Oliver . . ." Oliver reached for the Zapp-It and threw off his sleeping bag. It was just him and his sister; there wasn't anyone else to protect them. Oliver knelt and listened. The growl came again, this time from somewhere in front of the door. The sound wasn't very loud, but it was ferocious.

Oliver shook his head. "It can't be a very big animal," he said, but his voice cracked.

Tiffany watched Oliver clutch the Zapp-It tightly in his hand. "Maybe it's not growling as loud as it can."

Oliver turned to her anxiously. "Thanks, Tiff!" The growl was lower this time, as if in warning. Oliver looked toward the back of the tent. He could hear something moving in the woods behind them. The thing in front of the tent suddenly scurried closer and growled again.

The creature behind the tent was replying with higher-pitched hoots. They heard thumping noises, as if it was beating the ground in warning. Oliver shook his head. "What's going on out there?"

Tiffany cocked an eyebrow. "That sounded like a monkey."

"Yes, it did," Oliver said, bemused. He turned the Zapp-It on, and it began to hum. He started slowly unzipping the door to the tent, but jerked back as one of the creatures outside growled again. Finally he pulled aside the tent flap to see out. Where was it? He looked around; the forest was dark, but some moonlight had broken through the clouds above, casting eerie shadows into the clearing. Then he saw it.

In the light from the lantern, he saw a brown furry squirrel sitting next to the base of a wide oak. It was larger than any squirrel he'd ever seen, but it was definitely a squirrel. The animal sat on its haunches with its little paws in front of it. Its tail was bushy and twice the size of its body. Several more thumps came from behind him, and Oliver pulled his head back in.

"What is it?" asked Tiffany.

Oliver smiled. "A squirrel, but it's bigger than I've ever seen."

"Have you seen the size of the nuts out there?"

Oliver nodded. "True."

"What is the other thing? Is it a monkey?"

"I don't know; it's behind us." Oliver moved back to the flap and looked at the squirrel. This time the squirrel noticed

Oliver and growled at him, baring little yellow teeth. He heard some movement from behind them. "Whatever it is, it's moving closer." Oliver raised the Zapp-It.

Unafraid of the growling squirrel, Oliver craned his neck to peer around the side of the tent. There on the ground was one of their packs. It was open, and things were spilt onto the ground. Oliver could see an apple with a bite out of it and several wrappers. The creature, however, was not in sight.

Oliver slowly crawled out of the tent. The squirrel growled and climbed partway up a nearby tree. Oliver looked around, but there was still no sign of the other creature. He checked the Zapp-It's charge meter, which showed full. He took a deep breath and stood up. The squirrel growled and turned in a circle on the tree trunk, clicking its paws against the wood. Oliver waved the Zapp-It at the squirrel and then turned back to look at the pack, but it was gone. He quickly scanned the clearing for the thief. Cautiously walking toward the remaining wrappers, Oliver heard a noise overhead—the same hoot as before.

Something heavy dropped onto his back. Something alive! He spun around, but the thing clung to him. It cried out in his ear, and a paw swiped across the back of his head. Oliver reared around and swung the Zapp-It over his shoulder, pressing the shock button. A miss! The creature dug its fingers into Oliver's neck and shoulders.

"Tiffany, help!" Oliver yelled, his voice higher pitched than he realized it could go. Tiffany scurried from the tent as Oliver spun around in circles. Oliver heard his sister break into uncontrollable laughter.

The thief, the attacker, the antagonist was nothing more than a little grey monkey.

Tiffany stumbled toward him, overcome with fits of laughter. She waved her arm at the monkey, but it clung to him tightly. Finally, Oliver dropped the Zapp-It and reached his hands over his shoulder to grab the monkey. He wrenched it from his back and over his head. The little creature stared into Oliver's eyes. For a moment, Oliver couldn't help but notice how innocent it looked. It would make a good pet.

"Yeow!" cried Oliver as the monkey bit into his thumb. Oliver released the monkey and it scurried over to a nearby tree and up to the lowest branch. Oliver held out his bleeding digit. He looked around at his sister with a shocked expression. "I was not expecting that."

Tiffany broke into laughter again. "It . . . you spinning. It's a tenth of . . . wow." Grabbing her side, she collapsed to the ground, giggling. "From your squeals I was expecting something . . . bigger!"

"Ha, ha—very funny." Oliver looked at her wryly. "I didn't squeal." It took a moment for Tiffany to recover, and Oliver pulled her to her feet.

"The pack—the monkey has it on the branch," Tiffany said, pointing to the tree. Oliver glanced at the tree and shook his fist at the monkey, who was now happily perched above.

"I think he gashed my neck," Oliver said as he reached around to feel for something.

Tiffany looked through the hair on the back of his head and pulled down the neckline of his shirt. "No, it doesn't look like he got you too bad. There are a few scratches, but nothing deep."

Oliver shook his shoulders. "Well, he did get my thumb. Look at that." He held it out—it was red.

"I'll bandage it in a minute, but the monkey still has our pack."

Oliver grabbed the Zapp-It from the ground and charged the tree.

"Mr. Monkey, you better run!" The monkey reached for the pack, pulled it up to a higher branch, and squealed at Oliver, who was standing at the base of the tree. Oliver waved his arms and the monkey started to climb higher, but this time it fumbled the pack, and it tumbled to the ground. Oliver swept it up protectively. Again, he shook a fist at the monkey with a laugh. "That's right. You'd better run."

Oliver turned and walked back toward Tiffany as she smiled and laughed. "You tell him, Ollie."

Eyebrows furrowed, Oliver glared at his sister. "Put this in the tent." He handed Tiffany the pack and then laughed. "I'll grab the other ones."

Somehow the monkey had managed to open the compartments. Of course, one of his classes at the Academy had been on evolution. He knew how close to humans monkeys were—just one step up the evolutionary chain according to his professor. Of course, his parents had never bought the evolutionary theory. "Too many gaps," they said. "Too much chance was needed to make it actually work." Oliver gathered the rest of the packs from the scooter and placed them inside the tent.

"Well, that was interesting," Tiffany said.

"You're telling me." Oliver and Tiffany heard the squirrel growl at the monkey again. The Wikks laughed together as they listened to the two animals bicker. "Well, let's try to get a bit more sleep before we go."

"Sounds good." Tiffany yawned and climbed back into her sleeping bag. "Good night and thanks for protecting me," she said with a giggle.

Oliver smiled. "Yeah, real funny, Tiff. Good night."

1.20

King

ustin stared at the set of arched wooden doors. A couple of soldiers in silver armor, armed with axes of all things, stood guard. The soldiers pulled the doors open at Feng's command. The twins entered a foyer that sat at the foot of a wide set of iridescent blue stairs, like the crystal Obbin had traded them. At the top of the stairs, they came into a long room with an arched ceiling that towered thirty feet above, supported by thick silver pillars. Fireplaces lined the sides of the room, each with an arrangement of plush couches and chairs resting on thick rugs. Great silver bowls with blue fires burning inside hung from chains, floating twelve feet overhead and bathing the room in a blue glow.

"This is the Great Hall," explained Feng. The twins followed the captain to the end of the grand room where they stood at the base of a small platform. A silver throne sat atop, and in it sat a jolly looking blue man dressed in dark fur robes. On his head of light blue hair was a silver crown, adorned with sapphires on each of its points. Feng bowed and motioned for the twins to do the same, which they did.

In response, the jovial man smiled and then spoke, "Greetings my young friends. My name is King Dlanod." The king's voice was low and friendly. "Welcome to the Kingdom of the

Blauwe Mensen." For a moment, the twins said nothing. They weren't sure what to do. They had never met a king before.

"Uhhh," Mason stuttered. "My name is Mason."

"And I'm Austin."

"Very good. It's nice to meet you," the king said with a laugh.

A man next to the king stepped forward, his hands clasped before him. He was short in comparison with Feng, but the stern demeanor of his face compensated for his physical stature. He wore a grey suit, with a black tie over a white shirt. On his feet he wore a pair of shiny, black shoes. His outfit seemed out of place, in comparison with the king's garb of fur robes and Feng's attire of just fur shorts and a sash. His hair was bright blue, and nearly matched his skin tone.

He turned to the king and bowed his head slightly. "My name is Alfred Thule and I've been tasked with your transition," he addressed the twins. Mason frowned. Transition? What did that mean? "When the king was made aware of your existence, he summoned me and would not sleep until he had met you," Mr. Thule said.

The king nodded. "Good night," he said with a smile. "I do look forward to talking with you tomorrow."

"Good night, sir," Mason said.

Austin made a half bow. "Night."

"Now it is time for bed," Mr. Thule said sternly. "Feng will show you to your room. Try to get a full night's sleep; you are in no danger here." Mr. Thule smiled, but it felt wrong to Mason. The man's tone was unnecessarily short and stern.

Feng led the boys toward a passage at the right of the Great Hall. The twins walked through an archway to the right of the throne. As they left, Mason could hear the king and Mr. Thule talking, but he couldn't decipher what they were saying.

Up several flights of a spiral staircase and then down a long narrow hall lined with ornate tapestries they went. Mason stopped counting the number of rooms after twenty. Finally, Feng halted and opened a door, motioning the twins inside.

The room was circular, with a large, domed ceiling. In the center, a small round table sat low to the floor, surrounded by several dozen cushions.

"Sleep well," Feng said as he pulled the door shut.

Austin looked at Mason. "That's it. We came, said hi, good-night, and then were sent to our cell?"

"This hardly looks like a cell," Mason contended.

Austin laughed. "True. But we are their prisoners."

Mason smiled as he looked around the room. Aside from not having the freedom to come and go, and being separated from all but his brother, this didn't look all that bad. A tray of crackers and fruit was laid out on the table, so the twins helped themselves to a snack. Mason looked up at the domed ceiling. Painted with stars and planets, it was clearly a galactic map.

Austin stepped over to a large stone fireplace, above which a window stretched up the remaining distance to the ceiling. Next to the hearth, a fountain poured into a basin mounted in the wall. Austin swirled his finger in the cold blue water and noticed two cups on a shelf. Taking one, he filled it and took a long swig from the cup. "It's cold and—sweet," Austin said. "Come and try."

Mason joined his little brother at the sink and filled a cup. He took a swig, and a wide grin crossed his face. "I could drink this all day—errr morning long." He looked around the room. "This room is huge. I wish Tiffany and Oliver could see it."

"Where do you think they are?"

"I don't know, but I hope they're better off than we are."

"Besides the fact we've been taken prisoner into an unknown place, we're living quite luxuriously," Mason smirked. Mason picked up a fluffy dark green pillow and tossed it at Austin. His brother caught it and laughed. Holding the soft pillow against his head, he yawned. "I think it's time for some sleep." He looked at Mason who also yawned. After gathering several cushions together, the twins fell asleep instantly.

1.21

Morning

Oliver yawned and stretched his arms. The sides of the tent were aglow from the sun outside. He looked at his mTalk. "Wake up Tiff! Wake up! We overslept." Oliver shook his sister's shoulders.

"What are you doing?" she mumbled.

"We've been sleeping for nine hours. We've got to go!"

Oliver unzipped the tent and yanked his sleeping bag with him. He shoved it into a compartment on the scooter without rolling it. Tiffany barely crawled from the tent with her sleeping bag when Oliver pulled a red wire and the tent collapsed. He folded the tent into an awkward square and shoved it in with the sleeping bag.

"Slow down, Oliver!"

He cut her off. "No! We wasted too much time sleeping."

"Oliver, what's wrong?" Tiffany had never seen him so frantic before.

"Nothing's wrong. Just pack up so we can go," he said. Tiffany looked into Oliver's brown eyes. She saw disappointment. The best thing she could do at the moment was help him. She noticed how much colder it was and quickly took a more insulated coat from her pack, along with some gloves and a hat that covered her ears. She got a warmer coat, gloves, and hat for Oliver as well. He was clearly too busy packing to think about the weather.

Before he climbed on the scooter to start it up, she handed him the stuff. He sighed and put the winter gear on. She knew he wouldn't say it, but he was thankful. She was already strapped on when he climbed into the driver's seat. "Ready, Ollie," Tiffany said cheerfully. He smiled and paused for a moment. The nickname had reminded him of when they were younger.

Tiffany heard him sigh. "What is it, Oliver?"

Oliver smiled. "I just thought of a vacation we were on with Dad and Mom. Those were the days—no responsibility, just all of us on a warm sunny beach."

"That's a good memory. We'll have that again someday." Tiffany smiled. She pulled her mom's journal from the pack and opened it up. Where was she in her searching? She remembered. She wanted to find out more about the man in black, Captain Vedrik.

"Here we go." Oliver turned the throttle and the scooter surged forward. The maglev rail ran straight for several miles, and judging by the map, led directly to the city. The ground sloped downward as they entered into a valley covered in trees clothed in orange and brown leaves.

"What's the temperature?" Oliver asked.

Tiffany looked at the journal's screen. "That can't be right. It's twenty degrees lower than yesterday at this time."

"Well, let's just hope we can find the part for the *Phoenix* in Brighton. I don't think we will have time to make it to Mudo before the planet freezes." Oliver cleared his throat. "And thanks for getting me out some warmer stuff."

"You're welcome," Tiffany said.

The forest became sparse over the next three miles as they flew onto an open plain. A large transparent dome appeared on the horizon. Brighton was in sight. "The dome over Brighton is a mile in diameter," Tiffany said. "It was built to protect the citizens from the harsh winter."

Oliver nodded. "I hope we're not here long enough for that."

"Me neither."

"I'm going to try to reach Mr. O'Farrell again." Oliver let off the throttle and the scooter slowed. He tapped in Mr. O'Farrell's contact info on the scooter's radio. Nothing happened, and then a message indicated that a connection could not be established.

"I can't reach him," Oliver said. "Are you sure you gave me the right contact information?" he asked.

"I'll check again." She searched the journal, located Mr. O'Farrell's information, and sent it to Oliver.

"That's what I was using." Oliver shrugged. "I guess we'll have to go in on our own. Since we don't know the protocol for entry into Brighton, let me do the talking."

"Don't worry, I will."

"Well, unless of course I don't speak their language."

"Thanks," she answered sarcastically.

As they approached the dome, several roads converged with the maglev track, all leading to one gate. A dozen vehicles were lined up waiting to enter, so Oliver flew to the back of the line. A squad of guards dressed in brown-and-white camouflage parkas was manning the checkpoint. They were stopping every vehicle and checking them over.

Minutes passed and Oliver was getting nervous. There were only four vehicles still ahead of them. He'd started to wonder whether the guards had a list, or whether he needed some sort of entry token. What if he couldn't get in the city or they couldn't get a hold of Mr. O'Farrell? They'd have to either try to go to Evad themselves, or risk calling Archeos. Neither option was ideal. If only there were someone he could turn to.

"Excuse me," a voice said from beside. Oliver was startled and throttled the scooter, nearly sending him and Tiffany into the back of the ship ahead. An old man with white hair, wearing an emerald tweed flat cap, hovered next to them on a scooter. He wore a brown tweed jacket, white buttoned-up undershirt, green tie that matched his hat, and brown dress trousers. The outfit didn't seem to fit the weather. His eyes were an emerald green, and he had a round nose. His cheeks were rosy and smile lines were evident on his face. In fact, at the moment he was smiling.

"May I ask you what department your parents work for?" the man asked in a thick accent that Oliver couldn't quite place.

"What do you mean?" Oliver asked, anxious about the sudden inquisition.

"You're on an Archeos scooter, so I assume your parents work for the Alliance. Either that or you stole it," he added with a chuckle. The vehicles moved forward and Oliver and Tiffany were now fourth in line. Oliver looked at the man curiously. The old man pointed to an emblem on the side of the Wikks' sky scooter. His scooter had the same emblem. Oliver turned the throttle, moving the scooter forward as another vehicle passed through the gate.

"I don't mean to sound rude, but we are in a bit of a hurry to find someone."

"I see. May I ask whom? I might be able to help you," the old man offered politely. The old man straightened his back and fixed the cuffs on his tweed jacket.

"No sir. Our business is our own and we prefer to keep it that way," Oliver said curtly.

The old man frowned, but nodded his head in understanding. "I see. Well then, I wish you success in your quest."

Tiffany tapped Oliver. "He sounds so familiar, but I can't figure out why," she whispered.

Oliver whispered back. "Just ignore him and maybe he'll go away."

"Yeah, but—"

"But we are running out of time, and we need to find the part and get out of here," Oliver interrupted. He twisted the throttle and the craft moved forward. There were only two vehicles ahead of them. If he could just get past the guards, he could get away from the old man, but right now, they had nowhere to go.

A guard walked toward them. "Tiffany, put the journal away," Oliver whispered.

"Pass please?" the guard asked as he approached.

"Uh, oh yeah," Oliver stammered. They didn't have any passes into the city. There may have been some aboard the *Phoenix* somewhere, since his parents had been here before, but that wasn't going to do them any good now. He couldn't waste time going back to the ship. They'd have to take their chances in the other city. "Well—"

"I have the pass right here," a voice said from behind them. It was the old man. "Yes, right here. Kids, kids, you got ahead of me!" the man lied. "Here is the pass, sir." The guard walked to him and looked at the old man suspiciously. He took the pass and glanced over it. Oliver bit his lip as they waited.

"How old are the kids?"

The old man looked at Oliver.

Oliver cleared his throat. "I'm seventeen and she's fifteen," he said, pointing to his sister.

"Do you have your own passes?" the guard asked.

"No, we left them at home. They aren't required to have them," the old man argued.

"You're correct, but we like to be extra careful this time of year," he said sternly. Then in a lowered voice as an aside, "Keep out all the Mudo riffraff, you know."

The old man nodded his head, "Yes, that's true."

The guard smiled and scanned the old man's pass. A minute passed. Nothing was happening and the guard looked flustered. Finally, the device emitted a soft beep. "All right, looks good, Mr. O'Farrell. Sorry about the delay. Eises is wreaking havoc on our communications systems."

Oliver gasped, and he felt Tiffany squeeze his shoulders. She whispered into his ear, "It's him."

The guard motioned to the guards by the gate. "They're clear." One of the guards waved his arm for the kids and Mr. O'Farrell to proceed. They had done it! They'd needed help, but they'd made it into Brighton. Oliver felt a bit calmer now. He followed Mr. O'Farrell through the gate and they pulled off to the side.

"Mr. O'Farrell?" Oliver asked intently.

"That's right," Mr. O'Farrell said.

"Phelan O'Farrell?"

"Yes, and who are you?" Mr. O'Farrell asked.

"I'm Oliver Wikk and this is Tiffany, my sister," Oliver explained.

Mr. O'Farrell's mouth dropped open; he appeared to be shocked by this revelation. "Where are your parents?"

"Well, that's why we're here," Oliver explained. "But can we talk somewhere private?"

"Yes, certainly. We can head to my place. But I must know, are your parents safe?"

Oliver frowned and he felt a lump in his throat. He had to be honest with himself. "We think so."

Mr. O'Farrell looked at Tiffany. Tears swelled in her brown eyes. "Dear one, please do not cry," Mr. O'Farrell pleaded with Tiffany. "Let's go to my suite, and quickly." He looked around them cautiously. "We must be careful. Follow me." Mr. O'Farrell throttled his sky scooter and headed down the road.

"Hold on tightly," Oliver told his sister as the scooter accelerated. "Why did you help us?" Oliver asked as he flew up next to Mr. O'Farrell.

"I could tell you didn't have passes by the look on your face," Mr. O'Farrell said, raising his eyebrows. "I wouldn't want two children to be left out in Eises." Oliver frowned. Children! He wasn't a child. He fought back his desire to clarify.

"Eises?" Tiffany asked.

"It's the name of the ice storm that is about to strike and lay waste to anything outside the protective barrier of the dome," Mr. O'Farrell explained.

"Oh, yes. I'd read about the storm before," Tiffany shouted. "I only hope Mason and Austin are inside."

"Are your brothers here as well?" he asked.

"Yes, we had to leave them on the *Phoenix*," Oliver explained.

"I'd read about the storm before we came, but we weren't sure when it would strike," Tiffany said.

Mr. O'Farrell looked worried. "I don't want to alarm you. But we have less than forty-eight hours." He looked at Tiffany. "But don't worry, we'll get what you need and get off this planet before then."

"Do you know anything of our parents, or the men who took them?" Oliver asked.

"You say someone took them?" the old man asked, genuinely concerned and seemingly shocked.

"Yes, soldiers," Tiffany said.

Mr. O'Farrell held up one hand. "I see—yes, I think it best we wait until we are inside," he said seriously. Oliver and Tiffany looked at him with concern. "Once we're inside, you can tell me everything that has happened, and I'll do my best to string together the pieces."

1.22

Awake

Austin stretched his arms and opened his eyes; he'd never slept so comfortably before. The warm fire crackling, the soft fluffy pillows, and the long day leading up to their capture had made for a deep, peaceful sleep. He looked at the window above the fireplace. It didn't appear to be any lighter outside; was it still morning?

Rolling over, Austin saw his twin. Still asleep, his mouth was open as he breathed rhythmically. A new cart of fresh food and drink had been brought in. He crawled across the pillows and grabbed something that looked like a purple apple, confirming it with a single juicy bite. Sampling the other items on the plate, he identified each of the blue foods: pears, sticky buns, and grapes. Austin tilted a pitcher, poured its contents into a glass, and took a sip. It wasn't cow's milk; it was thicker and creamier—oxen milk perhaps?

A snore reminded him that his brother was still out cold and at the youngest Wikk's mercy. He smiled as devious thoughts slipped into his mind. Grabbing a handful of grapes, Austin crawled back to where his brother lay. He tossed a grape toward Mason's mouth but it bounced off his forehead. Another grape ricocheted off his chin, and then one off his nose. Perfect! The third grape hit the target. Mason stirred and shut his mouth, chewing the grape inside. He opened his eyes and stretched. Austin threw a handful of grapes, peppering Mason in the face. Mason sat up and saw Austin laughing a few feet away.

"What time is it?" Mason yawned and wiped his cheek.

"I don't know, but I think it's late. Did you sleep well?"

"Yeah, I've never slept better. I was so tired."

"Me too. They brought in a new tray of food, if you want some."

Mason followed Austin back to the cart and the two began to indulge in the fruits, rolls, and milk. It was quite the spread, more than enough for two eleven-year-olds. After sampling the entire tray, they found they liked the sticky buns most.

"So what do you think they will have us do today?" Mason asked as he plucked a few grapes from the bunch and tossed them into his mouth.

"I don't know. We have to meet with the king," Austin said, refilling his glass of milk and reaching for another roll.

Mason held out his cup and Austin filled it with milk. "I just don't understand. They take us against our will and then they bring us before their king—"

"Who seemed very friendly," Austin interrupted with a sticky smile.

"Exactly. Look at how they've treated us. Why this awesome room and lots of food? I just don't get it. You'd think we'd be in a damp, smelly dungeon somewhere." Neither of them spoke for a moment.

"Oh well," Mason said as he picked up a roll and put it in his pocket. He licked his sticky fingers and smiled.

"What's that for?"

"Later. We might get hungry and we don't have any money."

"Good point." Austin stuffed some grapes and an apple in his pockets.

The twins walked over to the fountain together and splashed water on their faces, trying to get the stickiness off. "It's nice not having anyone telling us to take a bath," Austin said. After washing, the twins opened their door and saw a guard across the hall. A low, nasal rumble came from the blue man, who sat slumped in a chair.

"He's asleep," Mason whispered.

Austin rubbed his hands together and stepped into the hall. He looked each way down the hall. No one was in sight. "Think we can escape?" asked Austin.

"No. We're in the middle of their city." Mason frowned. "Escaping isn't going to be easy."

"True. Well, what should we do?"

"I guess wake the guard," Mason supposed. "You do it."

"Why me?" Austin asked.

"Because."

"Because why?"

"Fine. Rock, Paper, Scissors."

"Okay."

Mason and Austin slammed their fists into their hands three times and then revealed. "Paper beats rock," Mason said.

"All right," Austin conceded. He tiptoed closer to the sleeping man. The guard's spear was carelessly leaned against the wall.

Austin looked back at Mason nervously. "Do it," mouthed Mason. Austin reached out one hand and tapped the guard's arm, which lay across the blue man's lap. Nothing.

Austin looked back at Mason and mouthed, "What now?"

"Shake it," Mason whispered.

Austin crinkled his nose. "Fine." He grabbed the man's shoulder and shook it.

"Uhhh . . . what—huh?" the guard stammered as he awoke. "Yes sir. Right away sir." The blue man looked around and saluted to no one in particular. Rubbing his eyes, the man took notice of Austin and immediately got to his feet, knocking his spear over in the process. "Oh, you. What are you doing out of your room?" the guard asked as he bent over to reclaim his spear.

Austin shrunk back toward the door. "Um . . . we're awake and we're supposed to talk to the king today."

"Oh—yes—right. I am to take you to Mr. Thule in the Great Hall," the guard admitted. "Follow me."

When they entered the Great Hall, Austin saw Mr. Thule sitting by one of the fireplaces, reading a book. The twins recongnized the bound ream of pages only because their parents had uncovered a few through their expeditions. Otherwise, books didn't exist in the Federation. Some sort of Imperial purge decades ago.

"Mr. Thule, I have brought the boys to you as requested," the guard said. Mr. Thule didn't look up from his book immediately. He flipped another page and finished a chapter. He sighed as he looked up at the guard and his charges.

"You are dismissed," Mr. Thule said haughtily. The guard bowed his head and walked away.

"Hello boys," Mr. Thule said, setting his book on the round table next to his oversized chair. "How was your night?"

"Fine, I suppose," answered Mason.

"You suppose?" Mr. Thule asked. "Is that how you speak to adults?" Mr. Thule frowned as he looked over the twins. Mason felt like the man could see right through him. "Didn't you see the change of clothes I sent you?" Mr. Thule asked sternly.

The twins shook their heads in unison. "No," Austin said with an edge. Mason jammed his elbow into Austin's side, causing the younger twin to grunt.

"Our apologies, we did not see the clothing you made available to us," Mason said politely. "Would you like us to go change?"

The old man shook his head. "No, it won't be necessary at the moment." The old man adjusted his tie and then stood.

Mason eyed the book on the table. "Sir, what were you reading?"

"You know what this is?" Mr. Thule asked with surprise.

Mason nodded, "It's a book."

The old man nodded. "You know of these relics from the past?"

"Our parents—" Mason started, but was cut off with a kick to his shin while Austin coughed loudly. Mason glared at his twin.

Austin faked a smile. "Our parents showed us one in a museum once," he said, covering. Mason nodded. It was true; they'd seen one in the Archeos museum collection before. He didn't argue with his brother's interruption. Clearly Austin didn't want Mason to reveal their parents' career aspirations to Mr. Thule.

"So what were you reading?" Mason asked again.

"Just another one of the lineage books of the Blauwe Mensen." Mr. Thule sighed exhaustedly. "Their library is full of them," Mr. Thule said as he took his jacket from the back of his chair. The older man put his arms through the sleeves and shook his shoulders so the jacket fell into place.

"They have a library?" asked Mason excitedly.

"Yes, one of the few remaining ones," Mr. Thule explained. "I'm surprised you are so interested."

Austin looked at Mason warningly. "Yes, I am. I love reading," Mason explained.

"Well, there are some very old books in this library."

"Can we visit it sometime?" Mason asked.

"I'm not sure they would grant you access," Mr. Thule cautioned. "They are very protective of their past. I wasn't granted access until I'd been here for seven years."

"Seven years?" Mason asked.

"Yes, I came to live with these people nine years ago," Mr. Thule explained.

"What do you mean, 'these people'? Aren't you one of them?" asked Austin flatly.

"No, no," Mr. Thule stuttered, caught slightly off guard. "I am blue, but I am not one of them."

"But how come you're blue?" Austin asked.

"That was rude," Mason whispered, poking Austin in the side. He waited for the old man to scold Austin and give a terse warning on manners. Instead, Mr. Thule shocked him.

"Oh no, don't worry. I wondered the same thing at first. You see—" Mr. Thule started, but stopped as Feng approached.

"Good morning, Mr. Thule. Good morning, boys," Feng said with a slight bow of the head.

"Hello, Feng," Mr. Thule responded. An air of superiority had returned to his voice.

"Good morning," the twins said together.

"The king would like the boys to meet him in the Aqua Cathedral," Feng explained.

Mr. Thule frowned. "If they must go, they will need swim shorts. Can you get some from one of the princes?" asked Mr. Thule. "Perhaps prince Rylin or Branz would be the same size. I'll have these two wait for you in their room."

"Yes, certainly," Feng said, and then left.

"But, we want to know about the blue people," Austin said anxiously.

"Later. For now we must do what the king wants," Mr. Thule said with slight annoyance. "Now, go up to your room. Feng will bring you some swim shorts and then show you to the Aqua Cathedral." With those words, Mr. Thule took the book from the table and walked away.

Tea

Oliver and Tiffany followed Mr. O'Farrell down the road. Ahead of them, Oliver could see a tall tower, which appeared to hold up the center of the dome. The buildings got progressively taller as they neared the city center. The road curved to the right in a ring around the city. After a few blocks they parked their sky scooters outside an eight-story building with green windows. They took an elevator to the eighth floor. When the lift stopped, the doors did not open until Mr. O'Farrell typed a code into a small keypad. A voice came across a small speaker overhead, catching Oliver and Tiffany off guard. "Welcome home. The current temperature is seventy-two degrees and the time is 9:21."

The elevator doors opened and the kids stepped into a nicely decorated foyer. "While you were out, I watered the plants and cooked your lunch," the voice added.

"Thank you, Sylvia. I have guests, could you prepare two more meals and boil some water?" Mr. O'Farrell said as he removed his emerald flat cap and set it on the table.

"I will do as you have asked. Is there anything else you need?" the voice asked kindly.

"No, thank you," Mr. O'Farrell said. "Sylvia is my automated home assistant. I wouldn't know what to do without her," Mr. O'Farrell said absentmindedly. Oliver looked at Tiffany oddly. He knew about these types of systems but had never heard anyone converse with one in such a personal way.

"Can I take your jackets?" Mr. O'Farrell asked. "Come in out of the foyer." Mr. O'Farrell extended his arm toward an archway. They entered a large open room with a couple of couches and five chairs, surrounding a large oval coffee table.

"The water is ready, sir," Sylvia informed them.

"Ah, what would you two like? I have peach tea, green tea, apple tea, or Russian tea."

"Russian tea? What is that?" Tiffany asked.

"Oh, my dear, Russian tea isn't like anything you've had before. It's a special recipe passed down to me from my mother who got it from her mother, who got it from her father and so on and so forth. This tea can be traced back, well, I assume to my ancestors on Ursprung."

Oliver's ears perked up. "Well then does that mean you know where Ursprung is?"

"No, no, my dear boy. I can trace my ancestors back a long way, but not that far back," Mr. O'Farrell said, shaking his head somberly. "There is much about our past that is still a mystery." Oliver and Tiffany smiled back at him curiously.

"You two make yourselves at home. I'll make some Russian tea, okay?"

"That would be lovely," replied Tiffany, smiling.

"If you don't mind, I'll just have some water," Oliver answered with a shrug. He wasn't interested in small talk; he wanted to find out about his parents.

"All right," Mr. O'Farrell answered.

Tiffany watched Mr. O'Farrell walk around the counter and get some mugs from the cupboard. "What do you think?" she whispered, leaning toward Oliver.

Oliver looked out the window. "I don't know."

"This place is beautiful. It's decorated with so many artifacts and art," Tiffany observed appreciatively, sitting back.

"I don't care about tea," Oliver replied smugly, not paying attention to anything Tiffany said. "We need to find our parents." Oliver walked over to the window and took a deep breath.

"Yes, but he's our parents' benefactor. They were coming to see him. He can help us," Tiffany explained.

Oliver gazed out into the city. He could see all the way to the outer wall of the dome and even beyond it. Vehicles were still lined up at the gate to be checked by the soldiers. He frowned at having to venture out of the city and back into the dense forest, especially with the approaching cold. They were wasting precious seconds with this *tea time.*

"Yes, well, he had better not slow us down," Oliver finally answered.

Tiffany picked up a large, ragged-looking book and began to flip through it. It appeared to be a journal, handwritten and full of dates, maps, and detailed sketches. Oliver returned to the table and made himself comfortable in the chair at the head. The two couches lined the long sides of the oval table, with the four other chairs angled on each corner. Where he was sitting was a fitting place for him to be—in charge.

"Oliver, look at this," Tiffany said, holding the book open to her brother. "It's a sketch, and it's labeled Valley of Shadows. Mom and Dad were just there not more than a year ago," she said curiously. She put the book back in her lap and looked at it. "Well, at least I think it's the same place."

"Is it important?" Oliver asked carelessly, looking at the screen on his mTalk.

The smile on his sister's face dropped. "I don't know. I'll have to check the journal."

Realizing he'd been short and condescending to Tiffany, he sat on the couch next to her. "I'm sorry. I'm just so anxious."

"I know. It's hard; things are out of our control. We know so little, but Mr. O'Farrell can help us," she encouraged.

"It's just that we know where our parents are likely headed. I just want to get there before we miss them," Oliver confessed.

Tiffany smiled. "I know, but be patient." She began flipping through the book again, pointing at things she thought were interesting. For several minutes, she and Oliver looked through the book.

"I see you have found my book." The kids flinched at Mr. O'Farrell's voice. They turned to look at him as he set the drinks in front of them. "There is no hiding it now," he said, looking at the book in Tiffany's hand. Oliver and Tiffany's ears perked up at the possibility that a secret was about to be revealed.

"I have a lot in common with your parents." Mr. O'Farrell took a seat in the head chair. "As you have probably noticed, the work in that book is a collection of scattered pieces. Most have no visible common thread, but I do believe there is something that links them—Ursprung." A smile formed on his lips, and then he took a sip of the steaming liquid in his mug.

"Really?" asked Tiffany. "How long have you been searching?"

"Just over twenty-five years," Mr. O'Farrell answered. "I've been keeping my ears open for any hint of a clue that may lead me to the secret of mankind's origin."

"What made you so interested?" Tiffany asked.

Mr. O'Farrell's smile disappeared for a moment. Almost a minute passed before the old man spoke, and the kids became anxious in his silence. "Well, I found a relic a long time ago, when I was twenty-two and working for an exploration company. At the time I didn't know its potential value and so I—" he paused. "I don't have it anymore. That is why your parents' work is so important to me. They have discovered many clues and artifacts that may lead to Ursprung or even greater secrets."

"Greater secrets?" Tiffany asked. "Like what?"

Mr. O'Farrell hesitated, as if choosing his words. He cleared his throat. "That is a rather complicated question and we should wait until you have time to better understand my answer."

Oliver raised an eyebrow at Tiffany, but she shook her head so he wouldn't push the question. "So why do you think our parents have been taken hostage?" he asked instead.

"Your parents are quite well known in the archeological community; their fame spreads with each new discovery," Mr. O'Farrell explained. "While I am disturbed at their capture, I am not entirely surprised by it. There are many people after that *greater* something."

"Disturbed? I'm a bit more than disturbed," Oliver said, the frustration in his voice rising. "Men broke into our house and took my parents against their will; that's just slightly more than disturbing, wouldn't you say?" Oliver was nearly shouting.

"I understand that, and we will have justice," Mr. O'Farrell said. "But first, please tell me about these men."

"Well—" Tiffany started.

"They're called the Übel," Oliver interrupted. "They came two nights ago and broke into our home and captured our parents." The anger was still boiling inside Oliver.

Mr. O'Farrell sat straight back in his seat. "The Übel you say?"

"So you have heard of them?" Oliver asked.

Mr. O'Farrell's expression grew dark. "Indeed I have. They are a secret order that date back more than a thousand years. Some believe them to have existed at the beginning of the Empire."

"Empire?" asked Tiffany.

"Yes, before the Federation was formed, it was called the Empire," Mr. O'Farrell explained. "In fact it was the Empire up until little more than a hundred years ago."

"Tiffany, can you wait with the questions?" Oliver asked impatiently.

She looked at him apologetically. "Sorry."

"It's no problem," Mr. O'Farrell answered politely and raised a white bushy eyebrow at Oliver. "No one truly knows who the Übel are. However, they are dangerous and some believe connected to the Federation on many levels. It is said they are the wealthiest organization, save the Federation. It would seem they have become more active in the last few years. Rumors of a new leader in their order have circulated recently. Of course we have no proof of their existence, nor for that matter whether there was a change in power."

"Proof! I saw them with my own eyes," Oliver interrupted. He was furious. He could feel his body shaking involuntarily. His temples pulsed in anger. He would make these men pay for what they had taken from him. "It was late, just past midnight. I headed back to our home, and this captain had invaded the compound with his men," Oliver began.

"Was his name Vedrik?" Mr. O'Farrell asked.

"You know of him?" asked Tiffany.

"I do indeed. We suspected the Übel, your parents and I. Vedrik had been following them for some time."

"Yes, Mom said he was always there, lurking in the shadows. She called him the man in black," Tiffany explained.

"What do you mean Mom called him the man in black?" Oliver asked. "You said they hadn't told you anything about all of this."

"I found it in my reading," she defended. "I just hadn't told you about it yet."

He didn't look convinced, but he cleared his throat anyway and continued. "The captain and our parents spoke of an offer, and of a discovery at Dabnis Castle." Oliver added, "Our brother Mason suggested that there must be a mole in Archeos." Oliver saw Mr. O'Farrell's shocked expression. "It seemed that the book they had discovered was the final piece to the puzzle or something."

"I know of the book, but how did Vedrik hear of it?" Mr. O'Farrell shook his head. "Your assumption is correct; there must have been a leak. So what happened next?"

"I esca—" Oliver stopped. "I was chased away from the compound. I'd hoped for a chance to free them, but the captain saw me and called for his men. Dad commanded me to rescue Tiffany and the twins."

"We barely escaped," Tiffany added. "Star fighters pursued us through a canyon, and if not for Oliver's awesome flying we'd be captured this very moment, like our parents."

Oliver blushed and cocked his head to the side proudly.

"Well, what an experience. Your dad would be very proud of you, Oliver," Mr. O'Farrell said, and then looked at Tiffany. "Dear, do not worry. We will find your parents."

"Will you help us?" Oliver asked.

"I most certainly am going to. Not only are they my friends, but they are vital to the future of my quest." Mr. O'Farrell sighed. "This makes me also worry about Jen and Rand. They haven't arrived yet either, or contacted me."

"That's right. Mom mentioned them in her journal. They were all to rendezvous here with you," Tiffany remembered.

"Yes, they were," agreed Mr. O'Farrell. "I will try to contact them." He stood and walked toward the kitchen. Oliver saw him lift up a device similar to the journal and tap on the screen. The old man stared at the screen for a few minutes and then frowned. "Nothing," he said from the kitchen. "But lunch is ready. Roast turkey sandwiches with freshly fried potato chips and fruit salad. Yum, yum." Mr. O'Farrell brought a tray back to the table, and the three of them ate silently for a few minutes.

"How do you like your sandwiches?" Mr. O'Farrell asked.

Tiffany swallowed. "They're fantastic."

"Very good." Oliver took a sip of his water.

"When we are done, I will pack up some supplies and we can head for your ship. I don't have much to gather as most of the supplies we need are already aboard the *Phoenix*," Mr. O'Farrell said.

"Mr. O'Farrell, we do have another problem," Oliver said, looking down at his lap.

"What is that?"

The reason we didn't contact you before we got here was because the communication transponder and several other things are damaged on the *Phoenix*," Oliver said solemnly.

"That, and as the guard said, Eises has been interfering with communications. It's no wonder why the mTalks' or sky scooter's radios didn't work," Tiffany said, forcing a smile. "That's probably why the twins couldn't be reached." Oliver knew that idea was a relief to his sister, preventing her from being worried about the twins not responding. Oliver was convinced they'd removed the devices and left them somewhere in the ship. They were probably pigging out on snacks and digging through the supplies to see what cool gadgets their dad had packed.

"Yes, Eises can be very disruptive to the planet. Did you know that this planet harvests nearly twenty percent of the Federation's lumber needs?" Mr. O'Farrell said.

Tiffany shook her head, "I didn't know that. That has to be a lot of trees chopped down every year."

"Yes, but the corporation responsible, XPLR, takes great care to keep it sustainable," Mr. O'Farrell explained.

"That's great and all, but shouldn't we get going? We need to find those replacement parts," Oliver said impatiently.

Tiffany frowned at Oliver and shook her head, but Mr. O'Farrell nodded. "You're right, we should be off." Mr. O'Farrell walked through a door at the far side of the room.

Tiffany looked at Oliver, who was eating his last chip. "What do you think about what he told us about the Übel?"

Oliver took a sip of water. "I don't know. What do you think he meant when he said they were connected to the Federation on many levels?"

Tiffany shrugged. "I hope we can get more information about the history of the Federation. It sounds like what I learned at Bewaldeter varies significantly from what he knows."

"Yeah, it sounds like nothing is what it seems."

"To put it lightly." Tiffany took the last sip of her tea and sighed.

"I am ready," Mr. O'Farrell said as he entered the room. He was wearing a tan button-up shirt and brown pants. There was a very large pack strapped onto his back and he was carrying a duffle bag in his hand.

Oliver and Tiffany stood and went to the door to get their jackets. As they stepped onto the elevator, Mr. O'Farrell paused for a second. "Sylvia, please shut down the suite. I will contact you once we are in flight."

"Initiating shutdown. Be safe—I love you," the voice said.

Oliver looked at Tiffany curiously and whispered, "Did the computer just say, 'I love you'?" Tiffany nodded uncomfortably. The elevator doors closed and it started down.

"We're going to head for my friend's shop first. I've purchased parts from him before," Mr. O'Farrell said. As they approached their scooters, Oliver looked up at the transparent dome. There were very few pink clouds left in the sky. If what Tiffany had read was true, then all the warmth was escaping and it would be freezing in a few hours, not 48. He tapped his sister and pointed up.

She gasped. "That's bad, Oliver."

"I know."

Mr. O'Farrell loaded his supplies on his scooter and got on. "Are you ready?"

"Yes, we are," Oliver said as he and Tiffany mounted theirs.

Mr. O'Farrell told them about the city as they traveled. He explained why the dome overhead was constructed and that the city streets led either to the center of Brighton, dividing the city up like a pie, or in a perfect circle around the dome, like rings. "There were twelve slices and twelve rings," he said.

Mr. O'Farrell also mentioned that the center tower was surrounded by a large garden filled with fountains and that the Planetary Governor lived there. He explained the purpose of the colony and its large lumber processing facility that harvested and processed tens of millions of trees a year to meet the Federation's demands. "We are almost there," Mr. O'Farrell said.

"So what's it like being stuck inside for a year?" asked Oliver.

The old man shook his head. "I actually haven't been through a winter yet," Mr. O'Farrell answered.

"How's that possible?" asked Tiffany.

"The winter comes once every three years and then lasts for a year. I take up residence elsewhere during Eises," Mr. O'Farrell explained. "I was to leave with your parents when they arrived."

Oliver nodded. He knew that none of the planets revolved around its star in a single calendar year of three hundred and sixty-five days. Some took much longer and some shorter. The Federation had set three hundred and sixty-five days as a standard year, based on customs from the past.

Mr. O'Farrell stopped his scooter in front of a tall building, and Oliver pulled up next to him. The building looked a bit on the grungy side in comparison with the one Mr. O'Farrell lived in. "We are here," the old man exclaimed, taking his cap from his head and scratching his white hair.

1.24

Aqueous Cathedral

Feng arrived at the twins' accommodations shortly after they had. Austin opened the door and the guard handed him two pairs of silver swim trunks and took a seat on the chair outside the room. Austin closed the door and handed a pair to Mason.

Mason looked at the trunks Austin had just handed him, and then at the trunks in Austin's hands. "Seriously?"

Austin laughed and shrugged his shoulders. "We're twins."

"Why do people always assume we should dress alike? Just because we look alike doesn't mean we like the same things." Mason shook his head and exhaled.

After changing into the swim shorts, they stepped into the hall and followed Feng. The corridors were lined with ornate tapestries and paintings. A wide staircase led down and ended at two archways, one lit and one dark.

"You can either take the stairs with me or the other way down," Feng said, pointing to the dark tunnel. "Either way will get you to the bottom. One is just a bit more . . ." Feng paused and then smiled. "More *fun* than the other."

Mason looked at Austin with a smile. "Should we take the fun way?"

"Of course!" Austin shouted, raising a fist into the air.

Mason took a step toward the dark archway. He heard the sound of a babbling brook echoing off the stone tunnel. A shiver ran through his body and goose bumps covered his bare chest and arms as he glanced nervously at his brother.

Austin shook his head and sighed. "I'll go first."

"Be my guest."

"All right, here goes nothing." Austin took a step into the passageway and looked back. "But come close behind me, all right?"

"Of course."

Austin stepped farther into the dark passage and warm water splashed over his feet. "The water's warm. It looks like the passage curves down—" Austin's words trailed off.

"Ahhh! Whoa! Woo-hoo!" Mason heard Austin scream.

Mason ran into the arched passageway and found himself swept off his feet by the rushing water. Down away from the opening he slid. Warm water rushed all around him in complete blackness. Mason heard Austin still yelling. He couldn't contain himself any longer. "Woo-hoo!"

The passage curved several times in a spiral, then dropped steeply. Curving back the opposite way, it dipped suddenly before spiraling again. The darkness began to fade, and Mason heard the splash of falling water. The slide beneath him disappeared and he was free-falling for a second before his entire body submerged into warm water.

Mason bobbed above the surface and shouted, "That was awesome!" He looked for Austin to share the thrill with his brother. Hands grasped his back and pushed him under the waves. Mason resurfaced and turned to see the offender.

"Wasn't that a blast?" Austin asked, and wiped his wet bangs from his eyes.

"Amazing!"

Austin splashed water onto his face. "It's like a bath."

Mason nodded, then sent a wave of water at Austin. "This is great."

The twins splashed back and forth, submerging and reemerging behind each other to get in their next attack. After a few minutes, they called a truce.

"What next?" asked Austin.

"I don't know."

They looked around and saw the vastness of the cavern. It was the first time they'd stopped to take in their surroundings. Stalactites protruded from the ceiling like sharp teeth, and ropes hung from several of them. Waterfalls dumped from several holes in the cavern wall, marking the end of seven waterslides. Diving boards lined the edge of a patio where several tables and chairs also sat.

"Look, it's Feng and the king." Austin pointed to two men floating in two round tubes near the patio.

"Let's go investigate."

The king was in a large inner tube with armrests; a drink sat in one side and a bowl of fruit in the other.

"Greetings, boys," the king said with a smile. He opened his arms as if revealing the cavern to them. "How are you enjoying the Aqueous Cathedral?"

"It's amazing!" Austin exclaimed.

"Yes, it's magnificent," agreed Mason.

"I am glad you like it. I hoped this would be a good place for you to spend part of your first day. A place for you to have fun and relax. Is your room okay?" the king asked.

"Oh yes, we slept wonderfully," Mason said.

"Like logs," Austin added.

"Logs?" the king asked.

"It means to sleep soundly," Mason explained.

The king nodded his head in understanding. "I see. Well, I am glad to hear you like your accommodations."

"The king and I were just discussing a feast planned for tonight. You are both to be honored guests." Feng explained. He bowed his head to the king.

"Why, yes. My family is looking forward to meeting you tonight. I had hoped some of my children would have made it down here today," the king admitted. "But they have a wide variety of interests."

"These are the hot springs of the royal family," Feng said. The captain of the guard was clearly relaxed; either it was his day off or the warm water had thoroughly relaxed him. "Ah, one of the princes has joined us."

The twins turned around to see who Feng was speaking of. On the smallest island in the middle of the cavernous hot spring, a rope hung from one of the stalactites. A small blue boy stood on a platform holding the rope in his hands and smiling mischievously at them.

Without warning he took off at a run, lifted his legs, and clutched the rope. He swung down, then up, and when he was nearest the twins, king, and Feng, he let go. The boy maneuvered into the best cannonball Mason had ever seen and submerged beneath the water. A small tidal wave overtook the watching swimmers. The king laughed jovially and shook the water from his hair.

Mason cleared the water from his eyes and looked for the boy, but he was nowhere to be seen. He heard a stern voice coming from the patio. Mason looked and saw the boy treading water. Mr. Thule sat in a chair at one of the tables with a book in his hand. The blue boy pulled his arm back and swung it forward, creating a wave of water. The old man, still in his suit, tried to shield himself, but it was no use. He and the book were hit with a deluge of water.

Mr. Thule was clearly not pleased as he stood and reached for a towel, but to his chagrin, it too was soaked. He looked quite furious. The book in his hand looked floppy from the water.

The blue boy didn't seem to be concerned with the angry man, and climbed from the pool. The boy ran across the patio and disappeared into the stairway.

"He's probably going to come down a waterslide," Austin smiled.

"The king smiled too. "Go! Chase after my son. I am sure that is what he wants."

The twins started to swim away, but paused when Feng called out to them. "Boys, there are drinks and snacks on the patio by Mr. Thule." Mr. Thule had removed his jacket and tie and was heading for the stairs. Feng chuckled. "I suppose that means the treats are likely as soaked as he is." The blue captain cleared his throat, stifling what was sure to have been another laugh. Feng continued, "There are diving boards over on the patio, but I would suggest not going on the fourth or fifth one," he said cautiously.

"Their heights are twenty and twenty-five feet respectively. And as you have seen by the prince's display, there are many vine swings throughout the cavern. The hot springs are over fifty feet deep. In fact, the lower you go, the hotter it gets. The rock floor is heated by magma thousands of feet below us," the king explained.

Mason's eyes widened. "So we're over a volcano?"

"Yes, that is what creates all the steam in the valley and the bridge you crossed to enter. That is why when the deadly winter sets in on Jahr des Eises, the valley is still tropical. The heavy layer of hot steam becomes trapped between the mile-high walls of the gorge," the king added. "Our gorge is a paradise. I am very thankful that my ancestors chose to settle here."

What did he mean about a deadly winter, they wondered? It had been getting colder while they were out in the woods, and the leaves had been turning color.

"When does winter come?" asked Mason.

"It's setting in now," Feng warned. "You are actually quite blessed that we found you when we did."

Oliver and Tiffany were out in the woods now. Did they have the supplies they would need to survive? Did they know the weather was coming? Mason frowned. They must have known, he was sure of it. Oliver had packed cold weather gear for their journey to the towns. Why had they not told the twins? Maybe if they had told them, Austin would have stayed in the *Phoenix* and they wouldn't be prisoners.

The king smiled. "But enough of that for now. Enjoy your-selves. There will be plenty of time for questions and answers later." Mason smiled. Plenty of time indeed. He and Austin would escape before then; they had to. Their first priority was to find the *Phoenix's* cargo and dig out their cold weather gear. Then to get to the *Phoenix* and get out of this icy grave.

The king and Feng used their hands to paddle to the patio. Mr. Thule had vanished, probably to get dry clothes.

"Let's find the prince," suggested Austin. Mason was ready to enjoy the Aqueous Cathedral. It wasn't often he got to swim in an underground cavern pool set at 102 degrees.

"Cool, I want to try a different slide this time," Mason said. A swim sprint broke out. Austin was the faster swimmer and quickly pulled ahead. He even showed off by doing a backstroke to clinch his victory.

At the patio, they ran up the stairs. Several arched passageways were hewn directly out of the stone walls, apparently leading to the slides from the staircase. Mason took the sixth one they saw and Austin continued to the next. Mason's slide began with a wide curve, then grew tighter, and tighter, and tighter until it felt like he was falling straight down. It lasted only a few seconds and he fell into the hot springs from a hole near the ceiling.

He looked around for the boy. Surely he'd come down a slide already.

A loud yell told Mason that his brother was about to be launched into the air. He watched his twin's body fly from one of the holes and into a somersault. A splash erupted as Austin did a cannonball into the water.

"That rocked!" Austin shouted as he swam toward Mason. "There was a half-pipe in there. I wish I had my board. I zigged, then I zagged, and then I zigzagged some more."

"I felt like I was in a tornado. It just spiraled and spiraled."

"Let's try the rope swing," Austin said, pointing to a small island. "Race you!" But before Austin could take off, Mason dunked him and then raced for the island. This time he won.

"Hey, no fair," Austin teased. Mason stood on the island as his brother swam closer. He grabbed the vine swing and jolted forward, propelling himself out over the crystal blue water, but he didn't let go and swung back over the island. "Come on; see if you can go farther than me!"

Austin planted his feet back on the ground. He took several steps back and then sprinted forward. The rope pulled Austin out over the pool; he released his hold and dove into the water.

Austin reappeared. "Beat that!" he challenged.

Mason sat up and sneered at his brother. "Easy."

Treading water, Austin marked the spot where he had landed.

Mason looked. "Seriously? That's as far as you could go? This will be easier than beating you at chess," Mason teased. Mason grabbed the rope and took a deep breath. He darted forward and held tightly to the rope. When the vine was taut, Mason attempted to launch himself toward Austin. His body sprawled out, but he couldn't twist into a dive. His bare chest and arms smacked the surface with a stinging snap. Mason groaned as his head broke the surface. Small red bumps covered his body.

Austin was a few feet away, laughing. "That's one way to beat me," he said. Mason looked and noticed that indeed Austin was closer to the island than he was. He'd won, but at a painful cost.

The twins swam back to the island and took several more turns attempting a variety of dives and jumps from the vine rope. Mason climbed onto the island and lay back with his legs dangling in the water, the red bumps having long since disappeared. "Where did that boy go, I wonder? It's been almost an hour since we saw him last."

"Who knows?" Austin replied, lying next to his brother. "Maybe he didn't like us intruding on his private pool."

"Too bad for him, he's missing out," Mason said. He looked over and saw the king and Feng talking and laughing on the patio. He pointed in their direction. "Mr. Thule is still not back. He looked pretty mad."

Austin laughed. "He deserved it; he isn't the nicest guy."

"Sure, but he's still an adult," Mason retorted.

Austin shrugged. "Didn't the king say there was food over there?" He patted his bare stomach.

"Yah," Mason said. "I do feel sort of hungry. I wonder what time it is."

"Who knows, but swimming sure works up my appetite."

The twins swam over and found that not all the snacks had been soaked. They consumed a variety of fruits and pastries. In the ten minutes it took them to eat, the prince still had not returned.

Austin wiped his arm across his mouth, "Ready?"

"You know you're supposed to wait ten minutes after eating before you swim," Mason reminded Austin.

Austin glowered. "That's not true; it's just made up."

Mason cocked his head to the side. "I don't think so."

"Whatever." Austin ran across the patio and dove into the warm blue water.

Mason walked to the edge and watched his twin swim toward the island.

"Come on," Austin called.

"I don't think so. I'm just going to wait a bit longer."

Austin was nearly to the island. "Don't be a baby!" he called.

Mason frowned. "Name calling isn't going to work," he said matter-of-factly. "I'll come in a little while."

Austin scoffed and continued for the island. Mason was about to go back to his chair when Austin's head dipped under the water. Austin was now going to mock him, as usual. But when Austin's head broke the surface of the pool a moment later, he was gasping for air, his arms flailing in panic.

"Help!" cried Austin. "Something has me." This wasn't a joke. Mason couldn't see anything attacking him. Mason looked at the king and Feng a few yards away, but neither seemed to notice. "Help!" Austin screamed and then disappeared under the water. There was no time. Mason dived from the patio and sprinted for where Austin had gone under.

The younger twin resurfaced, sputtering for air, but he was no longer panicking. Mason felt his anger rising at what seemed to be a joke after all. But what he saw next made him freeze.

Austin wiped water from his eyes and stared at Mason. "What?" Mason pointed behind Austin. Austin spun around and blinked in disbelief. "No way!"

Gift

Hanging over the door, a sign read, KRANK'S PARTS AND SERVICE. Most of its lights were out, and all four of its corners were slightly rusted.

"This is it?" Oliver asked.

"Yes," Mr. O'Farrell responded.

Oliver groaned. "No offense, but it looks sort of run-down."

"Well, I agree it does. But this man knows his stuff. In addition, it is unlikely that any of the new shops would carry parts for a ship as old as the *Phoenix*. Sam actually helped me refurbish the *Phoenix* and her sister ship, the *Griffin*. I must warn you, Samuel has lived on this planet for most of his life and he is rather grumpy, especially this time of year. He doesn't usually leave Jahr des Eises during Eises. Be on your best behavior and call him Mr. Krank," Mr. O'Farrell instructed them.

Oliver smirked at Tiffany. "He's grumpy and his name is Krank." Tiffany grinned back.

A small bell rang as the trio entered the store. Shelves lined every inch of the walls, and crates were stacked on the floor. Nearly every inch of the store was cluttered with something. After a few minutes of looking around, there was still no sign of Mr. Krank. Mr. O'Farrell walked up to the counter opposite the entrance and leaned over it. "Samuel?" he called.

"One minute," came a grumpy voice from somewhere through a doorway behind the counter. "I heard the bell!" Mr. O'Farrell gave the kids a hopeful smile.

"I hope he has our part," Tiffany whispered anxiously and then added, "I'm beginning to worry about the twins."

"What do you want?" A tall, slender man with grey hair and a small mustache appeared in the doorway behind the counter. He appeared to be in his late fifties and wore a black-and-red plaid shirt with grey suspenders and grey trousers. A small smile crossed his face as he saw Mr. O'Farrell. "Phelan," he said, reaching out his hand to shake. "Phelan, Phelan, how have you been?"

"Fine, fine. You know how it is being sixty-one," he said.

"Well, not quite. I'm still just sixty, you old man," Mr. Krank teased. "Who are these children?" Oliver's cheeks burned. If Mr. Krank had the slightest inkling of what Oliver had accomplished in the last day and a half, he wouldn't be so quick to call him a kid. This guy was no different from Mr. O'Farrell.

"This is Oliver and Tiffany, and they are visiting me for a short while," Mr. O'Farrell answered. Oliver winced at his name, his fists clenched. The old man shouldn't have been telling just anyone who they were. Clearly, there were spies everywhere for the Übel. As far as Oliver knew, this Mr. Krank worked for them too.

"Hello, Mr. Krank. It's nice to meet you," Tiffany said in her sweetest voice, and then squeezed Oliver's shoulder.

"Yes, hello," Oliver replied smoothly.

Mr. Krank nodded in acknowledgement. "Hello."

"We need to find a part for a ship, and I was hoping you might have it," Mr. O'Farrell said.

"All right," Mr. Krank said hesitantly. "What part, and what type of craft?"

"Oliver, go ahead and tell Mr. Krank what you need," Mr. O'Farrell said.

"The ship is NT-Class and we need a communication transponder."

"NT-class? Isn't that the same type of ship you had, Phelan?" Mr. Krank asked inquisitively.

"Yes. In fact, the ship we need to repair is the *Phoenix*," Mr. O'Farrell said. "Do you have the part?"

"Well, it's an older type of ship and I'm doing less servicing these days." Mr. Krank rubbed his left hand with his right. Oliver noticed Mr. Krank's hands were large and rough as if they had seen many days of work. His left hand was missing a couple of fingers. Mr. Krank must have noticed Oliver's attention, because he suddenly lowered his hands out of sight and behind the counter. "Plus, we used most of what I had to get those two tubs flying again," Mr. Krank continued. "And with the third still need—"

"Yes, yes," Mr. O'Farrell interrupted. "But if you did have one . . ."

"It'd be somewhere on those shelves over there, I suppose." Using his undamaged right hand, Mr. Krank pointed to a large shelf with parts that looked old and disheveled.

"Thank you, Samuel," Mr. O'Farrell said with an uncomfortable smile. "Let's get started."

Tiffany looked through a few parts and sighed. "I don't know how to tell if any of these are correct, and only a few of these have tags on them," she said, holding a round piece of metal with several rust spots on it.

Oliver looked at the stacks of parts on the shelves and nodded his head. "It's all right, Tiff. Why don't you read more about Dad and Mom's past archeological digs to see if there is something that can help us?" Tiffany pulled out their mom's journal and began reading. Oliver noticed that Mr. O'Farrell eyed what Tiffany was doing very closely.

Mr. Krank kept coming and going, seemingly checking up on them. He would step into the room and look over at

Oliver and Tiffany nervously, but as soon as Mr. O'Farrell looked toward him, he would leave. Several times, Mr. Krank walked over to Oliver as if to say something, but ended up giving him an awkward smile and walking away. After an hour had passed, Mr. O'Farrell excused himself. "Oliver, I am going to call some of the other shops in town and see if they have the part."

"All right," Oliver nodded.

Mr. O'Farrell went outside to make the calls. Once again, Mr. Krank appeared behind the counter and made his way over to Oliver. Tiffany took notice of the old man's awkward approach and gave Oliver an amused look. Mr. Krank walked up to them with a slight smile and then in a quiet, anxious voice said, "My boy, I have something for you—please take it quick." Extending his unmarred hand, he offered a small package wrapped in brown paper. Oliver looked at Mr. Krank questioningly. What was this man giving him and why? Oliver, unsure of its contents, was leery of taking it. However, something about Mr. Krank felt right. There was kindness in his face and his pale blue eyes were honest and hopeful. Oliver reached out and accepted the bundle.

The bell on the door rang and Mr. Krank jerked away abruptly and spun around. Mr. Krank made a motion for Oliver to hide the parcel. Oliver obeyed and stuffed the small package in his pack. Tiffany looked at her brother with a curious smile. "That was strange," she mouthed.

"Samuel, I hope you weren't bugging the boy with any stories of fantastical adventures," Mr. O'Farrell said with a laugh as he walked toward a slightly shaken Mr. Krank.

"No, of course not, Phelan." Mr. Krank looked back at Oliver nervously to make sure the package was out of sight.

Oliver spoke up to alleviate the uncomfortable tension now heavy in the room. "Everything all right?"

Mr. O'Farrell shook his head. "None of the stores have the part or anything that will work. Any luck here?"

"No, not at all, and I'm nearly through all the parts." Oliver set down a wooden crate.

"We may have to make for Mudo," Mr. O'Farrell admitted.

"You're going there? But it's dangerous this time of year, especially so close to the storm," Samuel interjected.

"No need to worry, Samuel, we'll be fine." Mr. O'Farrell turned his attention to Oliver. "Have you checked this stack?" Oliver shook his head and Mr. O'Farrell went over and began digging through the crates.

Mr. Krank took the opportunity to whisper one last warning to Oliver. "Don't open that until you're rid of O'Farrell." Oliver gave him a grave look, and Mr. Krank turned and left.

Tiffany, who had been in earshot the entire time, leaned toward Oliver and whispered, "What could he have met by 'rid of'?"

"I don't know. Let's keep quiet until we get the part, all right?"

"Agreed," promised Tiffany.

After another ten minutes of searching the remaining shelves, Oliver stepped down from a small stepladder and wiped sweat from his brow. "It's not here. I think it's time to get going to the other town."

"I guess we have no choice." Mr. O'Farrell set down a box of small rusty parts and took his emerald flat cap from an empty shelf. "I'm going to let Samuel know." He headed to the back of the shop. A moment later the two men reappeared.

"Are you sure the part isn't here?" Mr. Krank asked apprehensively as he followed Mr. O'Farrell out.

Oliver started to speak, but Mr. O'Farrell spoke first. "Unfortunately, yes."

"I'm quite sorry about that," Mr. Krank apologized and gave Oliver a nod. "You both take care."

Oliver patted his pack as he picked it up. "We will."

"Thank you," Tiffany said with a smile. "Goodbye."

"Until another day." Mr. O'Farrell embraced Mr. Krank, and as he did, Oliver thought he saw Mr. O'Farrell whisper something, but Mr. Krank didn't look pleased at whatever it was. Then Mr. O'Farrell turned and opened the door, motioning for Oliver and Tiffany to exit. They waved as they walked out the door and then mounted their scooters. Mr. Krank stood at the large glass window, but didn't wave. In fact, he had a defined frown on his face. But whether the frown was a result of what Mr. O'Farrell had said, or just Mr. Krank's general demeanor, Oliver couldn't be sure.

"It's much darker than it was when we arrived," Tiffany observed.

"Yes, it is. No worries though. We will be halfway to Mudo before nightfall," Mr. O'Farrell said encouragingly.

Sold

With the clouds dissipating, Tiffany could see the sun, small and high in the sky. The glowing orb was reddish in color and darker than the bright white star of her home planet Tragiws. The difference didn't surprise her, but it did make her think about how many undiscovered stars and planets might be out there. She shivered at her next thought: How many would they have to visit to find Ursprung? If they missed a rendezvous with their parents on Evad, she wondered, where would they meet them again? She watched the now orange and yellow trees flash past. Tiffany yawned. The past day's events had worn on her. She laid her head back and dozed off.

One thing was on Oliver's mind: rescuing his parents. His mission was clear and nothing would stop him. Oliver and Tiffany's newly found companion led the way. The two sky scooters screamed along the maglev track. Oliver was relieved that Mr. O'Farrell seemed to be set on finding Mr. and Mrs. Wikk as quickly as possible.

The scooters were cruising along at a good clip, but daylight was fading fast. Too much time was wasted looking for the part in Brighton and Oliver had nothing to show for it, except for whatever Mr. Krank gave him. It had been very strange, how Mr. Krank had given Oliver the package—and it even seemed out of character. He hadn't seemed like the gift-giving type. Mr. Krank's words echoed in Oliver's mind. What did the old man mean? Oliver shook off the distracting thoughts; he wanted to open the package now, but he had to focus.

The sky scooters zipped past where Oliver and Tiffany had emerged from the woods that morning. Not only was it getting dark, but Oliver's eyelids were heavy. Too little sleep in the last few days. His muscles were sore and his back felt knotted. He needed a break. Oliver sped up next to Mr. O'Farrell and motioned for him to slow down. The old man eased off his throttle.

"How much farther?" Oliver asked over the hum of the engines.

"What?"

"How much farther to Mudo?"

"Oh, an hour or so. The maglev track doesn't take us directly to the outpost." Mr. O'Farrell pointed at the rail. "We're going to have to navigate through some forest."

"Can we stop and take a break? Maybe even eat dinner?"

"Of course we can stop. I was only pushing forward because you were very adamant about not wasting any time on anything," the old man said. "But if you need a rest, I understand."

Mr. O'Farrell's comment felt like a punch to the gut. He didn't like being the reason they were stopping. Neither Tiffany nor Mr. O'Farrell had complained. This sixty-year-old man didn't look the least bit worn, and yet Oliver was seventeen and felt like he was about to fall apart. "Let's take a break and get a bite to eat. I'm sure Tiffany is starving," he said as an excuse.

Mr. O'Farrell gave Oliver an accusing look. "All right, we will pull off up here." They flew into a clearing just off the rails and parked next to the trees.

"It's just as well we stop. We may want to set up camp for the night. It wouldn't be wise to arrive in a place like Mudo this late, especially not this close to Eises," Mr. O'Farrell said, dismounting his scooter.

Oliver sighed. Mr. O'Farrell was probably just saying this to make him feel better. However, if he wasn't, then Oliver wanted to know what they were up against. "Is it not safe in Mudo?"

Mr. O'Farrell removed his flat cap and scratched his head, then put it back in place. "Mudo is a hard town, full of . . ." his voice trailed off. His tone was more compassionate when he spoke again, "Full of less fortunate people."

Oliver dismounted his scooter and woke Tiffany. "Get up, Sis. We're stopping to eat and probably sleep."

Tiffany stirred and opened her eyes. "Where are we?"

"Somewhere between Mudo and Brighton," answered Mr. O'Farrell as he untied a pack from his scooter.

Tiffany looked at her mTalk. "I didn't mean to sleep that long."

"No worries," said Mr. O'Farrell. "It's probably better you did. The two of your sleep banks must be quite depleted." Mr. O'Farrell pulled out a kettle, some potatoes, several carrots, a stalk of celery, and a can of some type of juice. "Oliver, would you mind getting some wood for a fire? I feel like cooking some Irish stew."

"Irish stew?" asked Oliver. "We have automatic cook cans in our packs."

"I'd love to try some homemade Irish stew," interrupted Tiffany, hopping off the scooter. "Oliver, go get some wood please," she said pointedly.

"You're in for a real treat," Mr. O'Farrell promised.

Oliver gathered wood, while Tiffany and Mr. O'Farrell sat down on an old fallen tree. The old man poured the can of juice into the pot and then took a knife from his bag and started peeling the potatoes and carrots.

"Can I help?" asked Tiffany.

"Certainly, you can chop up the celery, potatoes, and carrots as I peel." Mr. O'Farrell handed her the celery and a knife and resumed peeling the potatoes.

Oliver returned with the wood and piled it in front of Mr. O'Farrell and Tiffany. "Is right here okay?"

"Yes, that will be fine," answered Mr. O'Farrell, tossing potato skins over his shoulder. "Some little critter is going to enjoy those tonight."

Oliver took out a fireball and threw it onto the pile of wood, igniting it instantly. He brushed his hands together and took a seat on a stump across from his sister and the old man.

"So, Mr. O'Farrell, where do you fit into our parents' work?" Oliver asked. Tiffany gave him a cautious look. He knew she probably thought he was being blunt and rude. But there wasn't time for fuzzy feelings and getting to know one another. For all Oliver knew, this Phelan guy was the spy.

Mr. O'Farrell scratched the back of his neck. "Well my dear boy, I have been able to support your parents and their team financially. I am what you would call an investor." Oliver knew that Mr. O'Farrell was a key benefactor to his parents, donating millions of credits to Mr. and Mrs. Wikk's work. The old man had mentioned Ursprung and greater secrets as his drive for supporting them. But it was one thing to support monetarily; it was another to be physically part of the expedition. Clearly that had been Mr. O'Farrell's plan, and the likely reason for the planned rendezvous on Jahr des Eises.

"Isn't that why they have the Archeos Alliance?" Oliver asked. "You know, to provide funding." It was obvious the old man didn't know how little or much that Tiffany and Oliver's parents had told them.

"Well, yes, but Archeos can't provide the sum of funds that I do," Mr. O'Farrell explained. Oliver grunted unintentionally at the conceited statement. "What would make you want to spend your money on our parents' digs? I mean beyond the search for Ursprung." Tiffany started cutting the celery more quickly. Oliver's very direct questions were clearly making her uneasy.

Mr. O'Farrell's smile wavered a moment. "Over the life of the Federation many things have changed. For example, as we discussed earlier, it was once an Empire. For years I have been trying to learn about the truth to our past. It hasn't been easy. It seems to me that pieces of our past were erased, wiped out. During the years of the Empire, someone or some group didn't want the truth to be known."

"You're talking about a cover-up?" Oliver asked incredulously. "A conspiracy?"

Mr. O'Farrell's eyes lit up and he smiled. "Exactly!"

Oliver shook his head. "That's ridiculous."

Raising an eyebrow, Mr. O'Farrell asked, "Is it? You see, I would have never thought twice about the history of the Federation, until one day while I was working for XPLR Corporation." Mr. O'Farrell grinned as he remembered. "I happened upon some ruins and therein found a page from a book, an ancient book. It was made of paper, yellowed and frail, but paper. I'd found it sealed in a container. I believe it was someone's hidden treasure, a last remnant from the past we no longer know."

"An alternative history?" Oliver asked suspiciously.

Mr. O'Farrell looked toward the dark trees for a moment, not speaking. An eerie shadow crept over his face, turning his expression to stone. "I didn't know what I was holding in my hands then." He paused again. "I saw it as a ticket to wealth. I knew an artifact like that could sell for millions of credits, so I snuck the page back onto the XPLR ship and hid it in my bunk." He sounded miserable. The old man took a deep breath and exhaled as if releasing years of heartache. The fire popped, filling the air with the smell of burning wood.

"And then what happened?" Tiffany blurted, embarrassed at her insistence but too curious to hold it in.

Mr. O'Farrell smiled wanly at her and stared into the fire. "When I got back to Centris, I began my search for a buyer. I couldn't do it on the open market because my company would grow suspicious. Therefore, I tried the Dark Market. It didn't take long and a purchase was arranged. The buyer remained anonymous, but sent some men to pick it up and paid me sixty-five million credits." Mr. O'Farrell went silent as he stared at the crackling fire.

Oliver stared at the forlorn old man. Why did he sound so sad? Oliver almost felt bad for him but thought better of it. He drifted off every few sentences as if lost in thought. What was he hiding?

"So I took the money and my wife and I traveled together. I invested most of it and it grew quickly as the Federation was in a great economic expansion at that time. That is why I am able to fund your parents' work." The old man gave a forced smile. "We should get the stew onto the fire or we'll never get to eat."

Tiffany tossed the last few pieces of celery into the pot and Mr. O'Farrell added some water and hung the kettle over the fire on a small wire stand.

"Do you know anything about the man who purchased it from you?" Oliver asked.

"No, I've had some leads in the past, but nothing solid," Mr. O'Farrell explained.

"What do you think was erased from our history?" Tiffany asked.

"Many things, but most of all where we came from," he answered.

Oliver leaned forward on the stump. "You mean Ursprung?" Mr. O'Farrell nodded.

"And as you said in Brighton, that is why you are so interested in Dad and Mom's work; to discover where we came from, the fabled planet of our origin," Tiffany said.

Mr. O'Farrell didn't speak for a moment as if deep in thought. When he finally answered, his voice sounded weak. "Yes, that is why."

"I heard you mention your wife," Tiffany started cautiously. "Where is she now?" Mr. O'Farrell looked at her quickly and then back at the fire in front of them. The stew had already started to steam.

The old man shook his head and cleared his throat. "Well, the stew should be ready soon. No more stories about me tonight." He looked at Tiffany with a smile. "I'd like to hear about you two. I have already heard some from your parents, but I want to know more about Bewaldeter and the Academy."

Tiffany looked at Oliver anxiously. He could tell she felt bad for asking about the old man's wife, but why hadn't he answered her? "Oliver is a great pilot," Tiffany started. "He not only took off from Tragiws and escaped two star fighters, but he also safely took us into and out of hyper flight, and then he made a miraculous landing here on Jahr des Eises, despite the nasty updrafts." Tiffany looked toward her brother with admiration.

Oliver blushed. "It really wasn't all that bad, I just wish the thing came with an instruction manual," he joked.

Mr. O'Farrell smiled. He lifted the mTalk on his wrist and tapped it a couple of times. "You should have something similar now," he explained. "I mean there is one programmed in the system to help you, but now you'll have it handy all the time."

Oliver looked at his mTalk; there was a new message and two attachments. He opened the first attachment, which was labeled, *The Phoenix Plans and Systems*. "Wow, thanks," Oliver said.

"No problem; you'll also notice the second one. It's something that can assist you in flying."

Oliver opened the second attachment, and a small application started to load. A menu opened and one of the options in particular stood out: Auto Launch. "Is that really what I think it is?" Oliver asked.

"Why of course. Just because the *Phoenix* is a bit older doesn't mean I haven't made some modernization modifications," Mr. O'Farrell said.

The new information had put the old man in a slightly better light in Oliver's eyes. This guy knew his stuff. Maybe he would be a helpful addition to the quest to rescue his parents.

For the next hour, they ate and enjoyed the stew. Oliver and Tiffany each took turns telling Mr. O'Farrell about the last few months of their lives. Oliver held back a lot, but openly spoke of the generalities of life at the Academy.

Prince

Austin stared directly into the bright turquoise eyes of Obbin.

Impossible. The boy had died. He'd fallen off a cliff into the blue steam. "Obbin?" stammered Mason, still treading water behind Austin.

The blue boy nodded with a wide grin. His green hair was no longer spiky, but clinging to his scalp. Otherwise, he looked the same as he did when the twins had met him.

Austin looked the boy over. This was the prince they'd been chasing? Obbin? Obbin wasted no time. "Want to have a contest?" he asked. Before the twins could answer, he dipped beneath the water. The only sign of the blue boy was the trail of bubbles leading toward a small island.

Obbin climbed from the water and motioned for the twins to follow.

"Is it really Obbin?" Mason asked.

"I think so. It looks like him."

"He's the prince?" asked Mason.

Austin nodded in disbelief. "I guess."

"What should we do now?" Mason asked.

"Play with him, I suppose," Austin suggested. "We can ask him how he survived later." The brothers swam toward Obbin.

The prince swung out and leapt from the rope into a backflip. As he bobbed back to the surface, the twins applauded.

"It's easy. Here, I'll show you," the prince promised. Austin and Mason watched Obbin grasp the rope and place it halfway up his body. The prince ran and jumped into the air, planting his feet on a knot at the end of the rope. When the rope stretched to its full length, Obbin let go with his hands and pushed off with his feet into a stunning backflip. The twins cheered as Obbin reappeared above the water.

"I'm next," Austin claimed, and went for the rope. For the next hour, the boys unofficially competed to see who could do the best tricks. Obbin showed them how to do twists, flips, and even a cool spiral back dive. Afterward, the three boys lay on the island, tired from the day's activity. They laughed about some of the bloopers from their jumping and diving, especially about Austin losing his trunks.

The king's voice interrupted their revelry. "Obbin, come my son. It is time to get ready for the feast," he called from the patio.

"One more minute?" Obbin pleaded.

The king shook his head. "No, my son."

Obbin frowned, but obediently swam to the patio. "I'll see you later," he called as he climbed from the pool. Obbin shook his head and body, again soaking Mr. Thule, who had only recently returned.

The king shook his head semi-apologetically at Mr. Thule and then handed Obbin a towel. "My son," he said jovially.

Mr. Thule frowned and wiped his face. "Boys, it's time for you to get ready for the feast as well." The twins jumped into the warm water and swam for the patio where they were handed towels.

"Did the two of you have fun?" Feng asked.

"We sure did," Mason said. "I hope we can come back."

"Anytime," Feng promised. "But six hours of swimming is plenty for one day."

"Six hours?" Austin asked.

"Yes, you have spent the entire day here," Mr. Thule said pointedly.

Once they were nearly dry, Feng led them back up the damp stone stairway, followed by Mr. Thule. "Well boys, I will see you at the feast. You should find a fresh set of dress clothes in your room. Get dressed quickly, as it would be very rude to be late to the royal feast." Mr. Thule left the boys with Feng. As promised, there was a fresh set of clothes for each of the twins when they arrived in their room. There were also more snacks.

Austin looked at Mason. "These people sure eat a lot!"

"No, you eat a lot," Mason teased. Austin shrugged it off. The boys began to change when they heard a knock on the door. Mason's left foot got stuck halfway out of his trunks, and he fell onto a pile of pillows. Austin looked at his older brother and laughed. Feng was arguing with someone outside. He sounded concerned, but respectful. The door burst open and in walked Obbin. The prince wore spectacular clothing: a silky silver shirt lined with blue stitching, light brown pants, and blue shoes. His green hair was spiked again, but his bone earrings were absent.

Feng followed him in. "Young prince, I was not told that you would be taking them to the feast." Obbin turned to him and disrespectfully waved his hand. Feng turned and marched out, mumbling something.

"Are you ready for dinner?" Obbin asked, quickly pointing at the door and noticing they were still in their swim shorts. "Oh," he said, scowling.

"We need to change our clothes," Mason said, still half in and half out of his trunks.

Obbin folded his arms and sighed. "Well, hurry. I want to take you a special way." The twins dressed quickly. They had been given silver shirts with brown pants much like Obbin's.

Austin and Mason followed Obbin into the hall. Feng was no longer there, so the twins knew they were free to follow the prince. Not that there would have been much choice. Austin was learning that the prince was very persistent. Obbin led the boys down several corridors and abruptly stopped by a floor-to-ceiling painting of a waterfall. At first, Austin thought that it was the one beneath the palace, but this one was wider and not bright blue.

Obbin pointed at the painting and whispered, "Short cut." The prince pulled on the frame and it swung away from the wall on concealed hinges.

Mason's eyes lit up. "A secret passage!" Austin nodded. If there was one, there were others. If only he had a map of them, then he and Mason could easily escape.

Obbin raised his finger to his mouth and hushed Mason. "Yes, but be quiet. I'm not supposed to use them." He motioned the twins in and then followed, pulling the framed canvas closed behind him. The passage went pitch black. Obbin clicked something and a small beam of light lit the narrow passage. The ceiling was barely high enough for the twins to walk through without ducking. The tunnel curved and split many times, eventually leading to a dead end. Austin frowned. If the prince got stuck, there was no way he and Mason would be able to find their way through the labyrinth of passages.

Obbin slowly grazed his hand across the wall. "Found it!" he exclaimed as he pushed on a small white stone. Austin had an idea. He untucked his shirt and tore off a small strip from the hem. He stuffed the piece of silk between two of the stone bricks, leaving a corner of fabric exposed. If this were an exit, he needed to mark it. A section of the solid wall before them began to move. Light crept into the secret passage as the door opened into another hallway.

Obbin pushed the door shut; its concealment was another floor-to-ceiling portrait, this one of a tall animal the twins did not recognize. The beast was an orange color, with odd shaped black spots everywhere. It had a long neck and four spindly legs.

Mason looked at Austin with a puzzled expression. "What's that?"

"A giraffe," Obbin explained.

Austin nodded. "That would be awesome to see."

"I doubt that will happen," Obbin said sadly. "This picture is very old. It was painted from memory by one of my ancestors."

"I see." Austin frowned and looked at the lifelike picture. "I wonder why such amazing creatures don't exist anymore."

"Who knows?" Mason said. "Maybe they do somewhere."

"We need to go," Obbin reminded. "Voltan will be angry if I ruin his entrance."

"Who is Voltan?" Austin asked with a laugh.

Obbin sighed, "You'll meet him soon enough." Obbin led the twins down the corridor and onto a balcony overlooking a large circular room. It was smaller than the Great Hall, but still grand. A fresco of clouds and a sun adorned the domed ceiling. Ornately decorated tiles created a mosaic of trees and animals across the large circular floor. Many blue people stood near a door at the far side of the room. Obbin slid down the banister of the staircase, and although tempted to follow, the twins walked down the stairs. The prince waited at the bottom with a mocking smile.

"Good evening, boys," the king said when they reached the waiting people. The king wore a blue tunic under a long aqua robe with white furry trim. On his head sat his crown. The twins said hello in unison.

Mr. Thule stepped forward; he wore his grey suit again, only this time a small blue jeweled pendant was pinned to the left breast pocket. He looked the boys over and then at Obbin. "I see that the prince has brought you. I trust you saw much of the castle from his *guidance*." The old man's eyes drilled into Austin as he spoke. Austin looked away, feeling an unwarranted sense of guilt.

Mr. Thule cleared his throat. "Well then, since everyone is here we may begin." He cleared his throat. "Greetings," began Mr. Thule as he held his arms up and clapped politely to get the other people's attention. "Pardon me. At the king's request I have an introduction to make." Mr. Thule motioned to the twins. "May I introduce to your highnesses and members of the royal counsel, Austin and Mason. They arrived only yesterday as many of you know."

All of the blue people smiled and clapped. It was oddly frightening, like something from a nightmare. Blue faces, green hair, and bright white teeth all staring at Austin and Mason. The onlookers bowed their heads in unison and spoke together, "Greetings Nyankomme."

Austin swallowed the nervous lump that had formed in his throat. What did *Nyankomme* mean? He was interrupted by a sharp jab in his side. Mason was bowing his head in response to the blue people. Austin mimicked his twin.

Mr. Thule turned to the twins. "I will now introduce the royal family to you." Mr. Thule led the twins to a line of blue people, all dressed regally. The first was a lady who appeared to be the same age as the king. She wore a dress of deep purple trimmed with silver thread. Her green hair was tied into a bun and adorned with a delicate silver crown.

"This is her majesty, Queen Dotty," Mr. Thule said.

The queen curtsied to the boys, smiling as she did. "Welcome, my sons." Austin looked at Mason. His brother's face reflected the concern Austin was feeling inside. *Sons* was a weird way to acknowledge them. A young man stepped forward and bowed but did not smile. The tallest of the royal family, he looked Oliver's age, maybe slightly older. His hair was spiked, but instead of green it was jet black with only a slight blue tint. He wore a silky blue shirt with a silver cape draped over one shoulder. On his head sat a thin crown of silver.

"This is the Crown Prince Voltan," Mr. Thule explained.

"Thank you, Mr. Thule, for the introduction," the prince said with authority, his voice low and gruff. "I look forward to learning about the many gadgets that you have brought with you." Austin held his tongue, but he wanted to shout. Didn't he mean stolen? Voltan raised his chin slightly. "You will find that I reward those who serve me." His voice sounded arrogant and regal.

The Crown Prince stepped back.

"May I introduce Princess Grace," Mr. Thule said next. She smiled and curtsied to the boys. She looked to be close to Oliver's age also. Princess Grace wore a light blue dress that glittered with thousands of silver sparkles, like stars in the night sky.

"Welcome," she said in a sweet voice.

"Princess Mae," Mr. Thule continued down the line, the twins shuffling behind him. The girl curtsied in a lavender gown and smiled at the boys. She didn't speak, and oddly reminded them of Tiffany, both in looks and age.

Mr. Thule seemed to approach the next boy nervously. "Prince Rylin," the old man announced. The boy bowed to them, but did not smile. He was dressed like Obbin, wearing a silver shirt with blue stitching and brown pants, but he appeared to be older than they were. As Mr. Thule stepped toward the next boy, Prince Rylin stuck his foot out in front of the old man. Mr. Thule was cautious and avoided the obstacle with a small hop. He stared back at the prince and shook his head. "Yes, some of the royal princes will be repeating the intensive etiquette course I teach."

Before Mr. Thule had stopped, the next boy in line stepped out and bowed. He smiled largely. But a sharp elbow from his older brother, Prince Rylin, brought him back into line. He rubbed his side and scowled. "This is Prince Branz," Mr. Thule explained. He looked only a bit taller than Obbin and was maybe the twins' age. He wore the same silver shirt and brown pants as Rylin and Obbin.

After the introductions, Mr. Thule walked the boys off to the side. "In a few minutes we are going to walk out to the amphitheater. There you will be formally introduced to the entire populace of Cobalt Gorge." The twins exchanged nervous stares. Austin swallowed the lump in his throat.

Oblivious to their reaction, Mr. Thule continued. "A celebration has been planned in your honor, to welcome you into the Blauwe Mensen."

"Welcome us in?" asked Austin.

"Yes, welcome you in. The gorge is your new home." Mr. Thule's face turned solemn. "I'm sorry boys, but as I said, 'the king will protect his people at all costs.' That includes keeping you here indefinitely."

"What!" Austin cried. Austin wasn't sure what indefinitely meant, but the gorge being his new home was clear enough for him. The outburst caused several people from the royal party to look at Austin. Mason looked equally bewildered by the news.

"Boys, I am sorry. I can understand if you are frightened and upset. But they take their secrecy very seriously," Mr. Thule explained.

"They've kidnapped us?" asked Austin.

Mr. Thule held up his hands and gestured for the boys to keep their voices down. "No, no, not at all."

"Are you a captive?" asked Mason.

"Well, yes, I suppose I am," Mr. Thule stated. The blue man cleared his throat and started nodding. "Just try to enjoy the evening, and tomorrow I will answer all of your questions." The twins each started to speak, but Mr. Thule held up his hand to silence them. With a half smile, he turned and went to the king.

"Is something wrong?" Austin heard the king ask.

"No, nothing, sir. Let us enjoy the celebration," Mr. Thule suggested. The king nodded and then walked toward the door with Mr. Thule.

Austin got really close to his brother and whispered. "We really are prisoners."

"How are we ever going to get back to the *Phoenix*?" asked Mason.

"I think we need to escape tonight," suggested Austin. "Before it's too late."

"You're right, but how?"

"You remember that secret passage Obbin took us through?" asked Austin.

"Yeah."

"There have to be more of those passages."

"Yes, but someone could get lost in there, and the exits appear to be hidden. It even took Obbin a minute to find the button to open that door."

"I know, but I thought of that. I ripped off part of my shirt and shoved it between two of the stones. At least one exit is marked for us," Austin explained.

Mason shook his head. "I don't know. We may never even find that exit."

"Mason, we have to get out of here. These people are planning on keeping us prisoners forever."

Mason nodded. "But even once we get out of the castle and down from this fortress, how do we get through the cave. They aren't just going to open up the doors and put down the bridge to let us stroll out."

"No, but remember all the offshoots in the cave?"

"Yeah, there were a lot."

"Obbin must have used one of those tunnels the day we met him. He must have a secret way to get in and out of the gorge undetected."

"Of course! He wouldn't be allowed to roam freely if what Mr. Thule said about the secrecy is true," added Mason. "He must have snuck out."

"He must have," agreed Austin.

"Wait! I have a better idea. I bet we could make a deal with him, like he did with the crystal."

"But what if he doesn't like the idea? What if he rats us out?" asked Austin.

"If he does, we're still prisoners," Mason countered. "Besides, we still can launch the LOCA-drone."

"The LOCA-drone! How could I be so dumb? I left it in our room with my old clothes," Austin admitted.

"That's all right, we only need it if Obbin doesn't help us," Mason said.

"True," Austin agreed. "So what should we offer him? He has all of our stuff." Austin rubbed his chin. "Voltan made it very clear that he's laying dibs on it. Besides, we don't even know where the soldiers took it."

"I know what we could give him!" Mason shouted. A couple of the royal party turned and looked at the twins curiously. "I know," Mason whispered. "We could offer to let him fly in the *Phoenix*."

Austin furrowed his eyebrows. "Are you crazy? He can't fly the ship."

Mason shook his head. "I said *in* the ship."

"Let Oliver and Tiffany meet him?"

"Yes. Think about it. If they meet him, they'll know our story is true," Mason said with a nod.

Austin looked at the many blue people next to the door. "It might work. How mad could they be if they get the opportunity to meet someone from a lost tribe?"

"So we just have to find some time to talk to Obbin alone," Mason said.

"How are we going to do that?"

A wide, devious smile crossed Mason's face. "Let me take care of that."

"All right, then we escape tonight."

1.28

Package

The fire was dying down, and only a few flames still licked the charcoaled wood. The hot embers glowed orange, reminding Tiffany of the last sunset she'd seen on Tragiws. It had only been a few evenings ago, but it seemed like forever. Oliver had stopped his attempts to get more information from Mr. O'Farrell, and there was no more to say about school.

As the fire crackled, the old man stood and stretched. "Well, I suppose we should all get some rest. We'll get up early tomorrow and try to be in Mudo at daybreak."

"That sounds good," Oliver said.

"Then goodnight, kids," Mr. O'Farrell said. Even in the failing firelight, Tiffany could see Oliver bristle at being called a kid.

"Goodnight, Mr. O'Farrell," Tiffany said, and gave Oliver a warning look.

"Yes, goodnight," Oliver added.

The old man walked to his tent and climbed in. Tiffany caught his eye as he looked out at them once more before zipping his flap shut. He looked worried. There were a million reasons to be, but for some reason the expression gave her the oddest shiver.

"Well, Tiffany"—Oliver's voice startled her—"I think we should go to bed too." He stretched his arms and yawned.

Tiffany nodded. "I'm not tired yet. I think I'll enjoy the fire a bit longer. It's still giving off a lot of heat, and the crackling is relaxing."

"Suit yourself," Oliver said. "I guess you did have a nap." He tossed a small black ball to her. "Just throw this on the embers when you are done."

"No problem," she said, holding the sphere in the palm of her hand. Oliver disappeared through the tent opening. She could hear the unzipping of his sleeping bag.

The hooting of a bird caught her attention. She'd been so engrossed in the conversation that she hadn't taken a good look at their surroundings. The clearing they were in was much like the one they'd camped in the night before. Dark shadows cloaked anything that might be lurking just feet away. Tiffany shivered. The safety of the tent and her brother seemed pretty good. She walked close to the tent and tossed the small black sphere into the fire. The clearing went dark. Tiffany quickly crawled into the tent and zipped the flap shut.

Oliver was still awake and grinned at her abrupt arrival to the tent. "Tired?" he teased.

Tiffany couldn't hold back an embarrassed smile. She noticed a small, crumpled package of brown wrapping in front of Oliver. "What's that?"

"It's the package the old man gave me," Oliver said, shining the light from his mTalk on the gift.

Tiffany straightened. "His name is Mr. Krank."

Oliver scowled.

"Do you think this is the best time to open it?" asked Tiffany.

"We are currently 'rid of O'Farrell.' Those were Mr. Krank's only instructions," Oliver said.

"I'm not so—" she started.

"It'll be fine," Oliver interrupted and started to unwrap the packaging, freeing a small silver ball that rolled onto the sleeping bag before him.

"What is it?" Tiffany asked.

"I don't know." Oliver lifted up the wrappings from the package and a small silver control fell free. He took the flat, silver square in his hands. "Looks like a control of some sort."

"What are we supposed to do with it?" Tiffany asked.

"I don't know. Mr. Krank never said what it was," Oliver admitted, then yawned. "We'll just have to wait until we're back to the *Phoenix* to find out."

Tiffany agreed.

Oliver carefully wrapped the silver ball and remote back in the packaging and then slid it into his backpack.

"I'm going to get some rest," he said. "If you want to read, there is a small lantern in my pack."

Tiffany shook her head. "No, I'm going to sleep too." She set the e-Journal into her pack and slipped into her sleeping bag. A moment later she and Oliver were sound asleep.

1.29

Celebration

Obbin ran by the twins holding a blue feathered cap in front of him. Feng soon followed, chasing the young prince around the room. Obbin hid from the guard and laughed each time he was cornered. Several times Feng took back the hat but allowed Obbin to retake it.

Mr. Thule made his way back to the twins as a large silver gong was struck. "We are going to head down to the amphitheater now. The Blauwe Mensen are gathered and ready to meet you."

The doors were pulled open and several guards stepped into view. Feng snatched back his hat and corralled Obbin toward the rest of the royal family.

Mr. Thule guided the twins to a spot behind the king and queen. Mason looked behind him. Crown Prince Voltan stood proudly; behind him the other princes and princesses stood in two rows. The Crown Prince gave Mason a fake smile and then nodded for the twin to look forward. Mason looked at the king and queen. They didn't seem like the sort of people who were out to imprison him and his brother. Quite the opposite, they looked like loving parents prepared to welcome them, if not adopt them into their family.

Mr. Thule bent down to the twins' level. "Tomorrow we will spend the day with the king. I will explain to you about the gorge and the laws associated with living here. Because of your age, the king has decided that you will live here in the palace with the royal family."

"Gee, thanks," Austin said sarcastically under his breath.

"What was that?" asked Mr. Thule strictly.

"Nothing," Austin replied. Mason gave him a wary look.

"You two are the youngest captives ever," Mr. Thule said sympathetically. "If not for his responsibility as king to protect his people, he might have considered letting you go. But he is charged first and foremost with maintaining the secrecy of the gorge."

"Well, that is noble," Mason said. Austin looked at him quizzically.

"Yes, upon becoming king, he had to swear an oath of protection."

"I see," Mason said. He understood honor and that a promise was a promise.

The king and queen started forward and the entire party followed closely. They crossed out of the palace and into the gardens, which were now dark with the exception of a few lit torches. All of the towers that had lit the city were also extinguished, leaving the gorge draped in inky blackness. While the darkness was creepy, Mason smiled knowing it would provide the perfect cover for the escape.

Ahead of him, a blue glow flickered through the trees and reflected off the underside of the clouds above. Voices of thousands and music filled the air, growing louder with each step. Mason's stomach felt like it was rolling and his palms were sticky with sweat. Crowds made him nervous. He looked at Austin, who appeared calm.

The procession stopped at two tall pillars, capped with an ornately carved arch. Mason looked around. Before him, a long set of stairs led down into a large stadium, or amphitheater. The room was carved deep into solid rock, with rows and rows of seating. None of the seats were occupied at the time; instead, the throng of people occupied the large amphitheater floor. An enormous bonfire burned in the center and several stages and tents were set up against the outer walls. The smell of roasting meat, burning wood, and fresh bread wafted up the stairs to Mason's nose. His mouth began to water, and a different sensation entered his stomach. Hunger.

The king stepped out from the group, standing proudly as he surveyed his people. A drum thundered several beats and the people in the crowd looked at their king. King Dlanod motioned for the twins to step on either side of him. He cleared his throat and began to speak in a firm but kind voice. "Welcome, my brothers and sisters. Today we gather here to welcome two new members into our family. Their names are Mason and Austin, and they arrived only a day ago. Please welcome them." The king stepped back and stretched out his arms, displaying the twins.

The crowd broke into thundering applause. The clapping echoed off the empty rings of seats. Mason and Austin blushed at the wave of attention from the thousands of blue people below.

"Bow," whispered Mr. Thule from behind. The twins did, and the crowd clapped louder.

The king smiled and patted the twins' backs. "Welcome, boys. This celebration is for you. You need but ask one of our many citizens, and they will provide for your needs. Please enjoy and cast your worries aside. We will speak in detail tomorrow of your future here in the gorge." The king took his wife's hand, and they started down the stairs together.

For a moment, Mason's feet were glued to the spot. He didn't know what to think. Part of him felt ungrateful and guilty. This was all for them, yet they weren't supposed to be there. They'd been the ones who had disobeyed Oliver and encountered the

Blauwe Mensen. Now they were being welcomed with open and apparently loving arms.

Mason was pulled from his thoughts at Mr. Thule's prodding. "You can go now. You need not stay with the king. Just be—" But his words were interrupted when Obbin came from behind and passed them, and then the king. The blue prince ran down the stairs and disappeared among the crowd.

"Where's he going?" Mason wondered. "We'll never be able to find him."

Austin looked slightly anxious. "You're right. They all look alike."

When they reached the floor of the amphitheater, several fancily dressed men came up and began talking to the king. They had worried expressions on their faces, but the king didn't seem to be bothered by them. Mr. Thule stopped the boys. "When you hear the drum again, please meet back here for dinner," Mr. Thule said with a smile, but then turned stern. "Don't do anything that might get you into trouble."

"Okay, we won't," Mason replied, scratching his nose nervously. Mr. Thule eyed him suspiciously and then waved them off with a searching stare. The twins speedily walked away from the old man in an attempt to get out of earshot and sight.

"Do you think Mr. Thule suspects something?" asked Mason nervously.

"I don't know," Austin said. "But don't worry, with Obbin's help we'll be out of here tonight."

They walked around the amphitheater looking for the prince. As they moved about, people bowed their heads and greeted them happily. Several times, they were invited to try delicacies or listen to stories. They tried their best to keep from detouring too often, but the people were persuasive. They were all so kind and welcoming to the twins. Mason could imagine how he might find happiness in the city, how he might be able to live here. Eventually, after walking around for more than an hour, they saw Obbin standing in a circle kicking a ball with some kids.

"Obbin!" Mason called out to him. The prince looked away from the game and waved at the twins. At that moment, one of the kids kicked the ball, smacking Obbin square in the chest. He stepped backwards off balance. For a second, the prince looked as though he was going to tackle the offending kid. Instead, he sneered at him and ran over to the twins.

"What's going on," asked Austin.

"Just kicking the ball around with some friends," Obbin said, motioning to the group behind. "Want to join?" Austin looked at the circle of kids, who were now staring at them.

"No, we can't," Mason said. "But we wanted to make another trade with you."

Obbin cocked his head curiously. "Like what?"

"Well," Mason said as he motioned Obbin to come closer, "how would you like to fly *in* our ship?"

Obbin's eyes lit up and he stepped back. "Would I!"

Mason held his finger to his mouth. "Shhh." He looked around nervously to see whether anyone had heard the outburst. Only the kids in the circle seemed to be paying attention.

"And what do I have to trade you?" Obbin asked suspiciously.

"Well—we need our stuff," Mason said.

Obbin frowned. "All of it?"

"Yes, all of it," Mason said.

"Well . . ." Obbin was thinking. This part could get messy. If the boy were against them trying to escape, he would likely alert someone to their plan. To Mason's surprise, Obbin smiled. "All right. But where are you going to put it? You do know that after it's reviewed it'll be given back to you anyway."

Mason frowned. "Put it . . . well . . ."

"I mean, I'll be glad to help you hide it somewhere," Obbin said. "Especially since Voltan seems so interested in all of it. He deserves to be disappointed for once," Obbin explained.

Mason took a deep breath—here came the really tricky part. "We need you to help us take it back to our ship." Obbin frowned and shook his head. "Then you can fly *in* the *Phoenix*," Mason pleaded. Obbin smiled again. He must have been weighing his decision, Mason thought, so he interjected some more persuasion. "It'll be fun. I promise."

"I've always wanted to fly," Obbin said. "But I'll get in so much trouble. If I let you go, you may reveal the gorge to outsiders." Obbin's face was solemn. Mason thought for a moment. What could he possibly say? He looked at Austin.

Austin gave a nervous smile. "What if we promise not to tell?" The twins stared anxiously at Obbin. The prince put his hand to his chin and was thinking. He looked up at the sky, and Mason and Austin followed his gaze. They could see the low clouds and the blue light from the fires flickering off them.

"All right," Obbin said, but his face became stern, and blue firelight flickered off the whites of his eyes. "But you must take the blood oath of protection."

Mason and Austin looked at each other and mouthed, "Blood oath?" Obbin looked at them, waiting for their response. Austin nodded to Mason.

"We agree," Mason said.

"Yes, we do," Austin added.

Obbin smiled and rubbed his hands together. "All right, I'll do it." Obbin reached out to shake Mason's hand. It was evident to Mason that flying outweighed any punishment or recourse that Obbin would face for letting them escape. But Mason also wondered whether part of Obbin's decision to help weren't just a way to defy his older brother Voltan.

"Let's go," Obbin said, and started toward the bonfire in the center of the amphitheater. Mason and Austin looked around nervously. Seeing no sign of Feng or Mr. Thule, they quickly made their way through the crowd and toward the stairway. As they neared the stone staircase, their escape out of the amphitheater, Mason spotted Mr. Thule talking with several men. He grabbed Obbin's shoulder, stopping him, and pointing.

"Thule," Mason said. Obbin smiled and doubled back toward the fire in the center.

A few minutes later, Austin spotted Feng and told Mason. The guard quickly looked away, as if guilty. Mason grabbed Obbin's shoulder and motioned toward the guard. "Obbin, I think Feng is following us."

"I see him," Obbin said, and led the twins back to where he'd been playing ball with the other boys. He walked over to them and whispered, pointing in the direction of Feng, who was still following. The kids suddenly broke into a run, pushing through the crowd. They surrounded Feng and started jumping around him, blocking his view.

Obbin motioned for the twins to follow, and the three broke into a dead sprint toward the amphitheater stairs. They looked for Mr. Thule but didn't see him. They ran up the stairs and hoped not to draw too much attention. Obbin paused under the stone archway and looked out over the amphitheater one last time. Mason noticed a frown on his face; he hoped the prince wasn't reconsidering.

Oath

"Let's fly!" Obbin shouted, and sprinted toward the palace. The Great Hall was empty, and only a few torches remained lit. The fireplaces were cold and dark, and the overhead torches were extinguished. The twins followed Obbin through a door they'd not yet entered, up several flights of stairs, and down a long hall lined with paintings of wild animals, some of which the twins had never seen before. Obbin pointed to the floor as they walked. "We're above the Aqueous Cathedral now."

They went down another staircase and through another hall that ended at a large wooden door. The door opened into a four-story room, open from floor to ceiling. The topmost floor was all windows. Two narrow balconies skirted the second and third floors. Every inch of the first-, second-, and third-floor walls was lined with shelves—shelves of books! They'd entered the forbidden library that had taken Mr. Thule many years to get access to. Now Mason had gotten in purely by happenstance.

Mason stopped mid-stride, in awe of the architecture of the room and the thousands of bound manuscripts. He'd never seen this many books in his life. If only he could take a few hours, days, weeks to look through them. What information was contained among these pages?

"Umph," Mason gasped, stumbling forward as Austin ran into him.

"What're you doing?" Austin asked, recovering his bearings.

"Oh, sorry."

"What's wrong? Why did you stop?"

"Nothing, I was just admiring all the books. This must be the library Mr. Thule was talking about."

"Oh," answered Austin unimpressed.

"Come on!" Obbin shouted impatiently from a tapestry-draped archway ahead.

"Coming," Austin said, prodding Mason forward. Mason took one more sweeping look around the room. If only his parents and sister were here to enjoy it with him. What might they discover?

Obbin held back the tapestry and led them up several flights of rickety wooden stairs and through another arch. The hall they entered was lined with floor-to-ceiling tapestries of scenery: jungles, mountains, a seaside, and even a desert. The stitching on each was so intricate that the images looked like photographs. Mason imagined that these works took a long time to create.

The prince stopped and opened the last door in the hall-way. Inside they found a room similar to theirs, except larger and taller with a balcony rimming the second floor. A large hoop hung from one wall, and several balls were scattered across the room. A pile of books lay on the floor, looking as though they'd not been touched in a long time. On the right wall, several cages were stacked with small creatures in them.

"This is my room," Obbin explained. "I just need to get a few things, and then we can go." The prince grabbed three packs and started shoving clothes, tools, and other items into the packs.

The twins looked at each other curiously. "What are you doing?" Mason asked. He watched as Obbin stuffed the orange suit that had caused all of the mess into one of the packs.

"I'm just gathering things for our journey," Obbin said. "Things I might need." Mason crinkled his nose. Why was he packing so many clothes for just a couple-hour journey?

Austin walked across the room and looked at the creatures in the cages. There were three lizards, two snakes, a turtle, four frogs, two birds, and a furry creature that he didn't recognize. "What's this?" he asked Obbin.

"Oh, that's Milo, my hamster," Obbin explained, walking to the cage for a moment. "Yeah, they'll be fine; my brother Rylin will feed them."

"A hamster?" Mason asked, crossing the room to get a better look.

"Yeah, my second oldest brother breeds them. He gave me this one as a present on my last birthday."

"Oh, interesting," Austin said, looking at the little creature covered in aqua colored fur. It was sleeping and he really wanted to see it move. But shaking the cage would be rude. "So, Obbin, about how old are you?" asked Austin. He bent so the hamster was at eye level.

"I'm eleven—well, almost eleven. How about you guys?"

"We're eleven," answered Austin as he poked a finger into the cage, just touching the hamster, but it didn't move. He blew on the blue rodent; still no movement.

Mason smiled and cleared his throat. "Yeah, but I'm turning twelve this year and Austin won't be twelve until next year!"

Obbin stopped what he was doing and looked at Mason suspiciously. "I thought you were twins?"

"Oh, we are, but I was born December thirty-first, 1588, at 11:55 p.m., and Austin wasn't born until the next year, January first, 1589, at 12:08 a.m. So I was born the year before him."

Obbin raised an eyebrow, "Interesting."

Austin sighed, "Yes, he loves to point that out whenever he can. I'm still stronger."

"Are not!"

"Am so!"

Mason and Austin were suddenly face to face. Instantly Obbin was between them, pushing them apart. "If you guys make a lot of noise, one of the patrols might hear and come to investigate." The twins took deep breaths and Mason walked away. Austin still stood with his chest puffed out. He didn't like to back down, especially with Mason. Obbin went back to his pile and began shoving things into his packs.

Austin browsed Obbin's room, admiring the vast and varied collection of objects the prince had amassed: skeletons of small animals, several of the blue crystals, homemade weapons like arrows, and even a slingshot. He also found an odd golden tube covered on each end with glass.

"What's this," Austin asked, holding the cylinder up.

"Ah, that is a telescope," Obbin said proudly. "My father gave it to me. Odd really," he said. "It's for stargazing, but how would he expect me to do that in Cobalt Gorge? The clouds are permanent; that is as long as we keep making them." Obbin shrugged and went back to packing.

The prince finally finished and handed a pack to each of the twins, then placed the last on his back. "We have one more stop, but it's just down the next hall." Obbin turned to the wall of cages. "Goodbye, my friends." On his way out, Obbin grabbed the slingshot and put on a small belt with a sheath and dagger attached.

They started for the next destination when Austin remembered the LOCA-drone. The device was still in the twins' room. Austin had folded it up in his pants to keep it hidden. But of course they didn't need it now; they were on their way out. They were going to escape.

Around the corner and down another hall they walked, but this corridor was different. Portraits of individual men lined the walls, all with crowns on their heads. Austin noticed that the first couple of portraits were not of blue people.

"This is the hall of kings. These pictures date back to when we first arrived and settled in Cobalt Gorge," Obbin explained. The next room they entered was dim, and in the middle sat a large blue crystal statue of a man. He was wearing a crown and in his hand was a long silver sword pointing out toward the boys. A basin sat at his feet, and a long inscription had been etched into the stone with a peculiar number on it. Austin cautiously approached the swordsman. It looked as though the weapon would run you through if you got too close.

"This is where you shall take the blood oath of protection," Obbin explained, pointing at the statue. "You will promise to keep the secret of the gorge in your hearts and minds, but not on your tongues. You will then press your palm against the end of the sword and allow a few drops of your blood to fall into the basin below." Mason looked frightfully at Austin, who returned the stare. Obbin saw this and took a step back. "If you do not take the oath, I cannot allow you to leave," Obbin said solemnly.

Austin gulped and took a deep breath. "All right, I will." He looked at Mason and then the shiny sword in the statue's hand. He glanced at the basin below. If this was the only way they could escape, then he had to do it.

"I will too," Mason said.

"Repeat after me then," Obbin said. He walked over to the statue and placed his left hand on the sword hilt. "I promise to uphold the code of the gorge," Obbin said solemnly.

"I promise to uphold the code of the gorge," the twins repeated in unison.

"I will hold the secrets of this place in my heart and mind, but never on my tongue." Together the twins repeated the next line. "From this day forward, unless released by one of the royal family." The twins recited the verse again. "This I promise and seal with my own blood," Obbin finished and held out his right palm. The twins finished the last line and held out their right palms. "Now press your hand lightly against the end of the sword. It does not take much because the sword is very sharp," Obbin explained, still holding onto the hilt of the sword.

Austin took a deep breath and exhaled. He forced a smile, hoping the fear that raged inside was not evident on his face. He straightened his shoulders and stepped forward. Holding out his hand, he touched his palm against the sword's tip. He felt a small prick and watched a droplet of crimson liquid slide down his palm and drip into the stone basin below. Obbin smiled a wide grin and embraced Austin. "Welcome, my brother." Austin stepped back and Obbin handed him a small piece of cloth to hold over the cut.

"Your turn, Mason," Obbin said, placing his hand back on the hilt. Mason stepped forward and looked at Austin, who didn't appear to be in any pain. Holding out his palm, he pressed it against the sword. A small droplet of blood formed at the site of the prick and rolled down his hand and dripped to the basin below. "Welcome, my brother," Obbin repeated and embraced Mason. The prince handed him a piece of cloth and stepped away from the statue. "We are now bonded as protectors of the gorge."

Obbin patted them each on the back and the twins smiled. The cut hadn't really hurt, and their hands hadn't bled any more than the single droplet. "Now to your stuff and then to the ship. Adventure awaits us!" Obbin exclaimed as he hefted his pack higher on his shoulders.

Back down the hall and past the bedrooms they went. Instead of taking the passage they'd come up, they turned down yet another corridor. This palace had more passages than any place Austin had ever been before, and these were just the common paths, not the many secret tunnels he imagined coursed the labyrinth below.

Obbin led the boys through a small door and into a narrow dark passage that looked to be used only every few years. It smelled musty, and cobwebs hung throughout. It was nothing like the other secret tunnels they'd traversed. Obbin turned on his little source of light again and followed the dank passage. It curved and slanted downward. Austin had to lean back and use the walls for balance as the passage floor was slick with mold. It would be embarrassing to fall.

After a few close calls of nearly falling, the three made it to the bottom of the path, where Obbin paused and held his finger to his mouth. "Shhh." The prince pressed lightly on the door and a sharp creaking noise whined from its hinges. He stopped and waited, then pushed a bit more. Finally, there was enough room to poke his head through. The prince looked back and forth.

Mason tapped Austin and mouthed, "We're so close." Obbin nodded to the twins and waved them forward. They found themselves in what resembled a large barn. The walls were lined with animal stalls containing horses, cows, oxen, and a dozen others. The room smelled of hay, dirt, and fouler things.

They crossed into another area of the barn, where there were tall racks loaded with machines, tools, parts, and all sorts of miscellaneous items. In the center of the room stood a wagon filled with several crates. Austin smiled as he read the inscription on the crates, "E4:32 Phoenix." Obbin had led them to their supplies. The first part of the mission was over. Now they had to get everything back to the ship.

Austin looked around, but didn't see Obbin anywhere. "Mason, did you see where he went?"

Mason raised an eyebrow, "No." The twins looked around and then heard a loud creak as two doors began to open behind them.

Austin tugged on Mason's shirt. "Quick, behind the wagon!" They scrambled toward the crate-laden cart and crouched. To their relief, Obbin appeared with three oxen in tow. He took them to the wagon and one by one yoked them to harnesses. Obbin then motioned for Mason and Austin to climb aboard. The prince climbed onto the back of the middle oxen and took the reins in his hands. He removed his pack and tossed it back into the wagon. The twins followed suit and set down the packs Obbin had given them.

"We're off!" exclaimed Obbin, and with a single flick of his wrist, the oxen began to trot forward. Mason climbed onto the front rail of the wagon and let his feet dangle while Austin got comfortable on a crate in the bed of the wagon. As the wagon approached the end of the barn, Obbin called out, "Austin, can you get the doors?" Austin hopped off and pushed on the large wooden doors. They weren't nearly as heavy as he'd expected. He opened them just a crack and carefully peered through. There wasn't a person in sight. It was quiet, eerily so.

"It's all clear," Austin said as he pushed the doors all the way open, then climbed back into the cart.

"Everyone must be at the celebration," Obbin said. Austin looked around at empty fields and greenhouses. The air was fresh. It smelled of plants and rain, as if the fields had just been watered.

"What is this area?" Mason asked.

Obbin turned to look at them. "This is where much of our food is grown." Mason nodded.

They were nearing the edge of the cliff when Obbin pulled up on the reins, slowing the oxen. The wagon crossed from the solid ground of the cliff top onto the elevator platform. The prince dismounted his large blue ox. "I'll be right back,"

Obbin said, and then ran toward a low wooden wall, hopped over, and disappeared. The twins felt the elevator jerk and begin to lower.

"What is he doing?" Mason asked. "He has to come with us! We don't know where we're going!"

"I don't know, but I doubt he's leaving us. He really wants to fly!"

As the lift lowered farther, Austin wondered how Obbin would safely reach the lift. It was too far to jump.

"Woo hoo!" howled someone from overhead. The twins looked up and saw Obbin plummeting toward them. Was he crazy? But then Austin saw the harness around the blue boy's body. The prince hooted as his green hair flowed wildly in the wind. Obbin leaned back and slowed his descent as he neared the platform, then landed with a soft thump. The twins stood still, mouths open in awe.

"That was awesome!" shouted Austin. "I want to try that."

Obbin looked pleased at the twins' expressions. "I'm glad you liked that," he said, sporting a huge smirk. The prince hopped back onto the ox and took the reins. "Maybe you can try it next time you visit." Austin realized the foolishness of his desire. No, he wanted to get out of the gorge, to the *Phoenix*, and rescue his parents. That was what he wanted.

The platform touched down on solid ground with a hard thud. The noise it made was covered by the loud rumbling of the waterfall. Obbin flicked his wrist and the wagon moved forward. Austin stared back at the waterfall. It was really something, even better than the one Oliver had used to lose the star fighter in the cavern a few days ago.

The city's streets were empty of people, but of course they'd expected this. Everyone was at the feast. Austin's stomach grumbled; he should have had more to eat. Sure they'd sampled a bunch of stuff, but he needed a real meal. He hadn't eaten a real meal since the night his parents had been kidnapped. His mom had made pot roast, carrots, potatoes, and honey wheat bread. They'd dined as a family, talking, laughing, and sharing the events of the past few months. Austin felt his throat tighten, and his vision suddenly grew blurry. A small tear ran down his cheek. Austin turned his head to look toward the cliff. He couldn't let his brother or the prince see him crying.

Fortunately, it was dark, and Obbin couldn't light the torches on the wagon because it would create a beacon and announce their escape. He had only his small light to ensure the oxen were staying on the road and not driving toward the river. Then Austin had an idea: the mTalks! He started digging in the area that the soldiers had tossed the devices. He found both of them: his—the smashed one—and Mason's. Austin went to the front of the wagon and turned the mTalk's light on, shining the bright ray in front of them. It was stronger than Obbin's and made the going easier. The oxen picked up their pace, less nervous of stumbling into the river.

The light illuminated the dark blue steam that rose from the many vents lining the streets. The eerie mist sifted before them in the light, casting their escape in an ominous glow. Several times, Austin thought he saw someone in the shadows or heard a voice, but Obbin never seemed concerned. At the end of the gorge, they crossed the small bridge and came to the set of large doors that, once opened, would lead them into the caves and hopefully to their freedom.

Obbin dismounted his ox and pushed on the doors. They creaked but did not move. The twins jumped down and aided the prince. Together, the three pushed open the doors, revealing the dark tunnel. A cold wind swept around them. The sound of the small waterfalls filled the cavern with a buzz. The silver bowls that had glowed with blue flames were extinguished, leaving a dark, forbidding path before them. The damp smell of rock and water hung in the air. Obbin lit one of the torches at the front of the wagon and he and the twins climbed back into the wagon and drove into the tunnel. They rode for a long time without words.

Austin had found his inventor's pouch and was messing with the broken mTalk, trying to get it to power on. He needed to fix it. He had remembered that the working one was his twin's, and if Mason remembered too, then Austin would be left without an mTalk. Austin looked at his twin. He appeared to be lost in thought. "Mason, what's wrong?"

"Nothing, I was just thinking about what I will say when we see Tiffany and Oliver again."

"Oh, you mean how we explain where we've been when we've just sworn in blood to keep it secret." It was certainly a problem. His grandpa had always said, "Truth first, everything will follow after that."

"Exactly," Mason said.

Austin shook his head. "I'm not sure either. But at least we're going to be free."

Mason nodded. "I'm thankful for that. And we're almost there." The wagon suddenly turned sharply, nearly tipping and throwing the twins and the contents out.

"What are you doing?" Austin asked.

"We have to create a diversion and clear the fortress of soldiers," Obbin explained. The wagon was now facing a passageway that branched off to the right. Austin shined the light from Mason's mTalk ahead onto the blue waters flowing in torrents just inches from the oxen hooves.

"Hold on!" Obbin commanded and flicked the reins. The oxen charged forward and into the rushing water. The wagon jerked to the left as the rapids collided with it.

"Yah!" cried Obbin as the wagon began to fishtail. Austin caught Mason as he slipped and nearly fell over the side rail into the water.

A moment later and the wagon was safe on the far shore. The oxen pulled the wagon through the entrance of the side tunnel, and shortly afterward Obbin pulled back on the reins and the wagon came to a halt.

After dismounting, the prince took down the three packs he'd gathered in his room at the palace. He pulled a set of blue clothing from each of the packs. "Put these on. We'll need them once we get out of here." Austin looked at Mason and shrugged. A moment later the trio wore wool coats and thick pants. Already Austin was feeling warmer from the heavy wool. Obbin took out two more things from his pack. One was a long pipe with several darts attached and the other looked like handcuffs made of rope.

"What are those for?" Austin asked.

"You'll need them to stop the guard," Obbin explained.

Austin suddenly understood what "you'll" meant. "*I'll* need them?"

"Yes, but not yet. First come with me."

Before Austin or Mason could react, Obbin took the lit torch from the wagon and started down the tunnel. As Obbin led the twins down the dark side passage, Austin turned on the mTalk's light. He had not been able to fix his yet, so he was still using Mason's. The passage dipped and curved several times, growing smaller and narrower until Obbin and the twins were hunched over. The flames from the torch licked the top of the tunnel, and the smoke began to make it difficult to breathe. Sweat beads formed on Austin's brow, dampening his bangs as his skin itched from the wool and perspiration.

"I don't like this; I'm claustrophobic," Mason said, pulling on the collar of his coat. His hands were clammy and his breathing sporadic. He wiped his brow.

Austin looked back at his brother. "I'm sure it's just a bit farther. You'll be okay. We can always get out the way we came," Austin said reassuringly. "Besides, I'm here and I won't let anything happen to you. I promise."

Not a minute later, they arrived at a small metal grate through which blue steam poured into the tunnel. They'd come to a dead end. Obbin extinguished the torch against the cave wall and yanked on the grate. It slid away with ease. They were free!

1.31

Whispers

Oliver awoke. Sweat beads covered his brow; his hands were sticky with perspiration. He had been reliving the capture of his parents in his dreams. He was angry with himself all over again—he could have saved them, he just knew it. He sat for a moment, still and silent, taking deep cleansing breaths as he'd been taught at the Academy. Then he heard a whisper in the air. Someone was speaking quietly somewhere outside the tent.

He looked at Tiffany, who was sound asleep, tucked into her sleeping bag. The journal lay open beside her, its screens dark. Oliver listened intently. The voice was faint but speaking in conversation. He couldn't hear the other voice, but clearly there had to be two people. Oliver leaned toward the side of his tent in the direction of the voice. He couldn't make out what was being said. Oliver moved for the front of the tent, and slowly unzipped the opening. He could just see out toward Mr. O'Farrell's tent. It was dark, and the entrance flap was still closed.

The snap of a stick cracking caught Oliver's attention. It had come from behind the old man's tent. The dark shadows and tree trunks masked whatever lurked within the surrounding forest. Oliver listened for the voices. Nothing—they'd gone silent for the moment. Then he heard the sound of conversation again, but this time he heard a soft beep after the voice stopped talking. Whoever was speaking was doing so into a device, maybe an mTalk or a radio. Oliver could almost hear the other voice now. "We must have it. Without it we have nothing. Rendezvous in three days at . . ." The end of the last sentence was inaudible.

Oliver wondered whether he could slip to Mr. O'Farrell's tent and wake the old man without being seen or heard. It was worth the risk. Oliver crawled from the tent and across the ground. Every leaf that crushed beneath his palm seemed to scream to the stalker in the woods that Oliver was out of his tent. He got to Mr. O'Farrell's tent and waited. He listened for the voices. Silence.

Oliver jolted back. Another branch had snapped closer now. Then another. He looked around, frantically surveying the tree line. Whoever was out there was not being very cautious. Maybe they didn't need to be. Maybe it was Vedrik and his men. Maybe they had tracked Oliver and the *Phoenix*. Maybe the Archeos mole had been watching O'Farrell's home. Oliver felt a small prick in the back of his neck. His stomach felt woozy. His eyes started to close of their own accord. He forced himself to keep them open, but it was no use. Suddenly and uncontrollably, his face thumped into the leafy ground. Everything went black and then silent.

1.32

Blow Dart

The twins followed Obbin from the passage onto a small stone ledge protruding out over a deep chasm. Their hair and clothing billowed in the rising blue warmth. In front of them, a small bridge made of three vines rocked back and forth, stretching out into the mist. There appeared to be one vine for your feet and two for your hands. Without hesitation, Obbin started across the bridge.

Austin swallowed the lump that formed in his throat at the sight of the flimsy looking toe bridge, it looked as if Obbin had constructed it himself, and judging by the grate blocking the tunnel, this crossing wasn't supposed to exist. Mason's quickened breaths echoed behind Austin, like a runner after a marathon. Obbin bounced on the toe line with all his weight to show its strength. "It's strong, I promise," he said encouragingly. "I've used it a thousand times, at least." The prince took a few more steps and he was swallowed in the mist.

Austin took a deep breath and, with a step of faith, walked onto the rickety toe bridge. Mason hadn't moved. Austin gave the expanse a light shake. It felt sturdy. "Mason, come on. It's fine." Mason gave an unconfident smirk. "I promise," Austin said. "Come on, we don't want to lose him."

Mason tapped a foot on the main vine, testing its strength. He stepped out with his other foot and the toe bridge swayed to the side. The warm blue air swept around him, tussling his hair. Under Austin's watchful eye Mason slowly caught up to him. After many measured steps, the twins arrived at the end of the toe bridge and at the foot of a small rope ladder where Obbin was waiting.

"Once we're up the ladder, wait in the mist until I tell you that there are no soldiers. There could be a patrol," Obbin instructed, then turned and climbed up the ladder. Once on top, Austin soon realized they were at the place where they'd chased Obbin into the blue cloud of steam. Austin shook his head and smiled to himself. The prince had known exactly where he was going. Obbin ran toward the forest, and just before he was lost to sight, he motioned for Mason and Austin to follow. The twins ran across the open expanse of rock, which glowed in the moonlight. They ducked and looked around nervously as they ran, hoping Obbin was right that there were no soldiers about.

Obbin wasted no time in explaining his plan. "I'm going to cause a disturbance in the woods ahead. This should cause the soldiers on guard to lower the drawbridge and investigate. Meanwhile, you two will go back to the wagon." Obbin looked back toward the crevice. "The soldiers will send a rider back to warn the commander. We have to stop him!" Obbin looked at Austin, a grim expression on his face. "You must wait at the edge of the side passage with the blow dart pipe and shoot the rider before he gets away."

Mason looked horrified. "We can't kill someone!" he exclaimed.

Obbin held up his hand. "No, no, the darts are laced with a sleeping agent. They are attached to the pipe. Speaking of which, don't let them prick you—you'll be out before you realize what's happened."

"But what if Austin misses?" Mason asked.

Obbin looked at Mason and shook his head. "He can't. He has to stop the guard. Mason, once the guard falls, use the rope cuffs to bind him."

"But what if we do miss?" Mason asked.

"Run!" Obbin said. "And hope that somehow we can still escape."

Mason looked at Austin, who flexed his bicep. "I've got this," Austin promised.

Obbin started removing things from his pockets and piling them between two large oak roots protruding from the ground. He pulled out a string with several small black-and-grey cylinders attached along it. A large grin crossed his face as he looked at the twins. "Fireworks! I'm going to go a ways into the woods and light these, then I'll come back across the toe bridge and meet you at the wagon. We'll drive out of the tunnel and across the drawbridge before the guards get back." Obbin cocked an eyebrow.

"But won't they be waiting for us on the trail?" Mason asked.

"No, I'm going that way," Obbin said, pointing to the far right. "All right, let's go." He sprinted into the woods, ignoring the low brambles. He was on a mission.

Mason and Austin ran back through the mist, unsure of exactly where the toe bridge was. Austin crept toward the edge of the crevice, Mason holding onto the back of his coat. At the edge, Austin knelt and used his hands to find the top of the rope ladder. The twins climbed down the ladder and onto the start of the toe bridge. As he crossed, Austin looked down into the chasm. How deep was it? Was there magma coursing below, or ready to explode to the surface?

Suddenly, loud bangs, pops, and booms erupted from the forest. Austin stumbled and almost missed his step. He grasped the guide vines with a death grip. Mason let out a shriek behind him. Austin looked back to see his older brother hanging from one of the vines, his legs dangling into the mist.

"Mason, hold on!"

"I am!" Mason screamed. Austin regained his balance and turned to face his brother. He had to be careful not to shake the vines too much, but at the same time he had to be quick. He cautiously approached Mason. "My hands are slippery from the steam! I'm losing my grip!" Mason cried. Austin watched as his brother, white knuckled, desperately held on for his life. He wasn't sure how he would even be able to help. After all, the toe bridge was little more than three vines, and there was nothing for Austin to balance on or use to leverage his brother's weight.

With one hand gripping the vine like a vice, Austin bent over to save his brother. "You have to reach up and grab my hand!" he commanded.

"I can't!"

"You have to!" Austin watched as Mason winced, fighting to gather the courage to let go of one of only two slippery holds.

"I'll get you. I promise!" Austin saw hope in Mason's eyes. The older twin let go with his left hand and thrust it toward the younger. Austin reached, and their fingers touched and then slid over each other. Austin clasped his brother's hand and pulled, holding tightly to the vine with his other. His feet wiggled on the vine below. Mason let go with his other hand and grasped Austin's extended hand. In a swift move, without a moment to think, Austin yanked Mason up, and somehow they each found a solid footing on the vine rope at their feet. Both of the twins gripped the guide vines tightly. Austin's heart pounded in his chest, matching the rapid rhythm of Mason's panting breaths.

"Let's get off this death trap," Austin said.

"And we'd better hurry. The guard will be coming soon," Mason reminded him.

"Yeah, they had to have heard those explosions!"

Safely across the chasm, the twins ducked into the tunnel. Turning on the mTalk's light, Austin led the way. As they passed the wagon Austin grabbed the blow gun pipe and Mason the rope cuffs. Inching their way toward the main tunnel, they heard the sound of horse hooves pounding against the stone floor. Austin and Mason crept forward, just to the edge of the river that separated them from where the guard would ride past.

"Here he comes!" Mason said, fingering the binding rope in his hand. "Are you ready?"

Austin turned the mTalk's light off and loaded a dart. He lifted the blowpipe to his mouth.

He wasn't exactly sure how he would know where to aim, but then he saw the faint flicker of firelight. The horseman came into view, one hand wielding a torch and the other tight on the reins of his horse.

Austin aimed, then waited, tracking the rider as he got nearer. His knuckles were white as he gripped the pipe. He was ready. He took a deep breath and then felt something slide into his mouth. He felt a small prick; he let go of the pipe, and his knees gave way as his body dropped to the ground.

Mason watched in horror as his brother fell to the ground beside him. The horseman was before them and passing by. He had to do something quickly.

Mason dropped the cuffs and swept the fallen blow dart pipe from the ground, loading another dart. Then in defiance of his better judgment, he shouted after the horseman. "Hey, rider man! Aren't you looking for us?"

In the flicker of the rider's torchlight, Mason saw that his words had been heard. The soldier reeled the horse around and started back. He let go of the reins and pulled something from his back: a bow and arrow.

Mason would only have one shot at this. The rider leapt from the horse, tossing the torch ahead of him to light the way.

Bow drawn, he started forward. The river still stood between them, but it would not stop an arrow—or a dart for that matter. Mason took a deep breath and lifted the pipe to his lips. Before the man could react, Mason aimed and blew as hard as he could. The soldier dropped to the ground like a sack of potatoes.

Before attending to his brother, Mason took the rope cuffs, knowing what he had to do next. His adrenaline high from his successful hit, Mason broke into a sprint and leaped across the river. He started to bind the rider's hands, but jerked backward when the man snored loudly. Confident at last that he was out cold, he finished his work. The horse whinnied a few yards away. Mason had an idea, looking back at the river. He started toward the horse, speaking calmly to it. The animal did not back away and instead approached without caution.

"Good horsey," Mason said. He'd taken riding lessons at his school, Bewaldeter. With one foot in the stirrup, he pulled himself up and into the saddle. He pressed his heels into the horse and trotted it back toward the river and across it. The water from the waves surged against the horse, soaking Mason's shoes and the bottoms of his pants.

Austin still lay crumpled where he had fallen. Mason quickly slipped down from the saddle and approached his twin. He noticed the feathery end of the dart sticking out between his lips. He removed the dart, but wasn't sure how he would waken his brother.

Mason jumped as Obbin's voice broke the silence. "What happened?" Obbin asked.

Mason took a deep breath and held up the dart. "I think he inhaled it."

Obbin shook his head. "Probably." The prince shrugged. "Oh well, let's get him loaded into the wagon."

Mason took Austin's arms and Obbin took his legs. They set Austin's limp body into the back of the wagon.

"How long until he wakes up?" Mason asked.

"I don't know," Obbin admitted. "Could be twenty minutes, could be an hour."

Obbin climbed back onto his ox as Mason started to get into the wagon. "Did you ride the horse over?" Obbin asked.

"Yeah," Mason said.

"Do you want to take it with us?" Obbin asked.

"I can't; then I'd be stealing," Mason said.

"No, the horses, like everything else, belong to all of the Blauwe Mensen, and you are now one of us," Obbin reminded him. Feeling rather special, Mason hopped down off the wagon and mounted the horse again. "Follow me," Obbin called as he drove the wagon back across the river.

Obbin kept the trio of oxen at a quick run, which allowed Mason and the horse to cantor. The darkness began to fade. As they rounded another bend, the entrance, or in this case the exit, came into view. The huge, forbidding doors were wide open and blue light flickered against the tunnel walls. The guard towers were empty and the drawbridge was lowered. Obbin drove the wagon down the peninsula between the two rivers and onto the bridge, with Mason following.

Again the blue mist engulfed them and Mason could barely make out his brother's body lying in the back of the wagon. The chorus of oxen and horse hooves against the planks of the drawbridge sounded eerie. The steam thinned as they crossed onto solid ground. They were almost home free. Well, almost *Phoenix*-free. Home was another issue entirely.

They crossed the moonlit stretch of grey rock in seconds and followed a tree line onto a wide dirt road. Mason expected the darkness of the woods to cloak them, but it didn't. Moonbeams broke through the trees, which were nearly bare of leaves. The green foliage had turned brown and everything looked dead. The storm Mr. Thule had mentioned had set in, and it was sending all of the plant life into hibernation. Mason's feet had already been growing cold in the cave from being wet, but now they felt frozen.

As the wagon sped down the dirt road, they took a hard left at a fork in the path. "Yah, yah!" the blue prince screamed. Mason's horse was nearly galloping to keep up; he was impressed at how fast these gargantuan oxen could move. Occasionally Mason watched the wagon tip dangerously to the left or right as a wheel struck a rut or Obbin took a curve too fast. He worried that his sleeping brother would be tossed out.

A loud horn blew from either behind them or around them; Mason wasn't sure. He looked over his shoulder at the moonlit trail, expecting to see a horde of blue men coming after them on horses. But he breathed a heavy sigh of relief when he saw nothing. "What was that?" Mason asked Obbin.

"Don't worry," the blue prince said, but Mason could hear an undertone of uncertainty in Obbin's voice.

After several minutes, at least another mile by Mason's estimate, they came to a familiar place. It was where they had been captured. A few yards more and they passed over a makeshift bridge of split logs crossing a deep valley. Once over it, Obbin halted the wagon, hopped off, and took his knife from its sheath. A quick slice through each of the ropes securing the bridge and the bridge slid into the gully below. The sound of wood beams splintering echoed in the forest as the bridge met its end. "That should delay any pursuers," Obbin said eagerly.

Less than ten minutes later, they arrived at the *Phoenix*. The ship was sprinkled with brown, orange, and red leaves, which demonstrated the drastic change in temperature and its effects on the foliage. Several leaves had blown through the still-open cargo bay door and were scattered throughout. "That's weird. We didn't leave the large cargo bay door open, only the small hatch," Mason remembered aloud, and he wondered whether Oliver and Tiffany were back.

Mason dismounted his horse and ran in through the open door, but only the broken sky scooter remained, still lying on its side and tethered down. There was no sign of the working scooter.

Mason walked over to the control panel for the doors. "Looks like the blue soldiers tampered with the controls. Somehow they opened the door."

Obbin's voice startled him. "It was probably my brother Voltan. He is very good with electronics."

"But there were hardly any electronics in the gorge," Mason said.

"Yes, but that is only because my father and the council like it that way. You should have seen Voltan's room. It's filled with collected gadgets and electronics," Obbin sighed. "If he has his way, we'll be exploring the galaxy again."

"Again?" Mason asked.

"You don't think we came from here?" Obbin asked incredulously. "No, we came from far away, as many of the books in the library say."

Mason shook his head. "I wish I could have spent some time in there."

"Maybe we can go back there someday," Obbin said.

"That would be really great," Mason started. "Of course we have a lot to do before we'd ever get to return."

"Like what?" Obbin asked.

"Well actually, our parents were taken by some soldiers a few days ago. We're here with our brother and sister. Oliver is the one who flew the ship here," Mason explained.

"There are more of you?" Obbin shouted. He looked angry.

"You didn't think Austin and I knew how to fly, did you?" Mason asked, but he knew the answer. They'd been slightly misleading to the prince.

"Why shouldn't I have thought you could fly?" he asked with his hands on his hips. The prince looked as though he'd been deeply betrayed. "Well, where are they?" he asked in frustration.

"We don't know," Mason said. "But they should return soon. They went to the nearby towns to meet with someone and get spare parts for the ship."

Obbin's scowl disappeared as he thought for a moment. "Will we fly when they return?"

Mason sighed. "Yes, then we will fly."

Obbin didn't look entirely convinced, but he changed the subject on his own. "We'd best get your brother into the ship and get everything unloaded before the soldiers get here."

Mason nodded; he knew all too well that they were coming. He only hoped Oliver and Tiffany would make it back in time.

Missing

awn came more quickly than Tiffany would have liked. Rubbing her eyes, she sat up and pulled the long strands of her brown hair into a ponytail and wrapped a tie around it. Outside, she could hear someone, probably Mr. O'Farrell, whistling and a fire crackling. The smell of burning wood wafted into the tent. According to her mTalk, it was 5:00 a.m.

"Oliver, wake up," she said softly. But his sleeping bag was empty. She appreciated that he'd gotten up and left her to sleep. She stretched her arms and then crawled to the tent opening. Tiffany climbed out of the tent and saw that Mr. O'Farrell was flipping eggs over the crackling fire. As the cold air enveloped her, she involuntarily shivered. She pulled her arms tightly around her body and rubbed her forearms. She looked around but didn't see Oliver. Maybe he'd gone looking for more firewood, she thought.

Mr. O'Farrell smiled at her. "G'mornin'. I was about to wake you two. Come on over and have some eggs and potatoes. I've made 'em up specially."

"You two? Where's Oliver?" asked Tiffany.

Mr. O'Farrell frowned. "Isn't he in the tent?"

"No, I thought he was out here with you."

"No, I haven't seen him all morning."

Tiffany looked at the sky scooters, but both were still there. "Have you been up for a while?" she asked.

"A half hour, maybe," Mr. O'Farrell said.

"He wouldn't just go off without telling us," she said in disbelief. "Oliver!" she called out. "Oliver, where are you?"

Mr. O'Farrell reached for his mTalk. "Let me try calling him."

He tapped something into the device and waited. "It must be Eises, still causing interference."

"Oliver!" cried out Tiffany. "Where is he?" She walked around the clearing, and Mr. O'Farrell joined her. They slowly spiraled out farther and farther from the camp. At last Tiffany noticed something curled up under a bunch of leaves. She ran over with Mr. O'Farrell, and they found Oliver, unconscious and buried in a pile of red and golden leaves. Tiffany rolled him over and could see that his chest was moving steadily up and down. He was alive.

"Oliver?" she said and shook his shoulders, but he didn't wake up. "What's wrong with him," she asked as she started to cry.

"I don't know," admitted Mr. O'Farrell. "Let me run back and get a medical kit from the scooter."

Tiffany knelt over her brother. Tears streamed down her cheeks and dripped onto his shirt. What was wrong with him, she wondered? How had he gotten all the way out here? She'd never known him to sleepwalk. Mr. O'Farrell returned and opened the medical kit. First he leaned his ear to Oliver's chest and listened. He held his hand just an inch above Oliver's mouth and nose. "He seems fine."

The old man pulled out a small straw and snapped off one end. He swiped it back and forth under Oliver's nose. Oliver's eyes opened and he sat up instantly. "Wait!" he yelled. Then he looked around as if getting his bearings. He looked at Tiffany and then Mr. O'Farrell. Placing a hand to his head he asked, "Where am I? What happened?"

Tiffany looked at him curiously. "We don't know, we just found you out here in the woods."

"You don't remember anything?" asked Mr. O'Farrell.

Oliver shook his head. "No, not really." He looked around and then up at the early morning sky. "What time is it?"

"A little after five," answered Mr. O'Farrell. "Here, let me help you to your feet."

Tiffany and the old man pulled Oliver up. He wobbled a moment and then Tiffany put her arm around him. "Let me help you," she said. He certainly looked out of it, weak, and maybe dehydrated.

"Let's get you back to camp. Depending on how long you've been out here, you might have hypothermia," explained Mr. O'Farrell. "We need to get you into some dry, warm clothes and near the fire." They led Oliver back to camp, and after he had changed, the three of them sat around the fire together. Oliver had pulled the hood of his sweatshirt up over his head and had his hands in the front pocket.

"So you don't remember anything?" Tiffany asked for the millionth time.

"No, I don't. Sorry," he admitted. What bugged her most was that Oliver didn't seem very concerned about what had happened. He'd been unconscious in the freezing cold woods all night alone. She wanted to know how this could have happened.

"Breakfast is almost ready; sorry it took so long," Mr. O'Farrell said.

"No problem," replied Oliver, looking at the skillet in the old man's hand. Then he glanced upward at the dark sky. "Why does it have to be so cold?"

"It's because you're suffering from a mild case of hypothermia, and remember, Eises is setting in. Thank you for cooking, Mr. O'Farrell," Tiffany said properly.

"Oh, it was no problem, I like cooking when I can." Mr. O'Farrell smiled and then put a couple of pieces of potato and two eggs on a plate. "Yes, the cold weather is moving in very quickly now. I'd say it has dropped nearly ten degrees since yesterday evening." Tiffany looked overhead at the trees. She noticed that many of the branches were bare. Looking at her feet, she saw red, brown, and yellow leaves all around. They splattered the ground with color.

"How far to Mudo?" asked Oliver.

"Not far, not far at all. I would guess we'll be there in an hour or so," Mr. O'Farrell said.

"Good, I'm ready to get back to the *Phoenix*," Oliver said.

"Me too," agreed Tiffany. Her mind went back to Oliver and the morning's events. Yet he still seemed unfazed. For the next ten minutes, they sat and enjoyed a warm breakfast. Oliver's color had improved and he seemed to be almost back to normal. After they were through, they broke down the camp and packed all their things back on the scooters. It was time to head for the outpost and to find the parts they needed. Then they'd be free to head for Evad.

1.34

Schlamm

As they sped along the maglev track, Tiffany again thought about the twins. She tried to contact them again, but there was still no answer. Tiffany opened her mom's journal and decided to start chronicling the events that had occurred thus far. After all, the details of this journey may be valuable later. It was likely now that they were already knee deep in the quest for Ursprung. They might stumble across clues that at the moment would seem unimportant, but in hindsight when connected with other things might prove to be useful. That was why the journal was so valuable; so much of her parents' work was meticulously catalogued and cross-referenced.

To the untrained eye, deciphering the notes would be like looking up into the night sky and trying to gather information from the stars. Whereas Tiffany understood how to navigate the entries and decipher them, much like an astronomer could look at the stars and recognize constellations and galaxies.

Truly the code to this journal rested with herself and her parents. She was pretty sure that Oliver had never taken the time or shown any interest in learning their methods. She wanted to begin reading more about the previous months of her parents' work, but knew that she needed to enter the recent experiences she and Oliver had had first. She didn't want to forget anything.

They arrived on the outskirts of Mudo less than forty-five minutes later. Leaving the maglev rail, they followed a roughly cut trail through the trees. The path didn't appear to be in regular use as large brambles shrouded it. Had they been walking they would have been slowed considerably, but the sky scooters allowed them to fly over the shrubbery.

No more than a hundred yards down the trail, Mr. O'Farrell informed them that they would be walking the rest of the way. The scooters were parked to one side, and Oliver and Mr. O'Farrell felled some small branches to lay over the scooters. Oliver stepped back and admired their work; the scooters were very difficult even for him to see, and he already knew where they were.

Mr. O'Farrell handed Oliver and Tiffany each a set of ragged-looking clothes. "What are these for?" Tiffany asked as she held out a tunic that looked as though it had been dragged through mud and then pulled across glass shards. Oliver laughed at Tiffany's proposed outfit, but then frowned when he looked over his own. His was in very similar condition.

"This is a rough place at times, and with winter drawing so near, it's better to appear as if we have little to lose," Mr. O'Farrell explained. "The desperation of a man can lead him to do things he would not if his circumstances were better." Tiffany nodded and slipped the tatty attire over her clothing, as did Oliver.

"All right, now we walk," said Mr. O'Farrell, picking up a long brown stick. "Perfect."

The approach to Mudo was nothing like that of Brighton. No dome shielded Mudo from the approaching year-long storm. There was no gap between the trees and the city; buildings and trees sporadically intermingled and became blurred together. There were no clear roads either. Rust cloaked the metal buildings, while the many wooden ones appeared to be newer additions. A hazy smoke filled the air, accompanied by the smell of burning wood. Few people roamed outside and those who did quickly disappeared into the shadows at Oliver, Tiffany, and Mr. O'Farrell's approach.

Oliver was nervous; the town was so desolate and rundown. The evasiveness of the few people he did see gave him a funny feeling in his stomach that activated lessons from his Academy training. Contingency plans began running through his mind. He analyzed their surroundings and identified various escape routes.

"Stay close to me if anything happens," he whispered in his sister's ear.

She looked at him frightfully. "Like what?"

"I don't know, but something just isn't right here," Oliver said as he felt his sister clasp his hand. She didn't have the training he did, so he had to protect her. Oliver and Tiffany followed Mr. O'Farrell to the front of a large warehouse.

"All right, remember, let me do the talking," the old man reminded them.

"What is this place?" Oliver asked.

"This building was once the hangar for the colonization ships that originally discovered Jahr des Eises and established the human presence here," Mr. O'Farrell explained. "It's just filled with old parts now and run by a man named Schlamm. Needless to say, Schlamm is a bit gruff on the exterior, but don't worry—he isn't as scary as he tries to appear." Tiffany looked at Oliver again as he squeezed her hand and smiled.

Mr. O'Farrell knocked several times on a large, rusted door. They waited for several minutes but there was no answer. He knocked again, but still no one came. Finally he pushed the large door open and stepped inside. "Stay close to me," the old man said, as he led the way into the old, decrepit warehouse.

A musty smell mixed with burning iron and sewage hung in the air. Large beams crisscrossed the ceiling with several skylights inset in the tin roof. Trails of dripping brown water leaked down from areas where wood had been used to patch the roof. Oliver looked around at all the parts. Even if they found the right part, it probably wouldn't be usable. Half of the items he saw were wet, and the others were brown with rust. What could he possibly find that would be of use to repair the *Phoenix*?

A blue glow flashed off the piles of metal parts around them. A fountain of sparks shot high into the air from behind a pile of junk ahead. Someone was working on something, or there was a very dangerous electrical hazard. Oliver sighed; from what he'd seen so far the latter was likely. The smell of hot metal greeted them as the source of the flickers came into view. A large, burly man was bent over an old wing, cutting through it with a torch. Several pieces of scrap on a nearby pile suddenly tumbled to the ground as if something had disturbed them.

The man must have noticed the avalanche, because he shut off the torch in his hand and lifted the visor that shielded his eyes. As he turned to face them, Oliver noticed his size. He was several inches taller than Oliver with bulky muscles to boot, but Oliver knew of several ways to bring down an opponent larger than himself.

"What duh yah want?" the man asked in a harsh, irritated voice. He rubbed his face, smearing grease across his cheek and into his black beard. He wore blue overalls over a shirt that was stained beyond bleaching.

"We are looking for a part for a ship," said Mr. O'Farrell.

"Oh, it's you," Schlamm said.

Oliver knew that Mr. O'Farrell had met Schlamm before, but the tone seemed so casual, as if their interaction was a common occurrence.

"Yes, it is," Mr. O'Farrell answered.

"What you got to pay wit?" asked Schlamm rudely.

"Federal credits, of course," answered Mr. O'Farrell firmly.

"Credits, ha! I thought I told yah last time. Can't yah remember where yah are?" said Schlamm angrily. He set down his torch and removed his gloves, revealing two hands but just five fingers and two thumbs between them both. "The Federation!" he said and spat on the ground. "When they built duh blasted domed city, we became its sewer."

"I do know the plight you have here in Mudo, but it is all we have to trade with," Mr. O'Farrell said consolingly. "I assure you we will make it worth your trouble."

Schlamm seemed to be considering the offer. He scratched at his beard and then looked back at a pile of parts several feet away. "What model a ship?"

"The ship is NT-Class and we need a communication transponder."

"NT-Class," Schlamm said with a laugh. "You're in luck. I just traded with some Corsairs!" Schlamm exclaimed, looking at Tiffany as if to frighten her.

"Corsairs!" shouted Oliver angrily.

Schlamm's head turned quickly to Oliver. "What you say boy?" Mr. O'Farrell shot Oliver a frustrated look.

"I said Corsairs," Oliver admitted firmly. To Oliver, Corsairs were a group of pirates who constantly threatened commerce throughout the Federation. They went around stealing and pillaging from outposts and ships. Oliver knew some viewed the rebels as defenders of freedom. But that viewpoint was held only by a slim minority living in the farthest reaches of the Federation. At the Academy, Oliver had been taught of the Corsairs' defiance of the Federation and the selfish nature of their actions. One of the first training missions Oliver would have been assigned upon graduation would have been to patrol a trade route. It is highly likely that he would have had a run-in with Corsairs. He might have even had the chance for a dogfight with them.

"What about 'em?" Schlamm asked.

"It just surprised me they were around here," Oliver said truthfully. He decided not to say how he really felt and risk enraging the hefty parts dealer before him; it wasn't worth jeopardizing the purchase of their parts.

"Rather frightening, aren't they?" Oliver added for good measure.

Schlamm let out a devious laugh. "Not fer someone like me, boy." He looked back to Mr. O'Farrell. "So, your part. I've got it; well at least I s'pose I do. Them Corsairs needed several large Morgandrake engines for their flagship, the Black Ranger. They traded me an entire NT-Class ship for them." Schlamm acted as if his visitors should be impressed. "Follow me."

He led them around several large piles of scrap to the far end of the warehouse. There in front of them sat a large ship identical to the *Phoenix*. "Get the parts you need and find me. Then we'll trade. Don't try anything suspicious, or it'll be the last thing you do. Spike will be watching!" he said, pointing to a nearby pile. With a laugh, he turned and walked away.

Oliver looked at Tiffany, confused. There was nothing on or by the pile of metal. "Do you see anything?" he asked. Tiffany shrugged her shoulders, equally confused.

Oliver looked back to the ship in front of them. "Pirates! Lousy pirates!" Oliver exclaimed. "I should have known. I don't want to trade with someone who gets his supplies from thieves and filth. Why hasn't he been arrested by Brighton's security force? The Federation doesn't stand for trading with pirates."

Mr. O'Farrell interrupted. "Oliver, you could have ruined everything back there," he reprimanded angrily. "I'm not con-doning what pirates do or Schlamm's choice of suppliers, but you can't just spout off when you feel like it. I recall it was you last night that was concerned for our safety. Well, let me tell you that an outburst like that certainly risked our safety." Oliver looked at his feet, his face red from the old man's words.

"I don't think you get it. Did you see the Federation's flag flying over Mudo? No, you didn't, and that's because these people don't recognize the Federation's authority over them. Besides, the Brighton security force isn't interested in cutting off the fund source to their largest briber."

Mr. O'Farrell stopped his lecture and walked a few feet from Oliver and Tiffany. Oliver wasn't sure what to say. He hadn't known all of that. He'd been naïve to think that everyone obeyed the Federation perfectly and that justice was present at all corners of the Federation. A moment later the old man returned. He sighed. "I know you are under a lot of stress. I don't like what happened any more than you, but we must be careful." Oliver nodded. The old man was right; he had almost blown it.

"I'm sorry, Oliver; I shouldn't have gotten so angry just then. I know that pirates are rotten people. However, we need this part in order to save your parents," Mr. O'Farrell said encouragingly.

"I'm sorry too," said Oliver. "It was dangerous. He just caught me off guard. It won't happen again."

Mr. O'Farrell grinned. "It's all right; you covered well."

"Thanks." A moment of awkward silence passed.

"Mr. O'Farrell, what or who is Spike," asked Tiffany.

"Oh." Mr. O'Farrell turned to look behind him. "Spike is a seven-foot hybrid chameleon-iguana. Genetically engineered and bred by a company called RepFuse, he is virtually invisible. He can change colors and blend in to his surroundings. His camouflage is why you don't see him." Mr. O'Farrell pointed at the pile Schlamm had noted. "I only know about him because of my and Mr. Krank's previous dealings with Schlamm. The beast tried to take a chunk out of Samuel's leg." Tiffany scurried next to Oliver. "Don't worry, he won't do anything to us unless we do something erratic," he reassured them. "Mr. Krank made the mistake of knocking a large piece of scrap onto the beast's tail. Now let's find that part."

"Sounds good," Oliver answered. He'd been looking at the ship. It had been damaged in several areas, probably by whatever means the pirates used to capture it. He felt bad for whomever had been on board. They were now captives, he assumed.

Oliver walked toward the hatch and quietly read the ship's name and number to himself. *C1:4-13 Griffin*. He'd heard that name before, but where? As he boarded the ship, he looked back to ask Mr. O'Farrell and saw a look of shock on the old man's face.

"What? What is it?" asked Oliver. Mr. O'Farrell didn't speak. It was then that he noticed Tiffany standing next to the old man, tears welling in her eyes. "What's wrong?" Oliver asked again.

"The *Griffin* is Rand and Jen McGregor's ship," Mr. O'Farrell said quietly.

"Rand and Jen?" cried Oliver. "But if their ship is here—"

"Then, yes, they are captives of the Corsairs," Mr. O'Farrell finished. A sense of loss filled Oliver. No wonder Mr. O'Farrell hadn't been able to contact the McGregors. What could be done, now that so many people were involved? His parents, the McGregors . . . who else was caught up in this? He looked at Tiffany; she was crying. Oliver stepped out of the hatch and toward his sister, who collapsed in his arms and began sobbing on his shoulder.

"It's all right," he whispered, his voice cracking a bit.

Tiffany looked up at him, her face fearful. "What do you think happened to Ashley? I saw her at Bewaldeter. Her parents were still on their way at the time." Oliver shivered. Ashley was Rand and Jen's daughter. Was she with them, trapped on the Corsair ship, or was she confused and alone at the school? Ashley, Tiffany, and Oliver had been on many expeditions together. She'd been a childhood friend for as long as he could remember. Oliver fought back his own tears. He'd held it together to this point, but this was it.

"Tiffany, I'm sure she's fine. She's probably safe at Bewaldeter. They'll take care of her," he promised.

He felt Mr. O'Farrell's hand on his shoulder. "It'll be all right," the old man said reassuringly. "We will find your parents."

"But what about Ashley?" Tiffany asked.

"I'll call the school and then send someone I trust to retrieve her," Mr. O'Farrell promised.

A moment passed and Oliver cleared his throat. "We need to find the part," he said, trying to regain his emotional strength.

Tiffany stepped back and wiped her eyes. "Let's go."

Oliver made his way around the ship. "Mr. O'Farrell, we'll have to get this latch open; the transponders are in here."

Mr. O'Farrell looked at the *Griffin* sadly. "All right. I have some tools in my pack." He lowered his satchel to the ground and pulled out a ratchet for Oliver. Oliver loosened the nuts and opened the hatch. He retrieved a small silver cylinder with a green ball attached to one end and showed Mr. O'Farrell. The old man looked it over and smiled. "Looks good! Maybe we should purchase two."

"We don't have a lot of credits and we may need to buy supplies eventually," answered Oliver.

"Don't worry Oliver; I'm taking care of the cost. I'd buy the ship, but it looks like it was severely damaged in its capture. I am assuming Schlamm had to tow it back."

"All right," Oliver said, and started working on the second part.

"Are there any other parts that I should try to get while you work on that?" Mr. O'Farrell asked.

"Yes," Oliver answered. "Tiffany has a list on the journal."

"Right." The old man looked with Tiffany and then headed into the ship.

Once Oliver had the second part, he went inside the *Griffin*. He found Mr. O'Farrell in the bridge, working under one of the main computer consoles. "I wouldn't mind getting a few extra things not on my list from here and a couple parts from the engine room," Oliver said.

Apparently he startled Mr. O'Farrell, because the old man shot up and knocked his head on the underside of the dash. "Yeow!"

"I'm sorry," Oliver apologized. "I didn't mean to startle you."

Mr. O'Farrell rubbed his forehead as a large red mark appeared where he'd struck the console. "Get whatever you need. I'm just going to finish here. I've not collected all the parts you need, but Tiffany knows what I've gotten so far. She was headed to one of the cabins."

Oliver suspected he knew right where his sister had gone. Sure enough, he found her in a cabin that he assumed was Ashley's. The walls were pink, but there was no longer any furniture or personal items.

"Tiffany," Oliver started. "Are you okay?"

She turned, and he could see her eyes were red and puffy. "She's my best friend, you know," Tiffany admitted. "She has to be okay."

Oliver crossed the room and embraced his little sister. "She will be; we're going to find out where she is. I'm sure she's fine." Of course Oliver didn't know for sure, but he had to believe it—not just for Tiffany, but for himself.

Tiffany followed Oliver to the engine room where he gathered a few more parts. Several of the items were quite large and had to be taken out of the *Griffin* and stacked on a cart that Mr. O'Farrell had found. Once everything was collected, Oliver, Tiffany, and Mr. O'Farrell headed for Schlamm's makeshift office. Oliver had to work extra hard to maneuver the cart around the many piles of parts as well as through the floor that had become a mucky paste of mud and metal. When they found Schlamm, he was sitting with his grimy boots on the desk.

"Find what yah needed?" he asked as they approached.

"Yes, we would like to purchase all of these parts," Mr. O'Farrell answered.

Without even looking at what was there, Schlamm spouted off a price. "Ah, it'll cost you fifty thousand credits each," Schlamm commanded with a devious smile. Oliver couldn't believe what he'd heard. He knew Schlamm would do his best to rip them off, but this was ridiculous. The most expensive parts would have been the communication transponders, and they shouldn't have cost more than five thousand credits in new condition at a parts store.

"I'll give you two thousand credits each," Mr. O'Farrell bartered.

"Ha, you must be kidding me," Schlamm said. "Forty thousand each."

"Three thousand credits each," responded Mr. O'Farrell.

"Thirty thousand each."

"Five thousand credits all."

"Twenty thousand credits each."

"Seven thousand credits each."

"Fifteen thousand credits each."

"Eight thousand credits all."

"Twelve thousand credits each."

"Nine thousand credits all."

"Ten thousand credits all."

"Deal," said Mr. O'Farrell, smiling. He quickly pulled out a small black stick and typed in ten thousand. He tapped his stick on a silver square on Schlamm's desk and a screen displayed the transfer.

"Thanks for doing business," Schlamm said mockingly.

"No, thank you," Mr. O'Farrell replied and quickly led the kids out of the warehouse. Once they were outside, Oliver turned to Mr. O'Farrell. "You got ripped off. Ten thousand credits each was way too much. None of those parts would have cost more than five thousand at a dealer!" exclaimed Oliver.

"I didn't pay ten thousand credits each. I paid that for all of them," he said with a smile. "Now we must hurry before Schlamm realizes what has just happened. Granted, ten thousand credits for everything isn't cheap, but it's a fraction of what he thought he was getting," said Mr. O'Farrell. "As we talked, I switched the negotiations from each to all, and he continued to negotiate with me and even made his final offer as ten thousand all, which I quickly took. I'm guessing he won't realize his mistake for a little while, but we had better not take any chances."

"Sounds dishonest," Oliver said.

"Consider that he made the offer and accepted the terms. He got more than the fair value of the parts, and as you pointed out, his suppliers don't exactly have an honest reputation," the old man countered. Oliver nodded his head, unconvinced. Trickery was lying as far as he was concerned. The one thing his dad had always said was, "If a man isn't honest, he can't expect to understand the truth." Oliver smiled at the thought of his father.

They walked out of Mudo and headed for their scooters at a trot. Oliver placed the parts safely in the empty compartments on the scooters. A few of the nonessential pieces were placed in Mr. O'Farrell's scooter, but none that Oliver needed immediately. Tiffany climbed on and Oliver started the sky scooter. A red blip appeared on the radar screen. It was approaching quickly from the direction of Mudo. Mr. O'Farrell must have noticed it as well, because he looked at Oliver. "It's Schlamm," he said. "Quick, we must go."

Oliver turned the throttle in his hands and the sky scooter shot forward. Tiffany gripped her brother's waist tightly. They sped along the railway at lightning speed, but the blip was closing.

"He's gaining on us!" Oliver called to Mr. O'Farrell. The old man looked at him with concern.

"I know! We have to split up. It's the best way to confuse him." Oliver nodded his head confidently. "There is a dry creek bed up ahead. Take it and I'll meet you at the ship."

"All right!"

"If he follows you, cut into the woods. Don't take him to the ship!"

Oliver nodded again. "Hold on Tiffany!" He felt her grip tighten.

"I am!" she screamed over his shoulder.

Oliver saw the blip on the radar closing in on them. They curved around a bend, and Mr. O'Farrell pointed at a spot ahead. "There, turn there!" Mr. O'Farrell shouted. The creek bed approached. Fifty yards . . . thirty yards . . . ten yards . . . Oliver turned the handles hard and the sky scooter dipped off the railway and down into the creek bed. Seconds later, he heard a thundering noise. Oliver looked back and watched as a large mud cruiser flew past the opening in the woods. He could even see Schlamm's outline in the cockpit.

Oliver sighed in relief. "Tiff, I think he's past. He must have decided to pursue Mr. O'Farrell."

"Or he didn't think his ship could navigate this creek bed," Tiffany added.

"Possible," Oliver said. "Either way, you can loosen your grip," he said, his voice strained from her tight embrace. He felt her arms drop away and heard her sigh. "Now on to the *Phoenix*."

Oliver verified that indeed the mud cruiser had continued in pursuit of Mr. O'Farrell. They were free to proceed to the *Phoenix*. The dry creek bed was clear and easy to navigate, with the exception of a few downed tree trunks. Oliver watched the scooter's navigation screen as they neared the *Phoenix*. They were nearly parallel with the ship when Oliver spotted an opening in the woods. He revved the throttle and the scooter shot up the bank.

"Whoa!" screamed Tiffany as she wrapped her arms tightly around Oliver's waist. "Tell me when you're going to do that."

Oliver looked over his shoulder, his eyebrows raised. "Sorry." The cold wind howled all around them as it zipped through the barren trees. Tiffany shivered and looked up, then tapped Oliver and pointed. Small white flurries had begun to fall from the dark purple clouds overhead. Oliver could smell the crisp cold air. Winter was here, and based on the notes in the journal about Eises, they had little time left before things would start being coated with ice. Oliver hoped Mr. O'Farrell would make it back in time.

The last hundred and fifty yards to the ship took almost ten minutes, and although it was bitter cold, Oliver was sweating from the meticulous steering around every tree trunk. It reminded him of the start of his quest to Brighton. Then a beautiful sight came into view: the shining sleek exterior of the *Phoenix*. A white dusting of snow covered the top of the ship and its forward-swept wings. Its silver skin sparkled with the addition of small ice crystals.

Oliver flew under the left wing and toward the cargo bay. He was so excited to be back to the closest thing to home that he had left, that he hopped off the scooter before it came to a full stop. The smaller craft continued to float past the ship with Tiffany still on board. She glowered at Oliver as she dismounted, but he'd already gone to the airlock to gain access. Oliver typed in the code, but nothing happened. He realized the door must have been sealed from the inside, which was a good thing. That meant the twins were safe. To his surprise they must have obeyed his orders. He lifted the mTalk to his mouth and called for the twins to open the hatch.

1.35

Reunited

"Austin, Mason," called a familiar voice.

The younger of the blond-haired boys stirred and sleepily opened his eyes and looked around. Where was he? Austin rubbed his head; it hurt so badly. He'd just had the worst dream ever—his parents had been kidnapped by an evil society and he and Mason had been taken by blue soldiers.

But the voice came again, shouting over the speaker on his mTalk. "Austin, Mason, we're locked outside!" it shouted.

Austin fumbled for the mTalk on his wrist, but it wasn't there. It lay on the table next to the bunk. He stood from the bed and nearly tripped over some clothes piled on the floor. As he looked down, he noticed they were thick and blue in color.

"Open the airlock, guys!" the voice shouted again. Someone stirred behind him on his bunk. Austin nearly fell backwards as he turned around and saw a blue boy sitting up in his bed. His brother Mason was also stretching and waking.

None of it had been a dream. Everything was true. The blue boy in front of him was Obbin and they were on the *Phoenix*, far from home and on a mission to rescue their parents.

Mason had already climbed out from the bunk, taken one of the dark blue jackets off the floor, and put it on. "Glad you're awake," he said, and started to leave the cabin.

"What happened? How did we escape?" he asked, but Mason was already through the door.

Obbin laughed. "You were brilliant with the blow dart, Austin."

Oliver's voice interrupted them again. "Austin, Mason, if you're still sleeping you shouldn't be. Come let us in!"

Austin took the mTalk from the table. "We're coming," he said groggily. He motioned for Obbin to follow, but the prince shook his head. "I'll be there in a minute."

"Suit yourself," Austin said as he headed to reunite with his brother and sister, leaving Obbin alone.

Down the corridor and into the cargo bay, where he saw Mason at the airlock entering the code, he reached his older brother just as the airlock door slid up and open. Sunlight and cold air filled the entry, which didn't help his headache.

Two silhouettes appeared in the glow. The light wrapped around Oliver and Tiffany as they stepped across the threshold and into view. An unexpected sense of joy came over Austin, and he and Mason wrapped their arms around Tiffany. Her eyes filled with tears of joy. The boys released the bear hug on their sister, and to Oliver's surprise, embraced him just as they had Tiffany. This lasted a second before the twins let go and stepped back. A moment of silence passed as they all basked in each other's presence. There was no sign of the anger from the earlier disagreement when Oliver and Tiffany departed for Brighton. Austin seemed to be, at least for the moment, over his dissatisfaction.

"Well it's good to be back, but we need to get ready for takeoff. I want to be able to leave as soon as Mr. O'Farrell arrives," Oliver explained.

"You found him?" Mason asked.

"Yes, and he helped us find the parts we needed. He's coming to assist us on the rest of our journey," Tiffany explained.

"Where is he now?" Mason asked.

Oliver nodded to Tiffany and then spoke to Mason, "He's taking care of something. He'll be here shortly."

"Okay," Mason said.

Oliver smiled. "Tiffany, can you get the navigation systems up and running?" Oliver requested.

"Sure thing," Tiffany agreed.

"Can I help you, Oliver?" asked Austin.

"Yeah, but first help Mason get the scooter in."

"Okay." Austin smiled and watched his brother disappear around the back of the ship.

Tiffany wiped her eyes from the joyous tears she'd shed. "So was everything okay while we were gone?"

Mason's face flushed with warmth. "Uh—well—about that," he murmured. "Maybe I should go help Oliver."

Tiffany stepped back. "What are you wearing?" she asked.

Mason's shirt and pants had become considerably dirty and been adorned with a few tears, and they were clearly not his own.

"Uh, these?" Mason said evasively with a laugh as he tugged at his shirt.

"Yeah, those!" Tiffany said suspiciously.

Austin turned to Mason nervously. "We should get the scooter back into the ship like Oliver said." He grabbed Mason's shoulder and pulled him through the airlock. Mason gave Tiffany a guilty smirk and went with Austin.

As they disappeared, Tiffany shouted to them. "We'll talk about this later." She shook her head and walked up the stairs and down the corridor to the bridge.

Oliver opened the hatch and pulled out the damaged transponder. He set it on the wing and then worked on fitting the replacement in position. He'd pulled his hood over his head, but the frozen air was still getting to him. Even the gloves on his hands didn't seem to be enough to keep him warm anymore.

Austin came around the corner with Mason. The twins had found coats, hats, and gloves, and were now bundled up. They stopped to watch their older brother work. He was on the topside of the wing on his knees, twisting the replacement part into place.

Austin shivered. "It sure is getting cold."

"Yeah, two days ago the forest was thick and covered in green," Mason recalled. "Now look, only the firs have any covering and everything is speckled with snow. Oliver, are you cold? Do you want a hat?"

Oliver looked down at his two brothers. Unlike most people, he could tell them apart without looking at their eyes. "Yeah Mason. That'd be great. Thanks."

Mason left for Oliver's cabin while Austin stayed behind in the hope he might get to help Oliver. "Do you need anything?"

"Nope, I think I've got it all taken care of." Oliver stood up. "All right, that should be fixed."

"The sky scooter is in and all of the supplies and remaining spare parts are unpacked and secured in crates," Austin explained.

"Good, good," he said distractedly. Oliver nodded as he surveyed his work; everything looked in place so he closed the hatch. He looked over the rest of the ship. The *Phoenix's* wing tip was dented, probably from the impact to the cliff on Tragiws. Oliver looked at his little brother, who was eagerly waiting to help. "Austin, scratch not needing anything. Could you go to the engine room and get a rubber mallet?"

"Definitely," Austin said, and before Oliver could say anything more he'd disappeared into the cargo bay.

Austin ran to a door tucked beneath the cargo bay staircase. It led to a corridor that would get him to the engine room. As he opened the door, he heard Mason call to him from the stairs.

"Where are you headed?" his brother asked.

"The engine room. I need to get a rubber mallet," Austin said.

"Cool," Mason said as he headed out of the ship. Austin opened the door and entered the lower corridor. He turned right and stepped into the engine room. It was oddly quiet in there; he expected it to be humming with energy, but it wasn't. Austin shrugged and started to search for the rubber mallet. Drawers were pulled out and doors left open.

After some digging, he found one. As he shut the drawer he noticed that a ventilation vent cover had fallen off. Lots of things had probably come loose in the landing. Maybe he and Oliver would be able to spend some time checking the ship out and fixing the things that had broken or come loose. That would give them a chance to bond with each other. Austin set the vent cover back in place and then headed for Oliver.

Oliver was already wearing his blue stocking cap and talking to Mason, who was sitting with his legs dangling over the side of the wing. A twinge of jealousy surged through Austin. Oliver laughed at something Mason said, which only increased Austin's angst. Mason looked down at Austin. "Hey, I was just telling Oliver about the time you and I switched the chocolate syrup at the Bewaldeter ice cream social for BBQ sauce."

Austin scowled. That had been his idea, and now Mason was getting the glory for telling about it. Austin climbed up the ladder, and as he did he took his anger out on each rung. It didn't seem to help, but only increase his frustration.

"Here it is," Austin said as he walked toward the wing. He hung his legs over the top of the *Phoenix* and hopped down to the wing. He handed the mallet to Oliver and then crouched over the dent. "These look pretty bad, I might need to help you," Austin said officially. "Mason, why don't you get another rubber mallet, but don't confuse it with a regular hammer," Austin said mockingly.

"That won't be necessary," Oliver said. "This won't take me long at all." Austin grunted and walked to the opposite side of the wing. That hadn't gone as he had wanted at all.

Oliver started banging out the dents on the wing, producing a loud metallic thump that echoed through the desolate woods, cloaking even the howling wind. It was useless for the twins to try talking to him, so they just sat in silence while their brother worked. When Oliver finished, the wing looked almost new, with the exception of a few scrapes. He was surprised at how pliable the metal had been. He surveyed his work and bent down to make sure the latch on the hatch was secure.

"AHHH!" Mason's frightened yell caught Austin off guard and he nearly fell off the wing. Oliver and Austin both looked at the blue-eyed twin.

"What is it?" Oliver asked frantically. Mason pointed at the woods. Austin followed Mason's hand and saw what frightened him. Between every tree stood a blue man dressed in fur garments and holding a spear in his hand.

"What in the world?" exclaimed Oliver.

Austin assessed the tree line. Despite the cold temperatures, the blue warriors were still dressed only in their fur shorts. Each man held either a spear or torch in his hand. The blue firelight glinted off the increasing fall of snow like sparkling blue gems, reminding Austin of what had started the whole mess. A lump formed in Austin's throat.

"Guys, get over here!" Oliver commanded. Mason pushed himself up from the wing and ran for Oliver, but Austin stood his ground on the wing.

"We don't have him! He left," Austin cried out.

"Have who?" Oliver asked.

"Obbin, the prince," Mason explained.

Oliver stared at them and cried, "What?" Mason didn't answer. One of the soldiers stepped forward. Austin instantly recognized who it was, Feng.

"We cannot let you leave. We are charged with the secrecy and protection of the gorge," Feng explained. "There is far more at stake than you realize."

Oliver's expression hardened. "No one tells us we can't leave," he mumbled. "Austin, get over here!" Austin obeyed, but behind him the blue men began to advance on the ship. They moved slowly and cautiously, but with spears raised as if to attack. Austin spun around and shouted incoherently. The blue men shifted backward as if unsure what the crazy boy was going to do. They'd not been this timid in the woods, but here in the shadow of the *Phoenix* they seemed less aggressive.

Austin huddled with Oliver and Mason, as if they were on a sports team. "Both of you jump off the wing and get inside. Mason, close the airlocks; Austin, go to the bridge and start the engines. I'll distract them while you get safe." Oliver looked at his mTalk. "It'll have to work."

"What?" Mason asked with fright. Oliver didn't answer, but looked back at the blue men.

Austin could see only the slightest glimmer of fear in his brother's brown eyes. "Tell Tiffany I'll rendezvous with you at the place she and I camped the first night."

"But how are—" Austin started.

"No time! Go!" Oliver yelled. "I'll distract them." Oliver climbed onto the roof of the *Phoenix* and ran toward the bow of the ship, shouting as he did.

"Here goes nothing!" Austin said. The twins lowered themselves over the side of the wing, dangling their legs for a moment. Austin took a deep breath and let go, expecting his legs to buckle on impact, but they didn't. Mason dropped down next to him and they ran for the small airlock.

"Hurry boys!" called Oliver from overhead. The blue men were everywhere. They seemed distracted, and yet three of them were charging after the twins. Just as Austin stepped through the door, a spear whizzed past and slid across the floor of the cargo bay, carving a long scrape into the metal.

A scream pierced the air. Tiffany was standing on the balcony looking down into the cargo bay. "What are they?"

"Blue warriors!" Mason shouted as he pressed the button to seal the airlock.

Tiffany scowled. "I can see that!"

Austin was already up the stairs and running past his sister as the yellow warning light flashed and the airlock door lowered. A loud clang echoed in the cavernous cargo bay as another spear bounced off the side of the *Phoenix*.

"It's the Blauwe—" Austin heard Mason explaining to Tiffany, but already their voices were fading. He had one mission—he'd been tasked with starting the engines, which in his mind meant he might be flying the *Phoenix*. The angry, jealous thoughts from before were gone, at least for the moment.

Austin was standing at the dashboard with so much adrenaline coursing through his body he couldn't even sit in the pilot chair. The screen glowed before him, but it was blank with the exception of the swirling purple image of the planet they were on. He scratched his head. He looked out the windows before him. A light dusting of snow covered the glass, but at the same time he could see blue warriors just a few yards off the bow, their spears raised.

He had to figure this out. Austin tapped the screen, the rotating globe disappeared, and several icons appeared. The moving sphere had just been a sort of screen saver or something. Austin read through the icons. Engine Ignition Sequence was one of them. He tapped it, but nothing happened. Austin tapped it again and listened. Again nothing. Austin sighed and grabbed a tuft of his hair in his hand. "What's wrong!" he cried out. He was still alone on the bridge.

Outside the *Phoenix*, Oliver was doing his best to distract the blue soldiers and keep them occupied. He ran across the ship's roof, from the bow to the aft. He ran back and forth across the wingspan. The soldiers were shouting Oliver's location to each other. They'd not launched any spears at Oliver yet. Clearly they wanted him alive, which Oliver recognized as a major advantage for him.

The one who'd stepped forward and spoken to Austin was trying to coax Oliver down. Did the blue guy think he was crazy? "Can't let them leave," Oliver scoffed. No one was keeping him and his sister and brothers there. No one was stopping him from rescuing his parents. He wished that Mr. O'Farrell would arrive, and soon. If he didn't, they would have to take off without him. If he did, though, the old man would find himself in the middle of a swarm of blue warriors. It was just as well that he had not shown up, but Oliver hoped he had gotten away from Schlamm.

Oliver looked up into the sky. Snow flurries were falling ever faster. They had to leave soon. Why hadn't the engines started up yet? He couldn't activate the Auto Launch if the *Phoenix* wasn't running. Two blue men stood near the wing, one starting to hoist the other up. Oliver let out a battle cry, "AHHH!" He raised the rubber mallet over his head and charged them. The warrior doing the lifting shifted back, dropping the other onto his back. The fallen soldier let out a loud, painful grunt as he landed.

Tiffany followed Mason into the galley, her cabin, back into the galley, and then into Oliver's cabin. Each time they could see Oliver as he ran back and forth across the wingspan.

Tiffany noticed that the blue men seemed to be confused, but weren't backing down as a result of Oliver's sporadic behavior.

She'd tried to get Mason to explain what was happening, but only bits and pieces were coming out.

"It's the Blauwe Mensen," Mason explained between breaths as he ran from room to room.

"The who?" Tiffany asked in bewilderment.

Mason took a deep breath. "The Blauwe Mensen. We were in their gorge while you were gone." They were back in her cabin now.

"You were what?" cried Tiffany.

"We've been to their palace," Mason clarified.

Tiffany looked awestruck and confused. She shook her head. "How?"

"Obbin!" Mason shouted, but it wasn't an answer as much as a realization. Tiffany followed her crazed little brother from her cabin and across the corridor to the twins' cabin. Mason looked around. "He isn't here," he said, his blue eyes wide with worry. Mason looked at his mTalk. "It's been over an hour. Maybe he escaped."

"Obbin?" asked Tiffany.

"He's one of them. He helped us!" Mason admitted and turned to leave again. Tiffany grabbed both his shoulders and held him in place. "Help—them—what?" Tiffany asked.

"No time. I have to help Austin fly the ship," Mason replied, breaking away from her and running from the cabin. Tiffany stepped into the corridor, and Mason ran toward the bridge. Her brain was spinning from all the information and the sudden turn of events. Oliver was outside the ship, Mason was searching for some Obbin person, and Austin was attempting to fly the ship. Austin was attempting to fly the ship? Tiffany's legs felt numb. She wobbled forward as if she might faint. But for some reason, and to no one in particular, she closed her eyes and said, "Give me strength." A sense of calm passed over her like a breeze.

"I don't understand. The engines won't start up. The system acts like they don't even exist on the network," Austin explained to his brother who'd just arrived.

"I'll check the engine room," Mason said.

"Hurry," Austin said. "The soldiers have a huge log. I think they're going to try to break in." Mason ran for the engine room, barely missing Tiffany as he tore down the corridor.

"Where are you—" Tiffany started to ask, but Mason was already past the cabins and onto the landing in the cargo bay. He took two and three steps at a time, then turned and ran through the door to the engine room. When he entered, he noticed the silence of the room. None of the reactors were humming on standby. In fact, none of the monitors or systems were even on.

Mason looked around the compartment in confusion. The main cable to generator one was unhooked. He walked over and hooked it into its port. Looking around, he noticed that nothing in the room was connected. His heart dropped into his stomach; there was no way he'd be able to figure out what hooked where. He needed help. He put his hands over his face as if he might cry, but then took a deep breath. When he lowered his hands, he saw a large poster on the wall in front of him, but it wasn't just a poster; it was a flip chart of schematics for the ship.

Mason walked over and read the first label, "Cargo Bay Access." He read, "Bow Section Airlock," "Engine Compartment Airlock," "Exterior Side Airlock," "Cargo Bay Exterior Airlock," and "Exterior Belly Airlock." Each pointed to a different entry point of the cargo bay of the *Phoenix*.

It was interesting, but not what he needed at the moment. Mason quickly flipped through the remaining pages, but none of them said anything about the engine room. He let them flap back down in disappointment. But there in front of him was a schematic labeled, "Engine Compartment." It had been folded up; someone had been looking at the cargo bay schematic. Probably his dad before he was captured!

Perfect! Mason looked it over quickly and then, for the next five minutes, he started to reconnect all the reactors and systems. Several times he went back to the schematic to confirm what went where. When he finished he looked around. There were no blinking lights, nor was there the low hum of electricity. Nothing was on. What could be wrong now? All that work and still he hadn't fixed the problem. Mason slammed his fist against the nearby generator. He jumped at his sister's voice.

"Have you figured it out yet?" Tiffany asked as she entered.

Mason shook his head. "Everything was disconnected." He pointed at the flip chart. "But now it's all back as it should be, or so I think," Mason admitted. "And still nothing is on."

Tiffany put her hand to her chin and looked around the room. Her gaze stopped on a large control panel built into the wall. A myriad of lights dotted the panel, but none were on. Next to it was a breaker box, its hinged door open.

"Look," Tiffany said as she crossed to the panel. "The main breaker switch is set to open."

"Open?" Mason asked.

"Open is off." Tiffany switched it over, but nothing happened. She switched it back and stepped away to look. Next to the main breaker was a small grey button labeled "prime." Tiffany pumped the small button several times with her thumb. Eventually she heard a click and the button wouldn't compress anymore. Then with both hands on the flat grey switch she flipped it up to the closed position, or on. The room buzzed to life, humming with millions of volts of electricity. The set of lights on the control panel lit up green, signaling that the systems were all operational.

"Let's get back to Austin," Tiffany began. "He said that we had to rendezvous with Oliver some distance from here.

But I think I might have a better idea." Her smile gave Mason a sense of confidence he hadn't had a moment before. Tiffany's ideas rarely failed. Satisfied, sister and brother headed back up the stairs to join Austin on the bridge for takeoff.

1.36

Escape

Oliver heard the engines start up at a low hum, but that quickly grew to a steady rumble. Oliver lifted his mTalk and loaded the application Mr. O'Farrell had sent him. He looked around the clearing; there was still no sign of the old man. They'd have to leave without him.

Suddenly Oliver's body tumbled forward. The rubber mallet, his only weapon, flew from his hand and fell to the wing below with a loud thump. Oliver landed on his belly and slid across the slick silver surface, twisting quickly to his back to look at his offender. A young man about his age stood before him. Oliver shifted away from the attacker with his hands.

The blue soldier must have climbed up the access ladder on the aft of the *Phoenix*. The young man wore a blue shirt and pants that looked to be heavy and made of wool. Over one shoulder was a silver cape and, on his head, Oliver saw a thin silver crown. This was getting weirder by the moment, he thought to himself. "Who are you?" Oliver asked as he started to get to his feet.

"Who am I?" the man scoffed. "I am—" The *Phoenix* jerked violently as one of the engines misfired with a thunderous burst. The young blue attacker was thrown off his feet and slid toward the edge of the ship's roof. Oliver took the opportunity and sprinted for the bow of the *Phoenix*. As he ran, he tapped the Auto Launch option on his mTalk. The ship began to shudder under his feet. Oliver's body was trembling so much that he couldn't keep the mTalk screen still enough to read it. Something was happening, but he wasn't sure what.

Oliver felt the ship lift up. The echo from the engines' rumble was getting louder. He knew he had to get off quickly or he'd be too high to jump. He looked back and saw the blue man sliding off the side of the roof and onto a wing, where he was helped down by several blue warriors. Oliver dashed across the roof of the bridge. He sat and slid over the windshield and down the nose. This would be just like his escape from the compound.

Oliver hit the ground running, but the blue horde surged forward. He was far more outnumbered than when he'd faced the dozen or so Übel soldiers a few days prior. There was no path to the woods. The only opening was being created behind him, as the *Phoenix* lifted higher and higher off the ground.

Oliver stopped his escape, and began stepping backwards. The nose of the *Phoenix* was only a few yards above his head, but the ship was gaining altitude quickly. Oliver felt the wind from the thrusters rushing through his hair and wrapping around his body, pulling at his clothes.

The blue men had not advanced any farther; instead, they stood ten yards away like a stone wall enclosing Oliver. Their spears were no longer raised as if to attack, but several held their torches before them. The man who'd spoken to Austin crossed out from the line of warriors; he held no spear or torch. "Surrender, my son!" Feng shouted, but it was still difficult for Oliver to hear over the noise of the engines.

"Never! You'll have to capture me," challenged Oliver.

"That can be arranged," yelled the young blue man who'd attacked Oliver before. He walked a few steps ahead of the first man.

Another man, older than the other two and one Oliver had not seen before, stepped forward and placed his hand on the younger man's shoulder. "Patience, my prince," the man said in a loud but calming voice. He wore a grey suit, white shirt, and black tie. The older man smiled, although Oliver could tell it was very forced. "Son, you don't want to get hurt," he shouted. "I suggest you ask your brothers to land the ship."

Oliver looked up; the *Phoenix* was now more than fifty feet in the air. Light beams shown down from it, bathing the clearing in brightness. The firs, the only trees with any covering left, shivered from the ship's thrust. The dust of snow that had been on their branches was now circling in a whirlwind above. "No!" Oliver said over the rumble of the engines. He knew that there was little chance that his sister and brothers could continue on without him, but he had to let them go; he wouldn't risk them being imprisoned too.

He lifted the mTalk to his mouth to call Tiffany, to say goodbye. But Oliver noticed that many of the blue soldiers were looking up. Some were pointing with their free hands, and some raised their spears as if to attack. Oliver looked toward the *Phoenix*. A hatch had opened in the belly of the ship, near the cargo bay. Oliver covered his eyes to shade them from the blinding spotlights. A couple of silhouettes knelt in the opening. One leaned nearly all the way out. Something began to unravel and drop toward the ground. A rope ladder!

The end of the ladder landed between Oliver and the three blue men who'd come forward to talk. Oliver wasted no time and dashed for the lifeline. So did the youngest of the three men. It was a sprint to the finish. Yards became feet, and feet became inches. Oliver grasped a rung on the rope ladder, but the young man went directly for Oliver and grabbed at his arm. Oliver thrust his knee forward and struck the blue attacker directly in the chest. The young man stumbled backward. The *Phoenix* had already climbed another five yards, and Oliver was quickly moving out of reach of the swarm of blue warriors that were surging forward.

Looking down, Oliver saw the man in the grey suit standing near the fallen boy, but staring up at Oliver. The third man, the first who'd spoken to Oliver, was bent over trying to help the young man up, but he was shoved away. The young man looked humiliated, but also angry. Oliver had definitely made an enemy. At least he would never be coming back to this icy grave of a planet.

The *Phoenix* was still rising steadily. Oliver climbed the rungs of the rope ladder; it swung wildly in the wind, but he was able to hang on. He'd climbed many ropes and ladders at the Academy, and this was no different. Two hands greeted him when he reached the top of the ladder, one Mason's and the other Austin's. The twins pulled Oliver in, and the belly hatch started to lift closed as Tiffany touched a control screen nearby.

"You made it!" Austin shouted.

"Thanks to you guys," Oliver commended. "I thought I was a goner."

"It was all Tiffany's idea," Mason admitted.

Tiffany blushed as she joined her three brothers. "We're not in the clear yet."

"Right!" Oliver agreed and smiled at Tiffany. "Everyone to the bridge!"

Tiffany's hands shook as she tapped the NavCom screen in front of her. Although they weren't at ground level, she knew that a horde of blue warriors were gathered below them waiting to take them prisoner. She forced herself to swallow the lump in her throat. They were unlike anything she'd ever seen. Somehow the twins were responsible for the blue men coming; the boys had brought this danger on them. Their whole mission could have ended and they could have been taken prisoner. That hadn't happened, but she didn't know exactly why yet.

The coordinates for their destination on Evad appeared on the screen. They flashed and she touched them; the message "confirmed" flashed in green below the numbers. Tiffany avoided looking out the front windshield as she looked toward Oliver. "Destination set," she said.

"Excellent. Is everyone strapped in?" Oliver asked. The *Phoenix* was now hovering level with the top of the tree canopy. The snow fell more heavily and the wind whipped up the flurries, creating a no-visibility whiteout. Oliver adjusted the angle of the thrusters and flew low over the trees. They seemed to be free of any threat from the blue men.

"Whoa!" cried Austin. He was staring out the window. Tiffany looked, and a large spear-like thing hurtled through the air, barely missing the *Phoenix*. The weapon was as long as a normal-sized pine tree on Tragiws, maybe twenty feet in length. Her stomach dropped as Oliver yanked the controls back and the *Phoenix* pulled up. Another spear followed. A loud crunch resounded and the ship shook. Clearly the spear had impacted the ship; where, she didn't know. She looked at the screen in front of her, but there were no warnings of damage. Before she looked up her body jerked again to the left as Oliver twisted the controls.

"Wow!" Austin screamed. "Did you see that one? It almost hit us too."

"I know," Oliver said through gritted teeth. His hands were clenched on the controls.

"Take us up!" Mason cried.

"I am!" Oliver yelled. A second later the *Phoenix* was gaining altitude. Tiffany pulled up the radar screen, but there was no sign of any new projectiles.

"Are we clear?" she asked.

"I don't think so. We need to get a bit higher," Oliver admitted.

"Why don't we just leave?" asked Austin.

"Because we need to pick up Mr. O'Farrell," Oliver said. "Tiffany, see if you can reach him. The communication transponder should work just fine now." Tiffany tapped the screen in front of her. She waited a moment, but there was no connection.

"Oliver, I'm not getting anything."

"Try again. The system says the communication transponders are working fine. I'm picking up all sorts of signals from Brighton." Tiffany frowned as she tried again and still couldn't get through.

"Do you think he's okay?"

"I'm sure he's fine. Maybe he turned it off or doesn't have a signal," Oliver suggested. "Remember Eises is causing interference." Tiffany nodded. The storm had caused all sorts of problems for them. She would have a lot to record in the journal. Suddenly, a message popped up on the screen and Tiffany put a headset on.

"Wait—I'm getting a communication from someone," Tiffany said, and looked at Oliver. "It's the Brighton security force and they want validation and serial tags."

Oliver cleared his throat nervously. "We can't wait for him any longer."

Tiffany's eyes widened. "They're launching an escort to bring us in."

"Awesome!" Austin shouted.

"Not awesome," Mason corrected. "Don't you remember the canyon?" His voice was rife with fear.

"Yeah, and it rocked," Austin said. Mason shook his head.

"It doesn't matter, we're out of here!" Oliver engaged the full power of the thrusters and pulled back on the controls.

"We've had enough close calls." The *Phoenix* shot upward and Oliver steered to avoid a dense section of purple clouds heavy with snow. Soon, as they climbed in altitude, only the deep-blue sky remained above them. A moment later the cold black of space engulfed the silver ship. Tiffany looked out at a growing number of white sparkling dots.

She looked at the glowing screens before her and noticed several small escort ships closing in. "Oliver, they're coming!"

"I see that!" Oliver exclaimed. "It'll be just a few more seconds before the *Phoenix* can hyper flight." Tiffany watched as Oliver tapped the screen. She hoped he could get them launched in time. "Everyone prepare for hyper flight," Oliver ordered. Tiffany looked down at the green globe rotating on the screen before her. The coordinates were set; all that was left was for Oliver to activate the hyper flight sequence.

Oliver took a deep breath and then pressed the flashing blue button to initiate hyper flight. A computerized voice repeated the coordinates and asked for confirmation. "Yes," Oliver responded. The overhead lights on the bridge dimmed and a red strobe began to flash.

"Confirm hyper flight sequence initialization. Projected course is clear," the computer stated. Oliver tapped the screen and large numbers began counting down on the console screens. "Ten seconds until jump," the computer warned.

Mason and Austin, sitting in the second row of seats, checked each other's harnesses. Mason brushed his shaggy bangs from his eyes and gave Austin the thumbs up. Tiffany pulled the strap over her lap tighter and then closed her eyes.

Oliver lowered the heat shields over the three sections of the windshield just like the first time.

"Eight seconds."

Austin gave Mason a cautious smile. "Here we go again."

"Six seconds."

Oliver smiled. "Evad here we—!"

His cry was interrupted as a warning siren wailed over the intercom followed by the computer's voice. "Warning: torpedo impact in five seconds." Oliver looked at the screen in front of him. The countdown continued to flash on his screen, and the computer's voice continued.

"Five."

"Oliver!" screamed Tiffany.

"Four."

"Do something!" yelled Mason.

"Three"

What Oliver didn't know was whether the countdown was for the hyper flight or the torpedo impact. There was nothing he could do. It was too late.

"Two."

Oliver braced himself, but for what he didn't know. Escape or death?

"One."

Instantly the kids were pressed into their seats as a sharp whistling noise filled the air.

Oliver gritted his teeth. His knuckles were white from gripping the controls so tightly. The jump into hyper flight took only twelve seconds but the suspense made it feel much longer. The torpedo never hit. They'd made it.

Oliver breathed a sigh of relief, which was echoed by his siblings. The pressure from the hyper flight eased and the screeching noise ceased. "You can all undo your harnesses now."

Mason began unstrapping, but Austin hesitated for a moment. "Oliver said it was okay," Mason assured his twin. Austin gave him a half smile and unstrapped. Clearly he remembered being beaten against the bridge floor during the previous landing.

Oliver turned in his seat and gave a deep sigh. "That was close."

Tiffany nodded her head. "Too close."

"What a thrill!" Austin said.

Mason shook his hand out before him. "Whatever. You squeezed my hand so tight I thought you'd crushed every bone."

Austin frowned sheepishly. "Uh, how long until we reach Evad?" he asked.

Anticipating the question, Oliver had already checked the exact time. "Two hours and three minutes." Oliver glanced back at the screen once more.

Austin nudged Mason in the side. "All right, let's get something to eat."

"Yeah, I'm starving."

"I don't think so," Tiffany warned. "It's time to explain yourselves." The twins moaned. Austin laid his head to the side and frowned.

"But we're hungry."

"That's too—" but Tiffany was interrupted before she could finish.

"I agree, I'm hungry too . . ." Oliver started. Tiffany scowled while Mason and Austin smiled. "So we can talk while we eat. Let's all go to the galley," Oliver finished. The twins' and Tiffany's expressions swapped.

"Yeah, I want to hear about this Obbin character," Tiffany said.

"Obbin?" Austin started.

"I looked." Mason shook his head. "He's gone."

"You're still going to tell us about him," Oliver warned. The twins sighed and left for the galley, followed by Tiffany, who held the journal in her hands.

Oliver paused for a moment and took a deep breath as the others left. He'd kept his sister and brothers safe so far. The question was whether he could do so again. Each risk he'd taken could have unleashed disaster. His desire to protect his siblings and rescue his parents was his driver. The tangled web of secrets, villains, and the unknown needed to be unraveled, yet he wasn't sure where to begin. He knew, as he always had, that there was something greater guiding him. He hoped he'd discover what that was, but most of all he hoped he wouldn't get his siblings or himself killed along the way.

Visual Glossary

Academy, Federal Star Fleet: The Academy provides top-of-the-line education while creating future leaders for the Federal fleet. All males in the Federation must participate in the Federation's military service.

Archeos Alliance: An organization that exists to unlock the past that has been lost. Founded as nonprofit, but receiving both private and Federal funds, the organization has become a battleground for special-interest groups. Mr. and Mrs. Wikk often receive grants through this organization and are considered employees. They report their findings to Archeos, and then Archeos makes official reports available to the Federation and other groups.

Bewaldeter: A private boarding school and premier K–12 establishment. A majority of Archeos employees send their children to Bewaldeter. The school provides a curriculum that allows kids to focus on their interests. Tiffany, Mason, and Austin Wikk attend it, and Oliver studied there until he was selected for early admittance to the Academy.

Blauwe Mensen (*Blue People*): A mysterious group known to the people of Brighton and Mudo as "blue ghosts." No one dares enter their home in the Cobalt Gorge. Obbin belongs to the Blauwe Mensen's royal family.

Brighton: Established as the capital of Jahr des Eises when the Federation annexed the planet. A large dome was constructed over the city to protect the citizens from the harsh winter, called *Eises*. The city's main purpose is to act as a base for the large-scale logging operation on the planet. Because logging generates a lot of wealth, the people of Brighton have become snobbish and look down on the inhabitants of Mudo.

The governor of Brighton lives in a penthouse atop the dome, which is supported by "the governor's tower." He can view the surrounding woods unobstructed from his lofty abode. Within the dome, roads branch out from the tower like spokes, while crossroads form concentric circles. The pristine buildings are shorter and shorter the closer they are to the exterior of the dome.

Cobalt Gorge: Home to the Blauwe Mensen. The gorge is well protected from the weather and from outsiders. The

Blauwe Mensen devised a series of drains that dump water deep into the planet and create steam. The steam then rises into the gorge and forms thick clouds over the city. The clouds create a warm, humid environment that turns the gorge into a jungle, habitable through the time of Eises. The city's external protection from intruders consists of a drawbridge, a deep crevice, and a cave protected by large doors and guard towers. The gorge has been home to the Blauwe Mensen since they arrived on Jahr des Eises as the first settlers of the planet.

Corsairs: Also known as pirates, corsairs plague trade routes on the fringes of the Federation and are a constant burden to Federal forces. The corsairs captured the *Griffin* and traded it to Schlamm, a ruthless parts trader.

Cryostore: A refrigeration and freezing appliance in the galley of the *Phoenix*.

Dabnis Castle: An abandoned castle where several clues and artifacts were found during the Wikks' last archeological dig. The clues, located under a pavilion, on the roof of a tower, and within a catacomb deep below the library, provide what the Wikks believe is the missing step on the path to Ursprung.

Dark Market: A network of collectors and treasure hunters who trade in stolen artifacts. As a young man, Mr. O'Farrell used the market to sell one page from a rare book that he discovered. This sale is the basis of his wealth.

e-Journal: An electronic notebook where Mr. and Mrs. Wikk store all their archeological notes. The notes consist of maps, statistics, pictures, videos, reports, coordinates, contacts, and much more. The information contains clues that may help unlock the path to Ursprung via a complex tapping method that traces links and makes connections. This tapping method is known only to Mr. and Mrs. Wikk and Tiffany.

Eises: A harsh winter storm that turns the planet of Jahr des Eises to ice for an entire year. The storm releases its frigid breath after a two-year cycle of spring, summer, and fall. It occurs as the planet travels away from its star (sun) and becomes the thirteenth planet by passing Vor Eis. Two layers of clouds form: an upper layer that is heavy and purple, and a lower layer that is wispy and pink. When charged by lighting, gusts of warm air blast upward through the purple layer from the pink layer. This causes a drastic drop in the surface temperature of the planet.

Empire: The government preceding the Federation, ruled by an emperor of unknown origin. The Empire expanded, through war, annexations, and clandestine revolutions. This was also the time when the truth of Ursprung was lost.

Energen: The boys' favorite drink. It provides a jolt of energy and is 100% natural.

Evad: A planet previously explored by Mr. and Mrs. Wikk that became part of their search via a clue found at Dabnis Castle. The only habitable planet in the Rel Krev system, it is covered in lush green tropical plants, some of which are deadly. The atmosphere is breathable, but hot and humid. Wild animals are plentiful, and most are unknown species because of the loss of historical information.

Federation: Established when the childless emperor, Albert the XI, ceded rule to the Senate by declaring, "The people should decide their fate." The Federation consists of 1,983 planets, asteroids, or stations. Governed by a president and Senate, the Federation is enjoying a time of great wealth and expansion.

Federal Star Fleet: The militaristic arm of the Federation that stands to protect and serve its citizens. Half of the entire force is dedicated to the expansion of the Federation. Expansion occurs through either the colonization of uninhabited planets or annexation by a vote of the inhabitants of a non-Federal planet. The Federal Star Fleet has taken a peaceful approach to expansion. All males must serve five years in the federal service.

Griffin: The sister ship of the *Phoenix*, built as an identical twin. It was given to Rand and Jenn McGregor to use on the quest for Ursprung. The ship, attacked by Corsairs and traded to Schlamm, is currently at his warehouse in Mudo on Jahr des Eises.

Hyper Flight: Space flight navigation at extreme speeds, considered very dangerous for inexperienced pilots. The route of hyper flight must be entirely clear for the duration of the trip, or the ship will smash into another object and be obliterated.

Jahr des Eises: A small forest planet. Initially the planet was discovered and settled by the Blauwe Mensen. These people, however, remain hidden and are not officially known to the Federation. An outpost, Mudo, was established by a resource exploration company as a base for logging operations. When the planet was annexed by the Federation, the city of Brighton was established.

While covered in a thick forest of gargantuan trees, the planet suffers from ice storms called Eises every three years. In the two years of growth, the logging industry is in full operation. During the Eises, those who remain behind are sealed within the dome of Brighton. Phelan O'Farrell, a wealthy donor to Archeos and to the Wikks specifically, lives on Jahr des Eises in the city of Brighton.

Krank's Parts and Service: A parts and repair shop in Brighton owned by Mr. O'Farrell's friend, Samuel Krank. Mr. Krank assisted in the refurbishing of the *Phoenix* and the *Griffin*.

LOCA-drone: A small silver disc with a screen embedded in its top. The LOCA-drone uses magnetism and negative energy to propel itself to a position over a designated area. Often used for search and rescue, it can also be used to mark locations and coordinates. Each device is assigned a unique encrypted access signature code.

LOCATOR: An application used to track and find LOCA-drones. The *Phoenix*, the *Griffin*, and their corresponding sky scooters are equipped with the LOCATOR application.

Maglev: A train-type vehicle that travels along a magnetized rail using magnetic repulsion to reduce friction and reach high speeds. The maglev on Jahr des Eises is used for delivery of newly felled timber to the processing facility and then to the spaceport for distribution throughout the Federation.

Mud Cruiser: A crudely designed, but highly durable ship that has a maximum hovering altitude of ten yards. The craft is generally used for hauling goods or transporting a few people.

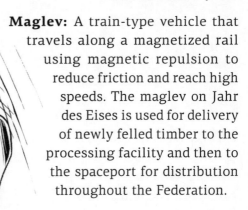

Mudo: An outpost established by the Resource Exploration Company XPLR Corp. The outpost quickly became a rough community of loggers and opportunists looking to make a quick buck. When the first winter after Mudo's establishment arrived, XPLR Corp. failed to provide the needed supplies to the workforce, and rather than evacuate, forced them to make do. Management quickly lost control and the workers revolted. Some attempted to flee the planet via the large colonization ships that were being used for housing, operations management, and timber processing. Only two of the twelve ships launched successfully. The remaining ships were either not in appropriate condition, or were not flown by workers with flight experience. The outpost was left in shambles, deserted by XPLR Corp., which moved its operation to Brighton once that city was established.

mTalk: Worn on the wrist like a watch, the mTalk has many useful applications, including a built-in video call feature, flashlight, navigation device, video camera, and other items still unknown to the Wikks.

Nanocook: A high-speed cooking appliance in the *Phoenix*.

Phoenix: A spaceship donated to the Wikks to facilitate research on their quest for the origins of mankind. The ship's sleek silver skin and forward-swept wings give it a unique appearance. But those features are nothing compared with the secret capabilities of the ship that Oliver will have to discover. The ship consists of a bridge (cockpit), four cabins (sleeping quarters), a galley (dining room/kitchen), three lavatories (bathrooms), a library/office, an engine room, an electronics suite, a two-story cargo bay, and an artifacts room.

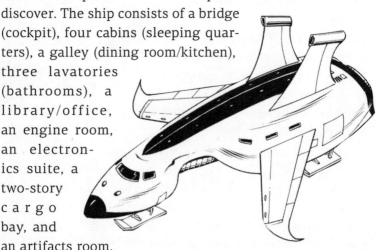

Rel Krev system: A planetary system with seventeen small planets, one of which is Evad.

RepFuse: A subsidiary of GenTexic, a genetics company that, while publicly known, is very secretive in its work. Schlamm's guard lizard, Spike, is a product of RepFuse.

Schlamm's Warehouse: A large structure built from the remnants of the ships that brought the first workers from XPLR Corp. to Jahr des Eises. It is owned and run by a man known only as Schlamm. A trader and mechanic, Schlamm has no guidelines about those with whom he deals; his only interest is in money. The huge warehouse is situated in the outpost of Mudo.

Sky Scooter: This small craft seats two and has multiple storage compartments. It can hover up to twenty feet above the ground and can reach speeds of one hundred miles per hour. The scooter is ideal for short commutes.

Spike: A seven-foot hybrid chameleon-iguana, genetically engineered and bred by a company called RepFuse. Spike is virtually invisible when he changes colors and blends in with his surroundings.

Thermaclean: An appliance to instantly sanitize the table and cookware in the *Phoenix*.

Tragiws: The planet the Wikks call home. Its climate is arid, but not a desert. The Wikks' home sits on the edge of the Plains of Yrovi near a deep cavern. The planet is small and sparsely populated.

Übel: A secret order/society composed of renegade forces. Captain Vedrik is an agent of the mysterious society. The society's handiwork is threaded throughout the history of the Federation and Empire, but is not publicly recognized. Their reach and influence are unknown, but thought to be vast. Their financial resources are second only to the Federation.

Ursprung: A fabled planet believed to be the birthplace of mankind. Its discovery is sought by many.

Vor Eis: Another planet in the same system as Jahr des Eises. Its position in relation to Jahr des Eises helps to tell when *Eises* winter season will begin.

Wikk Family Compound:
The Wikks' home sits on the edge of the Plains of Yrovi on a sparsely populated planet called Tragiws. Their compound is made up of seven domes con-nected by breeze-

ways. A large woods sits behind the home with a deep chasm coursing through it. This home is the only one the Wikk children have ever known.

XPLR Corp.: A large resource exploration company. Mr. O'Farrell worked for them in his early days. It has many outposts and subsidiaries operating within as well as outside the Federation.

Yrovi, Plains of: Location of the Wikk family compound on Tragiws. The plains are a vast area covering nearly 80 percent of the planet.

Zapp-It: A small defense device that uses an electric shock to either deter or stun an assailant.

Mr. O'Farrell's Family Recipe for Russian Tea

Mix the following ingredients together in a large bowl:

2 1/2 cups Tang
1 1/4 cups sugar
3/4 cups decaffeinated instant tea
1 teaspoon ground cinnamon
1/2 teaspoon ground cloves

Stir 3 teaspoons of Russian Tea mix into 1 cup of boiling water. Serve hot!

Brock D. Eastman likes to write, but his focus is on his wonderful wife and two daughters. They reside at the base of America's mountain and are learning to call Colorado home, but sometimes need a visit to the comfortable cornfields and hospitality of the Midwest, especially during spring and harvest.

Brock is product marketing manager at Focus on the Family, where he has the privilege to work on the world-renowned Adventures in Odyssey brand, a show his dad got him hooked on when he was a little boy. He also makes frequent appearances on the official Adventures in Odyssey podcast and has written an article for *Thriving Family* magazine.

He started writing the Quest for Truth series in 2005, and five years later, with his wife's encouragement, signed a publishing deal. He is always thinking of his next story and totes a thumb drive full of ideas.